Rosemary's Garden

By the same author

Daughter of Tremar
An Enchanted Place

Rosemary's Garden

Annie Marks

ROBERT HALE · LONDON

ISBN 0 7090 7763 7

Robert Hale Limited
Clerkenwell House
Clerkenwell Green
London EC1R 0HT

2 4 6 8 10 9 7 5 3 1

Typeset in 11/14 Sabon
Derek Doyle & Associates, Shaw Heath.
Printed in Great Britain by
St Edmundsbury Press, Bury St Edmunds, Suffolk.
Bound by Woolnough Bookbinding Limited.

Chapter 1

With ten days to go until Christmas, a sharp frost on the ground outside and a new fire, smelling sharply of fresh coal, catching in the grate to warm the tiny room, Edna Buddry idly watched her niece spooning porridge into her mouth and felt comfortable.

Dorothea was an undersized, mousy-haired little thing, who might one day grow to be quite pretty, but those were not the thoughts occupying her aunt. Edna was remembering finding her, as a vulnerable little waif, in a hideous Manchester orphanage slightly less than three years ago, and briefly comparing that shadowy, suffering child to the bright schoolgirl who sat before her now. There was no doubt that she had turned the child's life around.

Of course there was no doubt, either, that the child had turned *her* life around just as completely. Over sixty, childless, and widowed for so many years that she could no longer clearly remember what her husband had looked like, she had seen herself as simply continuing with her daily-help job for as long as possible, and then sitting in an armchair waiting quietly to die. All that was different now.

She sipped her tea as she sat at the table with Dorothea, and thought about her very much younger half-brother, invalided out of the war in 1944, and coming home with a shot up leg and a weak chest, looking for all the world as if he was on the point of death. She remembered him, too, meeting and marrying his delicate little Emily a year later and so hoping that their lives would improve, now they had found each other. But life was a cruel master when it chose to be. There had been such joy at the birth of their one little daughter, followed so quickly by the sorrow of Emily's death – and then, damn him, her brother's insistence that he was going to take his child away with him and earn enough money to keep them. He hadn't stood a chance.

Oh Lord, if she hadn't received that envelope full of her own unopened letters from a slum landlord in Manchester, with a note informing her that her brother was dead and the child housed in the local orphanage, Dorothea would have been lost . . . and this, the joy of having this child to cuddle, to have so much love in her life, would never have been.

Edna thought about it all the time – but she didn't tell Dorothea that.

Dorothea finished her porridge and looked up. In the beginning – for about two minutes – she had been frightened of Aunty; a big woman with iron-grey hair and a no-nonsense face, standing there in the governess's office, gazing down at her. Then she had been snatched up and hugged and had felt the woman's tears on her cheek, had felt the big bosom beneath her skinny body shuddering with sobs . . . and had understood her to be moved. Tentatively she had hugged her back then, and suddenly everything in her bleak little life had changed. It had been a turning point for Edna, but for Dorothea it had been much, much more and now, three years on, she never ceased to be grateful.

She tried it on though, when she thought she could get away with it. Well that was what ten-year-olds who were comfortable and certain they were loved were supposed to do, wasn't it?

'Aunty,' she said, offering a winning smile. 'Can we talk about Charlie?'

Edna threw her niece a baleful stare across the table and heard the coal spitting in the grate. She was a Cornish woman born and bred on an estate farm, and though she had been away from Cornwall for most of her life, she still kept the accent – and kept her farmer's daughter's ideas about animals, too. Unsentimental.

'I told you not to give that blessed cockerel a name,' she retorted. 'I said when we got him that he was for Christmas. He's a nice fat bird, and he's for eating – and you know that perfectly well!'

'Well I won't eat him!' Dorothea threatened. 'If you kill him I shall sit at the table and cry all through Christmas lunch.'

Edna felt a smile coming on and fixed her mouth to stop it.

'Get off to school you naughty girl,' she retorted. 'I ent going to do for him today, at any rate, so you still got time to persuade me to spare him, but you'm got to come up with better reasons than you have so far, I warn you. Only three days of school left and then we'll be going to Languard House every day and you can play with James. Now go on, run and find Rosemary.'

Dorothea gave her a huge kiss, pulled on her school coat, wrapped a scarf around her neck and bounced out into Boxgrove Crescent as Edna watched her from the window. It was a tiny little two up two down Council semi that she shared with this lovely child, and yet after five years of moving from slum to slum with her father and then four months of desolation in the orphanage, Dorothea behaved as if she lived in a palace now, and was the cleanest, tidiest, most caring child imaginable.

Aunty knew she wouldn't have to go and check that she had made her bed or tidied her room, it would be spotless, and after the child's brief foray into the back yard to the chilly outside toilet, she would have fed the chickens and put fresh milk down for Blackie, Edna's complacent old cat. It wouldn't be that way with James at Languard House, Edna thought. James was a rich child with too many toys and a boy's tendency to be grubby at all times, but he was a very special boy to Edna, and to Dorothea.

James and Dorothea loved each other with a simple, child's devotion that needed no explanation. It was just there, and it meant the world to them.

Edna had first gone to work as a daily-help for James's parents when he was five, and he had instantly taken an enormous fancy to her. He'd started to call her Aunty almost immediately and delighted in having her as a baby-sitter when he could.

It was at this time that one of life's mysterious coincidences had come about, and Anthea Webb-Goring had discovered that Edna Buddry – of whom her little son was so enamoured – had actually been born and bred on the very same Cornish estate now owned by her sister, Bella. It had been like a joyous home-coming, and suddenly Aunty was as near as damn-it, real family. So when the problems had arisen over Dorothea, two years later, Anthea had gone to Manchester with Edna, paid for their hotel accommodation and largely taken financial responsibility for the little girl.

It had been a delightful and charming bonus that James and Dorothea had taken to each other so completely.

Arthur Johnson stood in the small, neat front bedroom of his little house in Cheddar Close at the other end of Acacia Road, and checked his appearance for the last time as he listened to his three little girls running about and giggling on the landing. He heard their mother bark at them from the foot of the stairs, and knew it was time to set off for school: the usual morning routine.

Cheddar Close was a cul-de-sac of post-war terraced houses close to the railway line. They might have been extremely small, but Arthur was very proud of his home. It had a bathroom, which was more than Dorothea and Edna had, and a neat modern kitchen, and though the trains thundered by at the back, for Arthur it represented an enormous leap up in living standards.

Arthur had dragged himself into the suburbs from the very worst of pre-war London slum beginnings. He had been a reliable soldier during the war, and now had a good job as a travelling haberdashery salesman; which gave him an aura of respectability, and implied trust on the part of his employers, for he carried an expensive selection of their goods.

His wife, Edith, was generally acknowledged as an excellent woman and Arthur was proud of her, for she kept a spotless house. He was proud of his three daughters, too, for despite the fact that he was not particularly good-looking, Edith had always been quite a delicate, attractive girl, and the mixture of their genes had produced three very pretty girls. Shirley was a beautiful child of eight with a china-doll face and shiny golden curls, and six-year-old identical twins Katy and Monica were charmingly freckle-faced redheads.

Arthur loved his girls dearly and greatly admired the fact that Edith always dressed them alike and spent most of her life at her sewing-machine making clothes for them, but he never delved too deeply into the substance of his marriage, because he didn't dare. He and Edith had almost nothing in common, they shared a bed because that was what married people did, but there had been no physical contact between them since the twins were born, and they had long since run out of things to say to each other. Edith was fiercely loyal, of that there was no doubt, but in his darker moments Arthur sometimes wondered what her loyalties actually amounted to. He was husband, father and provider and she enjoyed life as a respectable married woman. She didn't look him in the eye any more, though, and he always had a nagging fear that she knew and understood him far better than she ever let on.

That she knew him for exactly what he was, and silently despised him for it.

For respectable as he struggled to be, Arthur had a flaw, a big one, which he fought against and strove to keep hidden – even from himself. When he saw his flaw through other people's eyes he knew how unspeakable it was, but seen from within himself it was a lustful need, clamouring all the time for attention, and these days it was oddly confusing because it didn't seem to apply to his own case. Arthur was irresistibly drawn to little girls. He'd been drawn to Edith in the beginning because she had been a strangely childlike seventeen-year-old, and now he wasn't interested in her because she was a grown woman. Crashing about as a soldier in war-torn Europe as hostilities had all begun to wind down, there had actually been opportunities – which he chose not to think about if he could help it – and coming home to try and take up a decent life had been bewildering.

Now there was something much more bewildering, and much

more threatening to this persona he had tried to carve out for himself, for he had found a little girl he absolutely adored. He thought that Rosemary Archer was the most beautiful child he had ever seen and whenever he thought about her his mouth went dry. He wanted her, he dreamed and fantasized about her – and he did everything he could to engineer meetings with her as often as possible.

It had seemed too good to be true when Shirley had started fighting for a little bit of independence and demanded to go to school without her mother and sisters. This created the perfect opportunity to spend time in Rosemary's company every day. Surely it had been the most natural thing in the world, to ask Rosemary and her skinny little friend Dorothea Sprake to wait for them at the bottom of Acacia Road, and then walk on to school with Shirley; how could they have refused?

And of course they hadn't, because to Rosemary and Dorothea it had seemed quite natural for Mr Johnson not to want Shirley to cross by herself into Franklin Road where they all went to school, but they wished they had known how to say no, for they didn't like Mr Johnson one little bit. He made them feel uncomfortable, only of course they were far too young to understand why.

Standing on the corner of Boxgrove Crescent Rosemary and Dorothea saw Arthur and Shirley coming down Acacia Road to meet them and exchanged glances. Arthur wore a raincoat, belted at the waist and a soft, brown felt hat, smartly tilted on his head in winter-time. He always looked the same, he smelled of cigarettes and carried his very heavy sample case when he went for the morning bus, and he always gave each girl a sweet to eat on the way to school. Rosemary and Dorothea took his sweets because he was Shirley's father, but there was something about him that made them wish like anything that they could refuse.

Now, as Rosemary hopped about, trying to keep her feet warm, she whispered to her friend:

'Only three more times and then we won't have to see him again for two whole weeks.' Dorothea pulled a face.

10

'I wish we didn't have to see him at all,' she retorted equally softly and paused, watching little Shirley skipping happily along beside her daddy. 'Maybe after Christmas he'll think she's old enough to cross the road on her own,' she suggested doubtfully. 'That'd be nice, wouldn't it?'

Arthur and Shirley came alongside them and they all moved off towards the corner of Franklin Road.

'Good morning, girls,' he said brightly. 'Not long till Christmas now, eh?'

Dorothea saw him fish in his raincoat pocket and come up with three mint humbugs which he handed around, before lightly touching Rosemary's shiny black hair. Somehow he always contrived to touch Rosemary.

'You are a lucky girl to have such lovely hair, you know, Rosemary,' he observed, chuckling softly. 'Black as crow's feathers, and so shiny. Bet you wish you'd got such lovely hair don't you, Dorothea?'

Rosemary looked uncomfortable; these were not yet things she and her best friend talked about and his talking that way made her blush.

'I'd rather have Shirley's hair, Mr Johnson,' she replied, turning her pink face towards him. 'So curly and golden. I wish my hair would curl like that.'

Arthur pulled a droll face at her.

'Just like a woman,' he observed. 'Never satisfied, eh? Honestly, you girls, you don't 'alf set about keeping us chaps on our toes, don't you.'

It was a highly inappropriate remark to make to a ten-year-old and both Rosemary and Dorothea were embarrassed and anxious to get away. There was something about Shirley's father that made them want to shrink, and they were always surprised that Shirley didn't seem to feel the same way.

Shirley appeared to love her daddy very much, and always gave him a big kiss before he went across the road towards the bus stop; but although he walked her to school every morning, he never, they had noticed, brought her up to the swings at the recreation ground, where all the local children congregated whenever they got the chance. He was always up there on his own, chatting to them through the chain-link fence as they played . . . but he never, ever brought his own children with him.

'Have a good day at school, then,' Arthur said as they reached the spot where he must cross the road to the bus stop. 'No chasing the boys in the playground. Or do they chase you, eh? Like being chased by the boys, do you, Rosemary?'

Rosemary swallowed and stared at the pavement, actually stepping back as he went to put his hand on her head one more time.

'I don't get chased by the boys, Mr Johnson,' she replied quietly and they heard him laughing heartily as he walked away from them.

As he reached the bus stop he put down his heavy case and glanced back at them once, acknowledging that his mornings would be less delightful for a while, once the school holidays had begun. They were just disappearing around the corner into Franklin Road and he reflected that if he was lucky he might catch sight of Rosemary again in the evening, for her mother always left the dining-room curtains open in their detached, three-bedroomed, mock Tudor house in Acacia Road, and often sent Rosemary in to lay the table for dinner.

Doreen would have been amazed and horrified if she had known that her deliberate act of leaving the curtains open to invite the envy of her neighbours had an entirely different and considerably more sinister effect on one member of the local community!

James Webb-Goring sat at breakfast with his parents, and was, just as Aunty had thought he would be, unwashed and tousle-headed. Fortunately his mother didn't worry about things like that and as she and his father sat across the breakfast table from each other, beautifully turned out to face the day, they paid no attention to their small son's appearance. It was, after all, the first day of the holidays for him, so if a bath was absolutely necessary it could be attended to after breakfast.

The Webb-Gorings were fabulously wealthy, even by the stan-

dards of the wealthy. Great-great-grandfather Goring had founded
a furnishing and fabrics empire during the Industrial Revolution
and now, generations later, it was flourishing. James's home in
Hampton Court was huge in comparison to Dorothea's tiny place
of residence; four floors with endless bedrooms and bathrooms
and sumptuous ground-floor rooms. But as is the way so often
with children, given the choice James would have plumped for
Aunty's every time.

Aunty had no bathroom at all, so when he went there to stay for
the weekend, which he did regularly because his parents enjoyed a
lavish social life, Aunty bathed him and Dorothea in a tin bath in
front of the fire. To James this was the culmination of a wonderful
time. He loved it beyond words.

When he went to Aunty's he and Dorothea would regularly go
up to the swings at the rec and meet up with other local children;
then sometimes they would follow a small, well-worn footpath
into a scrubby little copse, passing between some water board
buildings and the Cavendish Road allotments, and build dens or
play hide-and-seek for hours on end. James rarely ever mixed with
other boys from his prep school; he wanted only to be with the
children near Aunty's, and since Anthea really had little interest in
status and was happiest when he was happy, she was content to let
him.

James was a lucky boy, he lived a good life.

As his mother nibbled at her slice of breakfast toast and Charles
downed a hearty cooked breakfast, James idly sailed the sausage
on his plate across a sea of scrambled eggs, lost in a fantasy. She
was reading a letter, his father glancing at the headlines in *The
Times* and, as was the way at breakfast in Languard House, no one
was saying much.

Suddenly Anthea's eyebrows shot upwards and she glanced at
her husband over the top of her letter.

'Good Lord,' she exclaimed, 'this is from Bella, darling, and
she's inviting us to go to Pengloss for Christmas would you
believe? What on earth has got into her. I mean what a time to ask
– there's less than a fortnight to go! Honestly, she has no concep-

tion of living in the real world at all, has she?'

Pengloss, Edna's beautiful birth-place, was a perfect and cosy little manor house near the Lizard Point in Cornwall, where James and Dorothea went for six weeks every summer to play together and grow in the sunshine.

In the beginning, before Dorothea had arrived in her life, Edna had been simply delighted to re-discover this magical place of her childhood, and Bella charmed to accommodate her. The advent of Dorothea, however, had brought about much greater changes, for Bella was both widowed and childless. Not childless in the usual sense though. David and Bella Rosenthal's five year old son, Peachy, had kissed his mummy one summer afternoon in 1939, gone out to play in the sunshine and never been seen again. Almost twenty years, and officially Peachy was still missing.

For Bella finding Dorothea had been almost like finding the 'lost sheep' of the parable, and she had anxiously taken the child under her wing. Dorothea never went without, despite the fact that Edna had very little money. She had good, well fitting clothes and shoes whenever she required them, presents which Edna could never have afforded and the freedom of Pengloss. It was a situation which suited everybody.

It certainly suited Charles, who tolerated rather than liked his sister-in-law and who found it most convenient to let his wife and their daily-help take the children to Cornwall, whilst he stayed comfortably at home.

Now he eyed his wife nervously, finding the idea of Christmas there quite intolerable.

Trying to be tactful he said: 'It wouldn't be terribly convenient, my dear, and it's dreadfully short notice . . .' broke off and then, for something to do, flicked his napkin at his son and snarled, 'James, don't play with your food. Eat it or leave it, but don't swill it around the plate. It's a disgusting habit!'

'And don't leave it, either,' Anthea added with a chuckle, 'or Mrs Minns will corner you and force-feed you syrup of figs, as you know.'

James looked up at his mother and grinned. He wouldn't leave his breakfast, he never did, but he had one great hatred in the world: casseroled liver, which the Webb-Goring's cook, Mrs Minns, produced at least once a week for lunch, and he would do pretty well anything he could think of to avoid that. Once however, when he'd complained that he couldn't eat it because he felt ill, she had done precisely what his mother said, cornered him in the bathroom and fed him two huge dessertspoons of syrup of figs! For a very long time after that he had hated 'the Minns' with a vengeance.

Anthea watched her husband fondly for a moment as he concentrated on his breakfast, and then smiled at him reassuringly.

'Darling, I'm only telling you what she said,' she explained cheerfully, 'I'm not asking you to go. I don't want to go to Pengloss for Christmas any more than you do, in fact I can't think of anything worse. Supposing it rained every day, we'd go stark raving mad sitting there with nothing to do, and Peachy watching us from every flat surface in the room. Mind you,' she glanced at her son, 'no doubt James would like to go, given the opportunity, wouldn't you?'

'What? To Pengloss to spend Christmas with batty Aunt Bella?' James retorted. 'No thanks! Well, no thanks unless Aunty and Dorothea would be coming too, that is.'

Charles Webb-Goring turned on his son furiously. The idea of either of his family choosing to go to Cornwall for Christmas had filled him with horror, and now, relieved that they didn't want to, he could take refuge in a burst of anger.

'James, you are *not* to refer to your Aunt Bella as batty,' he snapped. 'It's very rude.'

'It's also very true, I'm afraid,' Anthea said cheerfully. 'But Daddy's right, darling, you shouldn't call her names . . . even if *he* does from time to time! She can't help being the way she is, you know, she used to be quite normal until Peachy disappeared and then Uncle David died. She's had an awful lot to put up with, one way and another.'

15

James piled scrambled eggs on to a piece of toast and began munching happily.

'I still don't want to go to Cornwall for Christmas though,' he observed. His mother smiled at him fondly.

'No, neither do I,' she agreed. 'Even though Aunty and Dorothea were invited too. We've already made our arrangements, so I think we'll stick to what we've got.'

She began a conversation with her husband about some Christmas party that was coming up and James, not remotely interested in grown-up talk, drifted back into his own thoughts as he nibbled round and round his toast. He was playing with his food again, but as neither of his parents seemed to notice he went on doing it and thought about Pengloss and batty Aunt Bella.

Pengloss was a centuries-old, romantically beautiful little manor house, all dark and mysterious with tiny windows and lots of dark wood panelling everywhere and it was a super house to play in, because it lent itself to enthusiastic fantasy games. Upstairs on the top floor there was a old nursery full of ancient toys which had been his Uncle David's, and there was a neat little schoolroom, too, but since David had been killed in the war James didn't remember him. He recognized him as a grown up only from the photographs Aunt Bella kept always on display. There were photos of Uncle David everywhere . . . and there were hundreds of photographs of the missing Peachy.

Charles finished his breakfast, gulped a last mouthful of tea, glanced at his watch and threw down his napkin.

'Got to go or I shall miss the London train,' he announced and bent to kiss his wife. 'Have a nice day, sweetheart,' he said and turned to James, 'and you, young man, do something constructive. Have a wash for a start, and then get some exercise. I don't want to hear that you've been goofing over your train-set all day. All right?'

'Bye, Daddy,' James replied happily and watched him go.

Anthea poured herself another cup of tea, and then folded her sister's letter between her fingers. Bella Rosenthal's handwriting was spiky and a bit strange. Witchlike, James had once unkindly suggested much to his mother's dismay. But James found it very hard to believe that Aunt Bella was only six years older than his mother. In fact it was hard to recognize them as sisters at all.

Anthea was so crisply neat and tidy with her short, fair hair and smart, expensive clothes, whilst Bella seemed so strangely ethereal with her long, dark hair, dark eyes and odd, flowing clothes.

It wasn't fair of David Rosenthal, James had once heard his mother remark, to set about getting himself killed in the Battle of Britain, leaving Bella to cope with the grief of their missing child and the grief of his death all by herself, and certainly Bella hadn't coped with it any too well. Over the years there had been a succession of mystics, mediums and fortune-tellers queuing up to part Bella from her money, and she had paid them handsomely to say what she wanted to hear. But if she still truly believed Peachy would one day come home, she was the only person who did.

Peachy had died, of that Charles and Anthea were certain. It would just be nice to know how he had died, and so far there hadn't been a single clue.

James looked at his mother steadily and suddenly he felt strangely guilty.

'Mummy, I'm sorry,' he said. 'I didn't mean to call Aunt Bella batty.' Anthea laughed at him fondly.

'Don't worry about it,' she replied. 'I've called her batty myself often enough. Well there have been times, let's face it, when she's been as mad as the first Mrs Rochester!'

'Yes, but since you and Aunty found Dorothea in that asylum,' James observed, 'she's actually been really nice and good fun.' He touched the edge of Bella's letter carefully with his fingers and conjured a picture of her sharply in his mind. No one ever talked much about the missing Peachy, and normally when he asked about him he was fobbed off, but he longed to put the facts together in his head. Well, no time like the present, he thought hopefully and murmured: 'Mummy, why was he called Peachy?' He waited. It was always gratifying to get a few nuggets of information, and now seemed a promising moment.

17

Normally Anthea would have said: 'Not now dear', and that would have been that, but this morning James thought she was feeling a bit guilty about not wanting to go to Pengloss for Christmas. And talking about Peachy just might make her feel better.

Taking a sip of her tea she smiled at her son.

'We found Dorothea in an orphanage, darling, not an asylum,' she corrected, and then stared at Bella's writing on the envelope beside her. 'Poor little Peachy,' she said, and James became very still in his chair, listening.

Anthea thought about Peachy, and thought about David and Bella, before the war, when their lives at Pengloss had been so idyllic. Handsome David Rosenthal; Anthea had envied her sister so much when she had become engaged to him. He had been tall and blond with a wonderfully clear skin; a dare-devil pilot who could have had the pick of any woman he wanted, and who really should have been a Hollywood actor, so marvellous were his looks.

She thought about their society wedding, with simply anybody who was anybody in attendance, and then she thought about the birth of Simon. The one child Bella would ever be allowed to have, for his birth almost killed her. Beautiful, smooth Simon.

'Your Uncle David nicknamed him Peachy,' she murmured, gazing at nothing in particular as she remembered the delicate baby in his mother's arms. 'When he saw him for the first time he said his skin was so pink and perfect that he was like a peach. He was really called Simon, but I'm not certain he ever knew that – well he was so small, wasn't he, when he . . .'

James pressed his lips together.

'Vanished?' he whispered.

She nodded.

'Oh God, five years old. He had such beautiful golden hair and great big blue eyes. He was overindulged, of course, and he might very well have grown into a monster, but then he was absolutely adorable. He went out into the garden to play with his ball one day in the summer of '39, and just . . . never came back.'

'But they looked for him?' James asked, trying to imagine how Peachy had disappeared from the grounds at Pengloss, since they were firmly fenced in. 'They did look for him – properly, I mean?'

Anthea shook her head at his innocence.

'Oh lord, they looked for him all right,' she replied. 'They searched in every conceivable place. For days and days. Everybody did. Bella and David and all the servants, all the gardeners and farm-hands, the police, everybody. Then a week later there was a ransom demand. A letter arrived addressed to David asking for a thousand pounds, and saying that if it was paid, they would be able to collect Peachy at a given time from a particular spot in the village. David did what he was told to do with the money, and they went in such excitement to collect Peachy . . . they stayed there all night, but he never came. No one ever claimed the ransom, either.'

James frowned. Rather unwillingly he thought about the photographs of the sunny, golden-haired Peachy scattered about Pengloss at every turn. It wasn't nice to think that Peachy was dead.

'So what do *you* think happened to him, Mummy?' he asked quietly.

His mother smiled very sadly.

'Goodness knows, James,' she replied. 'Your Aunt Bella has believed for years that the gypsies stole him, and that when he grows up he will somehow escape from them and return home in triumph, but let's face it, if he *is* still alive he's over twenty now. Anyway, gypsies don't go around the country stealing children – well they don't these days, anyway – and everyone knew there was going to be a war when Peachy vanished, so I doubt anyone was looking for an extra mouth to feed. I suppose the person who sent the ransom note had taken him, and killed him before the note was delivered . . . but . . . well the Rosenthal family are astonishingly rich; why only ask for a thousand pounds? Why not ask for ten thousand, or twenty?'

James stared at a spot of marmalade on the tablecloth and for a few seconds he let his mind flit about through gypsy caravans and swarthy men with red scarves on their heads and gold hoop earrings. Then he thought of Aunt Bella, of her strangeness and obvious loneliness, and he felt something which he thought might be anger. He actually liked her quite a lot nowadays, since he'd begun to grow up and she'd begun to be interested in him, and he felt resentful that someone had hurt her so much.

'David was devastated at the loss of his son,' Anthea continued, 'That's why they say that when fought in the Battle of Britain he simply didn't care if he died. He certainly earned himself a reputation for taking awful risks, and he'd shot down a record number of enemy planes before one finally shot him down. But his squadron always said he behaved as if life simply didn't matter. So Peachy was gone and David was dead – and that left Bella.'

'Poor Aunt Bella,' James murmured and was silent as the thought of her seemed to hang in the air around them.

'Poor Aunt Bella indeed,' Anthea agreed. 'But you're quite right about her. She has shown a huge improvement since Dorothea came into her life; fulfilling what David's parents always used to refer to as "their duty to the extended family of Pengloss". I just hope she doesn't imagine that the string of coincidences which brought Aunty and subsequently Dorothea into our lives won't suddenly bring Peachy back just as miraculously. Because believe me, James, he isn't coming back – I just wish his bones would turn up.'

James pressed his lips together tightly and gazed about the plush dining-room in which he sat, thinking as he often did about his long, long missing cousin.

'I wish I could find him, you know,' he stated. 'I wish I could make Aunty Bella happy.' To his surprise his mother bent and kissed him affectionately.

'Well, perhaps you should start looking within the pages of *Alice in Wonderland*,' she said softly. 'It was his favourite book in the world. Bella has a beautiful de luxe edition, all blue leather and gold tooling, which she and David gave him on his fifth birthday. She claims he could read it, but I imagine he needed some help, anyway he certainly knew the story inside out and backwards, poor little Peachy . . .' Abruptly she jerked herself out of her reverie, and smiled briskly at her son. 'Oh, enough,' she exclaimed. 'Aunty will be here soon. Go on, go and have a wash and clean your teeth. And don't forget your father's orders!'

Chapter 2

Arthur got lucky that evening, and needed something to brighten his day by the time he walked down Recreation Ground Road and entered the little all-purpose shop, Gregson's, on the corner. All day it had been damp and miserable, which had made the pre-Christmas shoppers he'd encountered during his working hours ill-tempered and fractious, and he was extremely glad to be home. The streetlamps made pools of light on the wet pavements and the rear lights of the occasional passing car reflected red. It was cold, and he was tired.

Gregson's smelt predominantly of cheese, with underlying smells of all sorts of other things: pepper, biscuits, un-smoked tobacco. After the continuing miserable hardships of the post-war years it was nice now that pretty much anything anyone wanted was on sale again, and as much of it as they cared to buy. Rosemary had come into the shop for bread and a packet of Players Weights cigarettes for her father, and was the only customer in the shop as he entered.

Arthur smoked Woodbines, and he had also come for cigarettes, but he had not expected to encounter Rosemary and felt his heart lurch with delight at the sight of her.

She was tall for her age though strictly still a child. She had narrow hips and long legs that promised to fill out into elegance, gorgeous almond-shaped eyes, and thick black hair that was cut to the level of her chin, parted on the left and held back from her face by a hairslide or sometimes a ribbon. In five years time she would be womanly . . . but Arthur wouldn't be interested in her then.

Her parents, Tim and Doreen, were justifiably proud of their one child, for she was not just pretty but clever as well, and at home she sometimes talked about being a doctor when she grew up. Tim regularly boasted about his daughter to bank customers; no empty headed aspirations to be a film star or an air-hostess for Rosemary, she wanted to be a doctor! A professional.

Arthur stood behind her in the shop. She wore a red coat and there were a couple of tiny mud splashes on her long white socks; when he moved a little closer he could smell medicated shampoo . . . and he could also feel the warmth of her. She was wheezing very softly, but everyone knew she suffered from asthma, and he supposed this cold, damp weather affected her. He would walk home with her in a minute, for he had to pass her house to reach his own.

When she had bought the items she required she turned and was faintly unnerved to find him standing so close to her. It made her take a small step backwards, but she still smiled at him.

'Hullo, Mr Johnson,' she said, gazing at him with her dark, beautiful eyes. 'Twice in one day. Have you had a good day?'

The Archers were very strict about their daughter's manners and Rosemary was always a credit to them.

'Very good indeed, thank you, dear,' Arthur lied. 'If you hang on just a moment I'll get my fags and walk back with you.' He looked up at Mrs Gregson, who was a hugely fat woman with a ferocious face, but who ran her shop with startling efficiency. 'Twenty Woodbine, if you wouldn't mind, please,' he said and handed her the money.

Rosemary was not that happy to walk home with him, and wished he wouldn't always find a reason to put his arm around her shoulders when they were alone, but she would never have dreamed of saying so. Outside, on the pavement, the drizzle was persistent, and the drops glistened in her dark hair. Arthur's hat, pulled forward slightly, showed dampness around the crown and the brim, his raincoat indicated that he had been outside for some little time, for the shoulders were quite dark with rain.

He lit a cigarette, cupping the match in his hands to keep it dry, and the child smelt the familiar whiff of tobacco smoke. For a fleeting second he eyed her over the top of his hands, then the match dropped and went out on the wet pavement.

'You know, you're such a pretty girl, Rosemary,' he observed as they began to walk up the road together. 'What do you want to be when you grow up?'

'A doctor,' she replied. He inclined his head, as if impressed.

'A doctor indeed. My, my, that's very ambitious.'

Rosemary smiled.

'Mummy and Daddy encourage me to be ambitious,' she said. 'I'm starting Guides just after Christmas, because I'm eleven in January.'

Arthur Johnson looked surprised.

'My word, it's a bus ride to Guides, isn't it?' he asked. 'Are your mummy and daddy happy to let you go on the bus on your own in the dark evenings? They must think you're very responsible.'

They were almost at the gate of Rosemary's house now. The porch light was on, and shone on the spot where her father's car would stand when he came home, and the windows of both the dining-room and the lounge were illuminated. The lounge curtains were closed, throwing out a rosy glow, but the dining-room curtains were still open and Doreen Archer could be seen laying the table for dinner.

It was very cosy and very suburban. The Archers enjoyed the space of three bedrooms. They ate dinner at 6.30 and always in the dining-room. There was no doubt that Doreen, anyway, considered them to be way above most of those who lived around them, and had Rosemary not been clever enough for the grammar school, she might well have bullied Tim into stretching their resources to the limit by finding a little private school for her, because her whole life revolved around their beautiful daughter.

Rosemary put her hand on the gate and had turned to say goodbye to Arthur when a coughing fit caught her and for a moment held her in its grip. Arthur watched her pull a hanky from her pocket and hold it against her mouth, looking at him all the time with her dark eyes as her shoulders shook with her coughing. His mouth was suddenly dry and he licked his lips. A tiny fragment of a fantasy licked like fire into his brain and was ferociously squeezed out.

'The damp and cold,' she whispered at last, tapping her fist against her wheezing chest. 'I must go in. Thank you, Mr Johnson, for walking me home. Only two more days of school now, before Christmas.'

Arthur threw down his cigarette and ground it beneath his foot, then he rubbed his hand across his mouth and smiled at the child.

'Shirley's after a walkie-talkie doll,' he observed with a smile. 'Very expensive they are too, I might say. So what are you hoping Father Christmas will bring you?'

'Mummy and Daddy are giving me a bike,' replied Rosemary seriously, and skipped up the little crazy-paving path to her front door.

Arthur pressed his fingers against his lips for a moment and closed his eyes as a warmth deep inside him made him forget the cold and the rain. He saw her for the last time with her mother framed above her in the open doorway and then she was inside in the warm and he was striding diagonally across Acacia Road on his way to Cheddar Close.

Two mornings later Aunty and Dorothea arrived at nine o'clock at Languard House, and James and Dorothea fell upon each other in great excitement.

It had been that way since the first time they had met; an extraordinary bonding between these two children from such vastly different backgrounds and, as it had turned out, it was a very satisfactory arrangement. To Dorothea, James's beautiful house always smelled rich and exotic; a mysterious mixture of leather, perfume, cigars and general affluence. Aunty's house usually smelled of Blackie's fish, but for all that Dorothea had honestly never envied James, nor ever lain in bed at night wishing that she could have a turn at living in Languard House. She was always delighted to visit, but home was Boxgrove Crescent.

'Mummy says,' James announced, leading her into the drawing-room where a large, bushy Christmas tree stood in the corner, bare and waiting to be glorified, 'that as it's raining, we can decorate the tree.'

The tree smelt deliciously resinous: that special Christmas smell which meant it would soon be the day and there would be presents. Anthea had left a couple of boxes of glass decorations on the table; they were old, pre-war baubles which had somehow, magically, survived the bombing, and they were all carefully wrapped in tissue paper.

Dorothea looked at them doubtfully and then looked up at the tree.

'Who's going to do the top branches?' she asked. 'We can't reach up there, not without something to stand on.'

Dorothea spoke very well, which sat at odds with her uncertain and occasionally brutal past, but was the legacy of her father, who had spent his life struggling to be an actor. When she and James were together they were often taken for brother and sister which pleased them hugely, but they weren't particularly interested in the mechanics of why. It was nice, Anthea thought; nice that they were too young to allow status, class and snobbery any place in their lives.

'Oh I'll stand on a dining-room chair,' James replied cheerfully, 'and you can hand them up to me, if you like.'

Aunty, who was still in the room, carefully shaking out Dorothea's little green coat, glared at both of them. It was a ferocious glare, but it didn't bother them. Aunty wasn't cross, just . . . Aunty.

'You just be careful with the decorations,' she warned balefully. 'I don't want to see no breakages, all right? You do a proper job between you, and when you comes to us for the weekend, James, you can help with ours, all right?'

'Oh yes please!' James shouted and Aunty allowed her lips merely to twitch with amusement as she carried Dorothea's outdoor clothes away. The next time the children saw her she was wrapped in a big white apron, polishing silver with such force that it wouldn't have dared not shine!

At Aunty's there were no glass baubles, it was do-it-yourself Christmas decorations: paper-chains, each link carefully glued together; and paper lanterns, painted with great care and then folded, cut and stuck together. Aunty's little front room was always a riot of coloured paper at Christmas.

The drawing-room at Languard House sported only the Christmas tree, and on the night before Christmas James's stocking would be hung by the fireplace and filled for the morning, with all the other presents beautifully wrapped and arranged beneath the tree.

James's enjoyment of Christmas Day was relative to how much he liked the presents he was given. Dorothea didn't care if Aunty didn't give her any presents at all, what really mattered was that she was warm, loved and well fed. The gulf between them was enormous, but neither of them cared about it, or even noticed it.

So on the following Saturday morning when James awoke he was in the place he liked best, the other twin bed in Dorothea's room. Dorothea was on his right, and between them stood a small brown locker on which was a very old-fashioned lamp. On the floor there was lino with a single, thin rug between the beds. The room was cold, but the children leapt out of bed without even noticing.

It was just a very few days to Christmas now: at last it was almost here. His mother and father were going to a huge evening-dress 'do' at the Dorchester Hotel that evening, and whilst his parents sped up to London in the Rolls, enveloped in a haze of Anthea's perfume, he would be sitting at the big old table in Aunty's front room, carefully choosing the colours for his paper-chains and lanterns. They would listen to the radio, there was bound to be a comedy programme, and they would stretch the paper-chains across the room, making a big starlike pattern from the centre light.

James knew where he'd rather be, and he was there!

Downstairs in the room below Aunty was moving about and listening to the news on the radio. James sat on the edge of his bed and looked across at Dorothea, and they both give little squeezes of excitement.

'Do you think Aunty'll give us a bath this evening?' he asked hopefully.

She grinned at him.

'I 'spect so,' she replied. 'I always get one on a Saturday. Wednesdays and Saturdays without fail and a wash in the kitchen sink on the other days. We'll ask her if we can go up the rec for a bit after breakfast, shall we? I haven't played on the swings for ages.'

The recreation ground was ten minutes walk from Aunty's, which gave them ten minutes to collect a crowd. And somehow they always did. Going to the rec was the local Saturday-morning pastime – as Arthur Johnson well knew.

'You can go to the swings till dinner-time,' Aunty told them, 'but I want you back here for twelve-thirty, sharp. And don't you be late!'

'Promise!' they retorted airily, and banged out into the street.

Outside Gregson's they encountered Rosemary, who said she would run her mother's shopping home and then join them at the swings. Then they met two more girls from Dorothea's school, and went into the rec by the bottom gate, racing each other across the field to see who could get to the swings first.

Ten minutes later Rosemary Archer came in at the top gate, with two local boys whom everyone liked.

Ten minutes after that, Arthur Johnson arrived.

Arthur had told Edith he was going to work, and Edith had smiled faintly and told him lunch would be at one. She, as usual, was running up little dresses on her sewing machine whilst his daughters played in the garden. He felt sure she knew he was lying to her, but the prospect of being in the house with her all day was suffocating and he had gone out simply to enjoy a walk. He had not intended to go to the swings, in fact he had told himself firmly that he wouldn't.

It was only when he'd seen Rosemary skipping down the street that he'd changed his mind. Well, he'd know perfectly well where she was going.

So James now had four female and two male companions in the playground and they were having a riotous time together. The boys spun the roundabout as fast as it would go whilst the girls hung on for dear life, all the time screaming at the tops of their voices; then they all grouped awkwardly at the top of the slide and came down together; and last of all James and the boys squashed into the front two places on the bouncy horse, pushing it down as hard as they could so that the back bounced upwards and the girls shrieked with delight.

Arthur stood outside the wire smoking a cigarette. Two girls sat astride the ends of the seesaw, bouncing up and down as it tipped backwards and forwards, their legs bare to their thighs and then . . . sometimes . . . higher. He watched firm, small bottoms sliding about on the horse, glimpsed white knickers as James spun the roundabout and the girls had to jump on. He smoked another cigarette, his hands thrust in his pockets as it hung from the corner of his mouth, and he made appreciative noises, laughing with the children – being like a father watching his children at play.

His mind: his feelings and emotions, they weren't watching children playing, and he itched to touch Rosemary's firm bare legs. She made him feel breathless, but he couldn't take his eyes off her and he didn't walk away when he knew he should have done. He stayed and stayed, unable to tear himself away as her beauty winged his imagination away into shameful fantasies. And he loved every minute of them.

In the end he didn't leave until the children did and then he walked back down the road with them to the little shop. He bought each of them a threepenny bag of sweets, and then, in pure delight, he walked along Acacia Road with Rosemary.

As James and Dorothea arrived home, Aunty's kitchen was hot and damp from the steak-and-kidney pudding steaming in the saucepan. She was mashing the potatoes as she told them to hang up their coats and wash their hands for lunch. As they did as they were told she saw them take their sweetie-bags from their pockets. Abruptly she stopped what she was doing.

'Where d'you get them sweets?' she demanded, her face red and shining from the heat of the kitchen.

James felt a tiny prick of unexplained guilt, as if he'd done something wrong. He said, uncomfortably:

'Er . . . Mr Johnson bought them for us.' He saw her frown.

It was a grown-up frown, like ones he occasionally saw on his mother's face but didn't understand. He had come to understand that they meant something significant that wouldn't be voiced out loud; only in his house they were usually to do with Aunt Bella. Clearly this one wasn't. Aunty went back to her potatoes.

'He was up at the swings, then?' she remarked. 'With Shirley, and the twins, was he? That'd be nice for them, I'm sure.'

Dorothea shrugged innocently.

'*He* was there,' she answered. 'He's often there, but not with the girls. He never lets his girls come up there, I think he thinks they're too young. He talks to us when we're playing.'

Aunty bit her lip and finished the potatoes. She appeared to be concentrating on getting the lunch to the table, but her body was tense and the children watched her warily. They knew there was something wrong, but they didn't know what.

'He don't go in, does he?' she asked at last. 'I mean, he always stands outside and watches you through the netting?'

'Oh always,' answered Dorothea. 'Well he's not allowed inside, is he, 'cos he's over twelve, an' it says on the notice that the swings are for under 12's only.'

Aunty nodded, accepting Dorothea's child's logic on that without comment.

'And has he ever bought you sweets before?' she enquired.

James and Dorothea shook their heads. Aunty lifted the bowl out of the steaming saucepan, ran a knife around the inside to loosen the suet crust, and then tipped the wonderful-smelling pudding on to the plate.

'Well, don't encourage him,' she said at last. 'If you want sweets you come to me, and if I can afford it I'll give you a few coppers, but if he wants t'buy you sweets again, you say no, all right?'

'Why?' Dorothea asked and then wished like mad that she hadn't.

For a moment there was a penetrating silence as they watched Edna thinking out her reply. It felt as if they were going to be in trouble, as if Aunty was going to be cross with them and not explain properly why, then abruptly she smiled and began piling mashed potato into a vegetable dish. In an unspoken way they knew the moment was past.

'Never mind why,' she replied cheerfully, 'just do as I say. Taking sweets off people . . . well it's charity, and I don't hold with charity. I buy you your sweets, not Shirley's father, all right?'

James and Dorothea dismissed Mr Johnson from their minds and followed Aunty to the lunch table.

They ate their sweets later while they were making their paper-chains, and by then they had pretty much forgotten who had bought them, but Edna Buddry hadn't. Edna had known Arthur Johnson ever since he had moved into the area and had never liked him. She liked Edith well enough and thought the three girls were both charming and pretty, but she'd never liked the look in Arthur's eyes, not where little girls were concerned. He couldn't be trusted, she felt certain, and she wasn't comfortable with him.

Had she known about Dorothea and Rosemary's morning rendezvous with him during term time she would have been extremely cross; and though the girls never said so out loud, it was for precisely that reason that they had never got around to mentioning it.

Sadly, though, it would have been Edna, not Doreen who would have expressed anger. Doreen was so busy with her ambitious longings for her daughter that she never looked closely at anyone else – especially not at anyone who had no prospects of being an influence on Rosemary's life. The Johnsons were socially inferior

– beyond that Doreen gave them no consideration.

On the other hand Edna, who had no social ambitions, paid considerable attention to everybody who touched Dorothea's life ... only by the time she came to consider deeply the fears she harboured it would, unfortunately, be too late.

Chapter 3

At lunch time on Christmas Eve a lonely figure wandered down Recreation Ground Road and turned into the rec. It was completely deserted, for it wasn't much of a day and apart from that it was Christmas Eve, and the local children were far to excited about the coming presents to want to be up at the swings.

The vagrant was a smallish, unkempt figure with ginger stubble on his chin and a very dirty army greatcoat on his back. He carried a knapsack which clinked as he walked, and having stolen a considerable number of bottles from a Christmas hamper left on a doorstep in Twickenham; now he was looking for somewhere to hole up for a few days and drink his haul at his leisure.

He passed the swings without interest and started along the little track that led into the copse, where he spotted the water board buildings and expertly kicked a hole in the fence which surrounded them, to get a better look. There were two buildings, one of which was obviously an old pumping-station and the other, apparently a brick hut. The hut looked promising, and fishing in his pocket he found a large screwdriver. Skilfully, he broke the padlock. Here was a perfect windproof retreat in which to get blind drunk.

Leaving his bottles then he went back on to the path and pushed his way into the allotments on the other side. Breaking into the sheds there was a simple matter, and after some moments he had helped himself to an old deckchair, two tins of spam left on a shelf, a number of candle-stubs and a rusty tin full of sixpences, three-penny bits, pennies and ha'pennies. Eight shillings and ninepence ha'penny in all. All he could wish for. An hour later he slouched into Gregson's and bought bread, cigarettes and matches.

Thelma Gregson frowned at him suspiciously as he paid for his purchases – apart from anything else he was stinking the shop out. He had rotten teeth and bad breath and the colour of his nails, as he slapped his money down on the counter, made her shudder.

She thought about asking him where he'd got his money from, and probably would have done had it not been Christmas Eve, for Thelma Gregson was ferociously community-minded; but she had last-minute orders to get out and then preparations to make for her own Christmas dinner, so in the end she hastened him out on to the street and forgot about him. It was only what he wanted, to be forgotten about. To be left in peace to get drunk. And he was confident he would be as he drifted back up Recreation Ground Road, because the only person he saw on his journey was a man in a mac and a felt hat, carrying a heavy case of some sort, and walking in the opposite direction.

They exchanged no greeting and the tramp didn't look behind him once as in the gathering gloom he headed back to his cheer-less little hut . . . so he was blissfully unaware that Arthur followed at a safe distance and saw exactly what he did.

And Arthur didn't forget about him. Arthur made a mental note not to forget.

On Christmas morning James leapt out of bed long before dawn and tore downstairs, minus his slippers and dressing-gown, to see what the day had come up with. It mattered greatly to him, because once lunch was over and the adults in his life were dozing in armchairs in front of the fire, he was expected to go away and play and not reappear before tea-time, so he needed plenty of new things to keep him occupied.

Beneath the glittering Christmas tree in the drawing-room there was an elegant pile of beautifully wrapped parcels. Judging by the shape and size of the ones labelled to him, there was new stuff for his railway and the much longed-for Bayko building set.

He was not allowed to open any of those presents until his

family were around, but his stocking, which he had carefully hung beside the fireplace the night before, was all his, and as he shook it on to the carpet out tumbled three Dinky-Toy army trucks, a small packet of soldiers, two tangerines and a handful of nuts. So it was set to be a good Christmas all in all, he thought, and settled down to play.

James was far and away the richest child locally, and almost certainly the loneliest on this day, but it was only what he was used to and he never thought about it.

Dorothea awoke about the same time as James, but she didn't go looking for presents, she crept into Aunty's bed for a cuddle. A familiar routine which they both very much enjoyed. Often the child would ask about her parents, and Aunty would tell her what she wanted to know – but always in such a way as to put them into the most favourable light possible. In fact Edna was still angry with her little brother for his pig-headedness, and always would be. She had been in service most of her life from the age of fifteen, and accepted it as the norm, but on that morning in the orphanage when she had first seen Dorothea, the child had been damp and pink-faced, and to her horror she had discovered her to be working in the laundry.

This beautiful little girl, working like a skivvy, at seven years old! Both Edna and Anthea had been scandalized, but the orphanage governess had seemed to be quite at ease with the situation.

Dorothea snuggled into Aunty's arms where it was warm and cosy, and Aunty brushed some strands of hair from her narrow forehead.

'You'm got some presents, my lover,' she murmured fondly. 'They're downstairs on the table if you wants to see them.'

Dorothea tightened her grip and settled more comfortably in the bed.

'Later,' she replied. 'It's warm here and I don't want to get up yet.'

Abruptly they both heard the sound of a cock crowing somewhere and Dorothea tensed. Many of the residents of Boxgrove Crescent kept a few chickens in their strips of back garden, and Aunty had been very quiet on the subject of Christmas lunch lately. This sounded like Charlie, but she couldn't be sure. . . .

'Aunty?' she said nervously at last, looking up into the big warm face, 'You never . . . did you?'

Edna burst out laughing and kissed her.

'No, I never!' she retorted. 'That's him bleddy crowing out there now; the only one in the street, and can't believe his luck. I went and bought us a chicken for Christmas dinner, 'cos I couldn't be doing with your threats, young lady!'

Dorothea squeezed her tightly with love and gratitude and then decided it was time to bounce out of bed. She would get dressed and go and give Charlie something really special, to celebrate Christmas.

Rosemary dressed carefully for Christmas Day. She had hung a pillow-case at the foot of her bed the night before, and had awoken early to find it full of brightly wrapped presents. There was a doll with hair that could be washed and styled, some lovely blue glass beads from an aunt, *Girl* and *Girl's Crystal* annuals and some bits and bobs for her doll's house, but the one present she really hoped for would be downstairs – if it had arrived.

The Archers went to church on Christmas morning, always. They went to church every Sunday and Rosemary was a leader in her Sunday-school class, but on Christmas morning there was no Sunday school, just wonderful carols to sing.

When she had politely asked permission she crept downstairs to the lounge and there it was. Leaning against the wall by the tree, a gleaming Raleigh girl's bike, painted green and with a lovely wicker basket on the front. Dressed in her new blue taffeta-and-velvet dress – which Mummy had bought her especially for Christmas Day – and wearing the blue beads she had received in her stocking, she touched the bike reverently and even sat on the seat for a few seconds; but she knew there wasn't any point in asking if she could go out on it, so she didn't.

Tomorrow, Boxing Day, then she would be allowed to ride her new bike.

On Christmas Day Doreen's parents and Tim's widowed mother always came for the day and Doreen served her Christmas meal at four in the afternoon, leaving the curtains open so that anyone passing could see them all sat neatly around the table, with space for everyone and matching glasses. Christmas for the Archers was about show and style, and only entirely dirt-free presents were allowed a place during the day, which did not include bicycles.

The Webb-Gorings, of course, didn't worry whether anyone saw them eating or not; didn't care about James going out on his bike, and went to sleep after lunch without any sort of feelings that they should be 'doing something special' because it was Christmas Day. Doreen Archer would never have understood their ways at all.

Arthur Johnson walked up to the rec in the afternoon, because he found his home stuffy and oppressive in an alarming sort of way. His girls were deeply involved with their presents, and with fires on in every room and having eaten far too much of the special lunch it had taken Edith an entire morning to produce, he needed space and fresh air.

He didn't like Christmas, and his discomfort with it went back to his childhood and his drunk and vicious father. He had known he wasn't welcome there; it certainly was not wise to stay around, and in consequence he had spent many Christmas Days wandering the streets with nothing to do. Now, although Edith was very careful never to say such a thing, he felt every bit as unwelcome in his present home, and the need to escape for a while was paramount.

Up at the rec the swings hung still and unused. Arthur poked a cigarette into his mouth as he passed them with only a glance. His interest was in the tramp and much to his satisfaction his nosiness was rewarded.

The man was relieving himself in a clump of horse chestnut trees that lay hard by the water board buildings, and since he was swaying dangerously as he peed, he was evidently pretty drunk. He didn't see Arthur, and tottered back into his little hut as soon as he had finished, but Arthur made a note of what he had seen and decided it might be a good idea to keep an eye on the situation. His thoughts were vague and fairly amorphous to begin with, but he was not very deeply into them before Rosemary surfaced and swam into his fantasy.

Maybe, just maybe, when the tramp was gone, the hut might come in useful, he thought. He smoked a second cigarette as he stood by some bushes, his mind drifting about amongst Rosemary's shiny black hair and almond eyes. She made him feel warm and he longed to catch a glimpse of her. He turned to go home as darkness was closing in at just before four o'clock . . . and then he waited in the shadows of Acacia Road, watching the Archer family take their places in their dining-room for Christmas dinner.

His heart beat tightly in his chest as he saw her lean across the table to kiss her granny, saw Doreen come triumphantly in with the turkey, and then saw the whole family fold their hands in brief prayer. He felt a spark deep inside him and abruptly hurried away.

Because he couldn't allow himself to analyse what he knew to be deeply wrong.

Rosemary had an asthma attack later in the evening and had to be calmed by her mother. Tim and Doreen had been told she would almost certainly grow out of it one day, but when she couldn't breathe her beautiful eyes became sharp with fear and Doreen was fiercely protective of her.

When at last her breathing became easier and her body began to relax she drifted off to sleep, and Doreen went back down to their visitors.

'Is she all right, darling?' Tim asked and the elegant, dark-haired, slender Doreen smiled and sat down beside her mother.

'She's fine,' she replied happily. 'She's sleeping now.' At once she began to wax lyrical on her favourite theme: the star that Rosemary would one day be. Finding a cure for asthma, perhaps, or winning a Nobel prize for medicine . . . no daydream was too high-flown for Doreen.

The others in the room eyed each other knowingly, and then patiently listened to her grandiose dreams. They were used to it. There was no doubt that Doreen was sniggered at by the people in the neighbourhood, but she wouldn't have cared even if she'd known, for Rosemary was the centre of her world, and her dreams were all part of it. Rosemary would go to grammar school, where she would mix with a much better class of girl. Then she would get invitations to tea with people who held positions of authority in the district, people who might even be able to guide her in her chosen career. And Doreen kept a spotless house, for Doreen would make the very most of return invitations.

Deep down inside, although she was inclined not to admit it, she disapproved of Rosemary's friendship with the skinny little Dorothea Sprake. All right, she was a nicely spoken child, and everyone knew Edna Buddry was a good woman, but she was not of Tim and Doreen's social set. Nevertheless Dorothea's little friend, James Webb-Goring was another matter altogether, and Doreen would have given anything for an introduction to the Webb-Gorings.

She found it hard to understand why they let the boy come to stay in Edna's council house so often, and why they didn't seem to mind him going up to the rec and playing with all the local children; she felt sure that if she had lived at Languard House she would have been much more careful in her choice of Rosemary's friends.

She watched the fire as she dreamed her familiar little dreams, and listened with half an ear to the conversation going on around her. She thought she might invite James and Dorothea round to tea the next time he was staying at Mrs Buddry's, and as she made her social-climbing little plans, she gazed at the expensive new bike they had given Rosemary for Christmas; standing exactly where they had left it last night, and still sporting the nice bow they had arranged on the handlebars.

Nothing was too good for Rosemary, she deserved only the best.

*

On the morning of Boxing Day, the obedient Rosemary was at last allowed to go out on the prized bike and being the generous little girl she was, she went straight round to Boxgrove Crescent, to offer to share it with her friend Dorothea.

Dorothea had read the two annuals Aunty had given her for Christmas (one of which was last year's and second hand), she had eaten the sweets she had found under the tree, sent with love from the cat Blackie, and she had played Chinese chequers during Christmas evening, gazing in delight at the fabulous box lid, with its huge, turbaned genie. Ranged on her bed were a collection of lovely clothes for her one beloved doll, and Charlie had nodded his beautiful head haughtily at her as she had whispered her love to him through the chicken wire. Now she was ready to use her big present.

The two little girls stood outside Aunty's council house and gazed at each other's spanking new bikes with awe. Rosemary's was green and Dorothea's was blue, other than that they were identical.

Anthea and Bella had bought Dorothea a bike because it was time she had one, and since Anthea would never have bought anything second hand, it was a brand-new one. Edna didn't allow herself to worry about the gifts the Webb-Gorings and Bella Rosenthal gave Dorothea, because there wasn't any point in worrying about something she couldn't afford herself. She just made sure Dorothea wrote the correct thank-you letters, and half-heartedly threatened her with the wrath of God if any of the gifts got damaged!

'How long can you stay out?' Dorothea asked, as the two girls gave little squeezes of excitement at the prospect of so much heaven-sent freedom.

'They never said,' Rosemary answered, 'so let's go!'

And they were off round Franklin Road and on up through the village, enjoying themselves enormously. Once or twice Dorothea thought of James, and felt a bit sorry for him because she knew he was being forced to go to a Christmas party in the afternoon and would have done anything to get out of it.

Had poor James known what the girls were up to he would have been furious! They were meeting friends and eating cake and sweets, whilst he, dressed in trousers, a white shirt and an extremely uncomfortable bow tie, was at the mercy of a suffocatingly attentive little girl called Camilla, who wore an extraordinary fluffy and beribboned yellow party-dress, and screamed all over him the entire afternoon.

In her company he was forced to play party games, expected to eat pink blancmange which he loathed and then be grateful for a highly unsuitable present, handed out by his host's father dressed in a Santa Claus outfit.

For him the afternoon seemed to go on for ever, but for Rosemary and Dorothea time sped by on wings, and before they knew it it was half past three, and subtly closing in towards evening.

'One more round before we go home?' Dorothea suggested as her cheeks glowed pink from the cold of the afternoon, and her breath came white and wispy from her lips.

'Let's go to the swings!' Rosemary shouted and they set off up Recreation Ground Road at full pelt, racing each other good naturedly.

Once there they stood their new bikes neatly against the chicken-wire fence, and then ran into the playground and leapt on to the swings. As they propelled themselves higher and higher they yelled to each other in delight; and the embers of the day grew colder. They screamed with laughter as they leapt off and then tore up the steps of the slide, coming down together, and then they jumped on to the roundabout and scraped their shoes on the Tarmac as they propelled it faster and faster.

Over in the gloom beneath the chestnut trees, the tramp stared across the grass at the swings in growing rage. He had finished his stolen drink that morning and was now shaking for more. His eyes were bloodshot, his head pounded unmercifully, he had no food left and he was cold.

He'd actually been dozing in the deckchair inside the hut when the girls had arrived at the swings, and the noise of their shrieking and shouting had penetrated not only the brick walls, but the deeper agonized recesses of his brain as well. Every squeal grated on his nerves like fingernails on a blackboard, and he watched them sourly, weighing up in his mind the pros and cons of scaring them off. If they ran home and told their parents, almost certainly the police would come looking for him and either arrest him or move him on, but the noise they were making was like an ever-present running sore, and nothing he did made any difference.

Finally a piercing shriek from Rosemary as the seesaw bounced her into the air crumbled his resolve, and kicking his way through the hedge he began to lurch towards them waving his arms in rage.

He was roaring and yelling insults as he stumbled towards them, and he was sharply black against the darkening red sky. When he reached the chicken wire he grasped it with his filthy hands and began to shake it furiously. Suddenly Rosemary and Dorothea were face to face with the stuff of their nightmares.

Scared out of their wits they began screaming again, but this time without the joy of play. They bruised their fingers wrenching back the bolt on the gate leading into the swings area and stumbled out in a panic, gaping at the tramp in terror as they grabbed their bikes with clumsy, shaking hands. Then they were gone, peddling furiously down Recreation Ground Road as if the hounds of hell were after them, never daring to look back despite the fact that at the speed they were going no one on foot could possibly have caught them.

Satisfied the tramp coughed thickly, spat a gob of sputum on to the path, paused to light the dog-end of a cigarette and turned back towards the hut, muttering to himself as he limped away. Now with any luck he could sleep off his hangover in peace, he thought bitterly, and kicking his way back on to the water board site he shuffled into the hut and banged the door shut behind him.

In the gloom, Arthur Johnson stood quite still, exactly where he had been standing for the past twenty minutes or so with his hands deeply thrust into his pockets. Hidden by a clump of bushes he had watched Rosemary Archer at play on the swings, lost in his delight, and the advent of the tramp had surprised him as much as it had surprised the girls.

Had he had any logical reason to be there, he thought, he might have intervened; as he gazed at the still gently moving swings, he told himself firmly that had the dirty little man actually laid a hand on either of the girls he would immediately have stepped in. Whether he would have done so was never to be known.

As it was he had rather enjoyed watching their fear – finding an odd extra thrill in it somewhere; but for all that it was time the tramp was gone. One or two more days, and if he was still there Arthur decided he would chase him off with threats of the police, because he couldn't risk the children avoiding the swings altogether.

Now he came out from behind his bush and lit another cigarette. He stuffed his hands back into his pockets and began to walk towards the road. It had been an unexpected and glorious surprise, Rosemary on the swings with Dorothea. It had quite made his Christmas!

Outside Rosemary's house the two little girls braked their bikes and skidded to a halt. They were wildly out of breath, and both cast terrified glances back up Recreation Ground Road, fully expecting to see their nightmare hot on their heels.

'Do we tell?' Dorothea whispered at last. Rosemary shook her head fiercely.

'Mummy'll never let me go out again if we do,' she replied. 'But we won't go up to the swings again for a while, just stay down this end, on our bikes, all right?'

Dorothea nodded.

'I know,' she said. 'James'll be coming to stay soon, and we'll go up there with him. If the man's still there then he'll chase him off. James is good at that.'

Rosemary nodded and the girls said goodbye, agreeing to meet again the following day. It was almost dark.

Doreen was very cross, and admonished her beautiful daughter for staying out so late, especially when Rosemary promptly had an asthma attack. Edna, on the other hand, was simply curious, for she could see Dorothea was afraid of something but was definitely inclined not to tell, so she said nothing. And the following afternoon it did not go unnoticed that both little girls were anxious to be on their bikes again, but were always close by whenever she glanced out. Evidently, wherever it was they had disappeared off to the previous day, they were not so keen to go there again, and Edna hoped that Dorothea would eventually want to tell her why.

In the meantime she simply kept a sharp eye on them . . . and wondered, half-guiltily, about Arthur Johnson. Well, they were safe enough for the moment at any rate, she thought as she watched them. But it was very difficult to get the man out of her mind, for all that, and she wondered uncomfortably if she was the only woman in the village who would have liked it very much indeed if the Johnsons were to move away.

Three days later Edna returned to work, and at last Dorothea could talk to James about the tramp. It was always possible to talk to James about anything, and for that she was grateful, for there were things grown-ups simply didn't understand, even Aunty – but she desperately needed to tell.

They lay on the floor in the attic of Languard House and played happily with James's wonderful train set. Built to cover most of the room, it had enough track to run five trains at once with stations and tunnels and a magnificent toy farm. Given a chance it was possible James would have spent the rest of his life routing and re-routing his trains, and though Dorothea never operated the switches, she adored the farm. Up there in the attic they were contented, occupied, and best of all, alone.

'But you never saw him before?' James asked when he had listened to her account of the Boxing Day encounter, and was not looking at her but concentrating on his switch-box. 'This tramp person. He's never been up there before?'

'Never,' Dorothea replied firmly, placing tiny sheep in a wooden pen and then moving the tractor up over the hill. 'He doesn't come from the village, that's for sure. And there's something else, too.' She glanced up nervously, lowering her voice. 'Mr Johnson was

44

there, James.' she whispered.

For a moment there was silence between them, then James halted one of his trains at a station, and looked across at her with a frown on his face.

'And he never did anything?' he said indignantly. 'You mean he was there when the bloke was shouting at you, and he didn't do anything about it?'

Dorothea shook her head and then bent her eyes to the farmyard. It was burned into her mind, just as it was, she knew, into Rosemary's, but she felt certain Rosemary hadn't seen Arthur. She'd only seen him briefly herself.

'He was behind the bushes at the side of the swings,' she murmured, 'and he was watching us. I knew he was there before the other man came, but I sort of forgot, I suppose, and I didn't think about him again until I was in bed that night. But he couldn't have gone away before we did, or else we'd have seen him, wouldn't we.'

James pulled himself up into a sitting position and allowed his trains to run round and round without stopping as he twisted his face crossly. He had been brought up with a strict code of rules, and one of those rules was that as a man it was his job to protect the ladies . . . in fact those were the very words his father used.

'You know something?' he declared at last. 'I don't think I like Mr Johnson.'

Dorothea widened her eyes at him and actually felt her face flush slightly.

'I didn't think you were allowed to say things like that,' she observed. 'I mean he's bought us sweets and things. I thought you had to like people like that.'

James shook his head slowly.

'Well, I remember Mummy once saying she didn't like someone,' he said, 'and Daddy said it wasn't fair, because he was a good man and gave lots of money to charity and so on, and Mummy said she didn't care, she still didn't like him – and that honesty was the best policy. So, I *can* not like Mr Johnson if I want to; it's allowed.'

Dorothea felt a strange wave of relief wash over her as she gazed in admiration at James. Whatever James's mother or father said it had to be right, because they were grown-ups, and important grown-ups at that.

'No,' she agreed, feeling a tiny thrill of wickedness at saying it, 'I don't like Mr Johnson, either, and I wish he wasn't Shirley's father, because I quite like Shirley. But I don't like him, and Rosemary doesn't either. She says she wishes he would leave us alone, and so do I. I just . . . I just *really* wish he would, that's all!'

When she and Aunty left Languard House that afternoon it was dark, cold and drizzly, and with the festivities over, there was a definite feeling of anti-climax creeping in. Dorothea was subdued, it was very noticeable, so when they got off the bus, they went into Gregson's to buy some tomato soup, which Aunty knew was her favourite thing in the world. Edna had had enough and she wanted the truth – and with any luck tomato soup would bring it forth.

The shop was warm and Dorothea breathed its familiar smell appreciatively. The enormous Thelma Gregson, vast behind her counter with arms akimbo, immediately unwrapped a penny bar of chocolate and handed it to the child and Dorothea thanked her as if it was the crown jewels. Dorothea was a particular favourite with Thelma Gregson mainly because she was so waiflike. The grown-up Gregson boys, Thelma's sons, were carbon copies of their mother – and Mr Gregson, who had died of a heart attack some years ago, had been like a barrel!

Dorothea ate her chocolate as Aunty and Mrs Gregson chatted, and was leaning against the counter, welcoming some sensation back into her feet and fingers, when the shop door clicked open to the familiar clank of the bell.

Unbelievably she saw the tramp!

He snatched up a loaf of bread and a tin of corned beef and slouched towards the counter, his foul smell creeping before him like an invisible cloud. Dorothea uttered a nightmarish little sound in her throat and threw herself against Aunty. Thelma Gregson pulled herself up to her full, vast size, staring at him ferociously.

'I hope you got the money to pay for that!' she snarled. 'I seen you in here before. Christmas Eve if I'm not mistaken, *an'* the day after Boxing Day. Well, I was too busy to watch you then, but you try stealing from me now and I'll 'ave the police on you.'

He sneered at her, showing rotten, blackened teeth and slapped his purchases on to the counter, enveloping everybody in his appalling stink.

'I got money, you fat old besom!' he retorted in a thick, Scottish accent. 'I'd no come in here if I hadnae, because I'd no get charity out o' *you*, I can see that.' Abruptly he stopped, gazing down at Dorothea who was clinging to Aunty and hopping from foot to foot in an agony of terror. 'And what's up with you, lassie?' he demanded sulkily, 'I've done nothing to you, I'm sure. Be still, for God's sake, you silly wee bairn!'

Edna pulled Dorothea tightly against her, and Thelma Gregson thrust out her hand to receive her money, but instead he threw it down, bouncing it all over the wooden counter-top contemptuously. Then he gathered up his bread and meat, swore violently and set off back towards the shop door, disappearing into the night.

Dorothea burst into tears and Edna and Thelma frowned at each other, recognizing an unspoken fear that needed to be shared. Thelma went to the door and flung it open, looking up and down the street carefully.

'He's gone, lovey,' she declared firmly. 'Quite gone, so you're safe. Just hold Aunty's hand and go home like a good girl . . . and Dorothea,' she touched the child's head with fat, soft fingers, 'be brave and tell whatever it is, eh? Much the best thing, I promise you.'

Dorothea was only too willing to tell now, because since Boxing Day she had been terrified to go outside after dark even to use the privy, and much too scared to go down the garden and close up the hen-house. She had hoped like mad that the tramp had gone, and had been devastated to find that he hadn't. Now she feared that he would never go away, and all this she told as tears trickled relentlessly down her cheeks.

Aunty took her on to her knee in front of the fire and cuddled her gently.

'You know what?' she whispered, nuzzling the side of
Dorothea's white face softly, as the fire crackled in the grate and
Blackie washed himself with concentrated care. 'He'm an old
soldier, that tramp, if I'm not much mistaken. Well, he'm wearing
a soldier's greatcoat, anyway, and army boots. I'm sure he did
frighten you and Rosemary, my love, but I don't think he'd've hurt
you, I really don't. In a way you has to feel sorry for people like
that, you know, 'cos I'll bet he lost everything during the war,
which is why he's on the wander now, but anyway, we'll nip in the
police station on the way to Languard House tomorrow morning,
and ask them to move him on, all right?'

Dorothea nodded gratefully and for a moment a deathly silence
hung between them, then a gust of wind sent a shower of raindrops spattering against the front window, and Dorothea pressed
her head against Edna's warm breast.

'Is there something else, sweetheart?' Edna asked very softly.

Dorothea closed her eyes and for the umpteenth time she
relived Rosemary's and her moments of terror in the playground
on Boxing Day. She saw the sky, coldly red as night closed in, and
she saw the sharp, black outline of the tramp clearly in her head.
And then she saw what Rosemary hadn't seen.

'Aunty,' she murmured, 'why do you think Mr Johnson didn't
do anything when the tramp was shouting at us? Why do you think
he just hid in the bushes? James says that it's a man's job to protect
girls.'

Edna pressed her lips together sharply, as her heart jolted in her
breast.

The following day, even before Edna and Dorothea called into the
local police station, the tramp wandered out of the village as
vaguely as he had wandered in on Christmas Eve. Arthur saw him
from the window of the bus, trudging along the Hampton Court
Road. Swiftly changing his plans for the day he bought a strong
padlock, made his way back to the water board buildings, cleared
out the worst of the tramp's unspeakable rubbish and sealed the
door.

When a police constable collected the key to the gate from the water board and went up there himself mid-morning, he found no sign of damage, and both buildings securely locked. Had he tried the key to the padlock, of course, he would have found it didn't fit. But he didn't.

So Arthur had a secret place known only to him, and no one else paid any more attention to the water board buildings than they ever had done in the past.

Chapter 4

'It's frightfully nice of this . . .' Anthea Webb-Goring glanced down at the letter in her hand to see the name, 'Mrs Archer, to invite James to her daughter's birthday party, Mrs B.' she said, ' I assume this is Dorothea's little school-friend, the one he talks about sometimes?'

They were enjoying morning coffee in the kitchen with Mrs Minns, and January would be giving way to February in the not too distant future. Rosemary was about to become eleven and Doreen was planning her birthday party as if it were a top-hat-and-tails wedding.

Tim had been a little embarrassed at Doreen's insistence on James being invited, and vaguely wondered if Rosemary had any notion of how pushy her mother could be when the mood took her, but Rosemary liked James very much and was happy to invite him. Besides, Dorothea had promised that James would make the rec safe for them to ride their bikes on again – unbeknown to Doreen or Tim.

Edna sipped her coffee and smiled at the invitation Anthea held in her hand. Written, she noticed, by Doreen herself. No doubt Rosemary had been expected to write the less important invitations!

'Nice little girl, Rosemary,' she replied, 'she'll go to the grammar school with Dorothea after they finish at Franklin Road juniors. I'm not so sure about Doreen, though, she'm got airs well above her station. I've known young Tim since he was a lad and he's bright enough, but he'm ent never going to set the world on fire, no matter what she wants.' She paused for a moment, then added cheerfully, 'Rosemary might though, if she ever escapes from her mother's social climbing!'

Anthea cast her eyes upwards.

'Oh lord, is that why she's asked James to her daughter's party?' she said and Edna chuckled softly.

'It's why Doreen's asked James, yes,' she answered bluntly, 'but not why Rosemary has. Rosemary likes James very much and he likes her an' all. The three of them spends a lot of time together when he comes to stay. I'd not be surprised if Rosemary finishes up doing very nicely for herself in the end, you know.'

Anthea poured them all a second cup of coffee.

'Dorothea must be in need of a new party frock by now, Mrs B,' she said thoughtfully. 'She has to have grown out of the last one Bella bought her.'

Edna wrinkled her nose uncomfortably.

Occasionally she felt slightly embarrassed by Bella Rosenthal's generosity, especially when it came to frivolous items, like party-dresses. Her inbuilt thrift rejected the need for them, however hard she tried.

'Oh I'll find somethin',' she said dismissively. 'Crikey, kids grow at such a rate these days, and Dorothea don't go to parties for a pastime. A party-frock is a bit of a waste of money I think.'

Anthea smiled without the least hint of patronage.

'Yes, but I don't,' she replied. 'In fact I've still got to get her a really decent Christmas present myself, so I don't want to hear any argument. I was planning to take her shopping sometime, so I shall pick her up on Saturday morning and take both the children to Kingston for the day. I've got shirts and things to get for James as it is, and he'll be much better behaved if he's got Dorothea for company, believe me!'

James said 'Shopping!' and gazed through the dining-room windows at the rain pouring down in the garden. 'But it's Saturday! Oh no, please, not shopping. I wanted to paint some soldiers today.'

Anthea sipped her breakfast tea and glanced at her son unemotionally. Charles, who had been going to play golf, but could see for himself that it wasn't going to be possible, looked up at his son sharply.

'James, I will not have whining!' he declared. 'I was looking forward to a round of golf this morning, but I'm not whining, am I? Now you're going shopping with your mother, and I don't want to hear any more about it.'

James blew an angry grunt through his nose and stared down at his boiled egg. He didn't fancy it any longer, in fact the only thing he fancied doing was going away and having a good sulk, then his mother coughed slightly and he glanced up at her from beneath his brows.

'I thought,' she said with calculated indifference, 'that we'd take Dorothea with us. I also thought we'd have lunch at Zeeta's on the bridge – as a treat if you fancied it. But of course if you'd rather stay here, I'll have to take Dorothea on her own, won't I?'

At once James's whole perception of the shopping-trip changed and he settled down to his boiled egg happily.

Dorothea was thrilled to bits. She loved going to Bentalls, she was going to get a party-frock, and then they were going to have lunch at Zeeta's, and it didn't matter how much it was raining, because the day was absolutely perfect.

'Now listen, young lady,' Aunty said as they sat at the table together and watched the rain through the front window, 'whatever Mrs Webb-Goring wants to buy you, you don't pass comment on it, all right? You say thank you and that's all. Don't you start saying you likes something else better – and if she asks you to make a choice, don't go picking the most expensive one.'

Dorothea nodded, packing the orders into her head and hoping like mad that she would remember them all. She was to say thank you every time Anthea spoke to her, she wasn't to run ahead or lag behind, wasn't to express any preference for lunch but eat whatever she was given and now had to be careful about the new frock. It was very bewildering, but it didn't stop her being excited.

When Anthea's car purred around the crescent and stopped

outside Aunty's front door, Doreen and Rosemary were just coming round the corner on their way to the bus stop. Doreen looked enviously at Dorothea climbing into the sleek, black Rover.

Dorothea didn't notice though, and fell excitedly upon James. She went very rarely to Kingston, and had never been to London in her life, despite living less than twenty miles away, but to her London couldn't be more wonderful than Kingston, and nothing could be more wonderful than Bentalls.

There was a sort of special smell as they walked through the heavy glass doors into the store, a heady mixture of expensive perfumes and new goods, and there, beyond the perfumery, were the escalators, beneath a coloured glass roof. Oh it was heaven, Dorothea thought, and was happy to hold James's hand and follow behind his mother because it meant she could concentrate on the beauty around her.

The first thing Anthea decided upon was a new pair of shoes. Something pretty but practical she thought. In the shoe department the assistant measured Dorothea's feet, and went off to get a selection of shoes, whilst Dorothea slipped on a pair of long white socks. The woman brought back some silver pumps and some white sandals, but she also brought the most beautiful pair of black patent-leather buckle shoes Dorothea had ever seen, and Anthea didn't have to ask, the look on the child's face said it all.

'And so much more practical than those silver ones,' Anthea observed, as the assistant went away to wrap them, 'You can have a pair of silver shoes when you grow up, can't you. I know they're a little bit too big, but we'll put an innersole in them for a while, then they should last you at least until after the summer.'

After the shoes it was the dress department and there, hung on the rails, was a bewildering and seemingly endless selection of pretty dresses. Anthea began to go through them with a practised eye, and much to her surprise, James was as good as gold; didn't complain, didn't fidget, didn't let go of Dorothea's hand and even seemed vaguely interested.

Anthea took down a blue taffeta-and-velvet dress and for the first time for ages Dorothea spoke.

Very quietly, almost apologetically, she whispered:

'That's the same as Rosemary's got.'

Anthea burst out laughing.

'Lord, that wouldn't be very tactful, would it?' she exclaimed. 'To turn up in the same dress as the hostess!' She pushed the dress back onto the rail. 'Heavens, what a *faux pas* . . .' Abruptly she stopped and closed her hand over a coat-hanger. 'Oh, now what about this,' she said in a voice of great approval. 'This is lovely. I mean, it's not a typical party-dress, but think how often you could wear it in the summer at Pengloss.'

The dress, of starched and crisp cotton, sported a pattern of very thin maroon stripes, and had a white, embroidered collar and a sash of dark-red taffeta. Abruptly Dorothea had a vision of herself in the dress, with her new black shoes, and put out her hand towards it in delight.

Anthea Webb-Goring smiled gently.

'You have very good taste, Dorothea,' she said. 'And what do you think, James?'

'I think it's heaps nicer than that blue velvet thing,' James replied honestly, 'and heaps and heaps nicer than that yellow thing Camilla was wearing at that stupid party on Boxing Day. She looked like a cake!'

Dorothea did look very nice in the dress. It was slightly on the big side, and since as yet she had shown no inclination to grow like a weed it would certainly last her through the summer. Neatly wrapped in tissue paper it was placed in a stiff, shiny-paper carrier-bag with Bentalls on it, and Anthea gave it to her to hold. New dress, new shoes, Dorothea was floating on a wave of happiness. Anthea went away then to buy some shirts for James, and James and Dorothea wandered through the children's department towards the stairs, to wait as they had been told.

They stopped by the door with the sound of shoppers' feet echoing as they came and went on the cavernous stone stairway, and watched people milling about. They were opposite the counter where winter accessories were on display, and amongst the other shoppers there was a tall man in a raincoat, fingering a red knitted wool scarf with large white flowers on it. It was a very pretty item, and the assistant showed him that it came with matching gloves.

Dorothea stared at the man in vague discomfort. She knew perfectly well who he was. She watched as he bought the scarf and gloves and then folded the little parcel to slip it into his coat pocket, and the tightness of her hand around his alerted James to her discomfort.

The man turned.

Arthur looked into the children's faces and for a few seconds he didn't see them. Dorothea's eyes were wide and dark and she was completely unable to tear them from his face, then recognition dawned in his eyes and he should have spoken to them. But he didn't. He pulled his hat down to partially cover his face, thrust his hands in his pockets and walked quickly past them on to the stairs, where he rapidly disappeared from view.

'That was a bit strange,' James murmured, frowning after him. 'Why d'you think he didn't say hello?'

'P'raps he didn't want us to see him?' Dorothea murmured. She heard the glass door on the floor beneath swing open and then shut behind him. 'Do you think we should tell someone?' she asked doubtfully and James stared at her, confused.

'There's nothing to tell,' he answered frankly. ' 'Cept that he's very rude!'

Arthur thrust himself through the store towards the escalators and the ground floor, feeling his face burning like a sky-sign. Damn those children, why of all people had they had to be standing there just then? He had felt warm, submerged in his dream as he had purchased the gloves and scarf. He had imagined giving them to Rosemary, and she looking shyly delighted . . . giving him a little kiss perhaps. . . . God dammit, and then to turn round and find that wretched little orphaned niece of Edna Buddry's watching him!

Arthur knew Edna didn't trust him, he'd seen it in her eyes. Something deeply knowing which had left him in no doubt that his soul was laid bare to her, and she knew him for what he was. And now, as he burst out into the miserable January day, he hated James and Dorothea. Hated them for spoiling his moment; for no matter how briefly, making him face himself. His day was ruined and with his lovely present weighing guiltily in his pocket, he trudged angrily towards the bus stop.

When James and Dorothea left Bentalls they had forgotten Arthur and went eagerly to lunch at Zeeta's restaurant on the bridge. After lunch Anthea did some personal shopping, during which James fidgeted most of the time, and finally they popped back into Bentalls on their way to the carpark, to buy a birthday present for Rosemary. Anthea chose a white, leather jewellery box which, when the lid was raised, tinkled out the waltz from *Swan Lake* as a pretty ballet dancer dipped and spun on a spindle in the centre.

'I thought that might do from both of you,' she observed.

James shrugged and blew out a sigh. It wasn't something *he'd* ever want as a birthday present. Dorothea gazed at it in such awe, however, that after telling the children to start off through the shop towards the carpark, Anthea secretly bought two, one to put away for Dorothea.

That night, in bed, after Aunty had been up kissed them goodnight and switched out the light, James and Dorothea whispered about Arthur, and both suddenly remembered how strange he had looked when he had seen them.

'I s'pose,' James said, 'it's not really our business, as Mummy would say, but I thought he looked funny when he recognized us. Mummy says there's a special way you look when you're guilty; she says she can always tell when I've been pinching biscuits from the larder.'

'But what would be have to be guilty about?' Dorothea wondered. 'Unless he didn't want us to see him buying the scarf and gloves. It couldn't have been for one of the girls, because Mrs Johnson always dresses them the same, so I wonder who it was for? Rosemary, p'raps, for her birthday? But why would he be giving Rosemary a birthday present? Shirley won't be coming to the party, she's only eight.'

However on the following Tuesday morning, their first day back at school, all that changed, because Rosemary and Dorothea were a few minutes early at the corner of Acacia Road, and Dorothea was busy passing on all the information about the weekend as Arthur and Shirley came down to meet them.

Arthur saw the two girls whispering together as they stood waiting, and suffered a stab of paranoia. What if they were talking about him? What if the wretched Sprake child was being spiteful about him buying goods on the children's counter in Bentalls?

He had put his purchase away carefully, hidden from Edith, in a big wooden box in the water board hut which he had now furnished with a table and another chair. On Sunday afternoon, all alone in his special place, he had looked at it again and dreamed of Rosemary smiling and saying thank you ... dreamed of touching her ... dreamed of being gentle and promising not to hurt her. Now he found himself angry, partly at the girls and partly at himself, and he knew he had to know what they were talking about.

'Whisper, whisper,' he said with a nasty, forced brightness as he came alongside them. 'What little girls' secrets are you telling each other, then? Want to share, do you?'

Rosemary blushed brightly and looked distinctly frightened. Dorothea felt herself shrink, as if she expected to be punished for something.

'We were just talking about my birthday party, Mr Johnson,' Rosemary murmured almost apologetically, for all the world as if she was guilty of something, which, of course, she wasn't. 'It's this Saturday and we're having a conjurer,' she added, and then realized what she had said. Golden-haired, doll-faced little Shirley was gazing up at her longingly.

Rosemary was an inherently nice child and hated hurting anyone. Even as she stood there, staring at Shirley and her father, she knew she had dug herself into a pit, and that there was only one way out of it – though she dreaded her mother's reaction.

'Would you like to come to my party, Shirley?' she asked, smiling. 'I'm sure Mummy would be delighted if you could.'

Shirley gazed up at her in adoration, her pretty little face a picture of humble delight. It made it worse somehow, because the two older girls had no understanding of the discomfort they felt, or of the look on Arthur's face. Rosemary was sure Doreen would be far from delighted, but it was too late now, and as Shirley skipped away from them across the school playground a few moments later, Dorothea pulled a face.

'What d'you do that for?' she demanded. 'She's only eight!'

'Well I didn't have much choice, did I?' Rosemary replied miserably. 'I couldn't say I was having a party and then not invite her, and now I have to tell Mummy, and she'll be furious with me. Oh I do *wish* Mr Johnson hadn't asked us to walk Shirley along Franklin Road in the mornings, don't you?'

'Or I wish we'd said we weren't allowed,' Dorothea retorted unhappily. 'I wish we'd said that.'

But Doreen wasn't furious at all. Doreen lived in a small, tight world that centred around Rosemary and Tim, and paid little or no attention to what went on anywhere else in the neighbourhood. She was happy enough for Shirley Johnson to come to the party, she was a polite little girl and very pretty. She had never given Arthur so much as a passing thought – and she knew nothing about her daughter's morning rendezvous with the man.

When Rosemary confessed it, because at that point she couldn't very well not, Doreen replied that it was very sensible of Mr Johnson to want a couple of older girls to see his little daughter into school each morning, and promptly dismissed it from her mind. In fact she was very proud that Arthur Johnson obviously considered Rosemary to be sensible enough to be entrusted with his daughter, and she never thought about it again.

On the morning of Rosemary's party, Doreen was almost as excited about James coming as Rosemary was about the conjurer. He was, James discovered to his horror on arrival, the only boy at the party, but fortunately for him there were no little girls like the ghastly Camilla from the Christmas party at Rosemary's; all her friends were Dorothea's friends as well, and James liked them very much.

He didn't much care, however, for the way in which Doreen seemed to fall upon him as he came through the door. He contrived to shake hands keeping a rigid distance between them.

'I don't normally go to girls' parties, you know,' he announced seriously, 'but I've made an exception for Rosemary, because we're close acquaintances.'

It was a wonderfully pompous little phrase and anyone else would have had trouble holding back their laughter. Doreen, however, was highly impressed.

'You see,' she murmured to Tim a little later, 'that's what a public school education does for you. Oh, I *wish* we could afford to send Rosemary.'

Tim Archer smiled patiently.

'I think it's more likely he was aping his father, actually,' he observed quietly. 'But he is a nice little boy, I grant you that.'

Dorothea had never felt quite so much the centre of attention as she did at Rosemary's party being the only girl in the room to have a male escort. Doreen complimented her at one point on her dress, and she was so proud to say it had come from Bentalls, because she knew Rosemary's dress had come from Bentalls as well.

After tea a conjurer entertained them for an hour, then Rosemary opened her presents. Anthea's choice of the musical jewellery box was a fabulous success – both with Rosemary and with her mother, but James and Dorothea were astonished to find that Shirley Johnson's present to Rosemary was a post office set. Not a sign anywhere of the scarf and gloves.

That night Rosemary put her blue beads and the little silver bracelet her grandma and granddad had given her for her birthday into her new jewellery box, watching the dancer spin to the music, reflected in a mirror inside the lid. The box smelt of leather, and was lined with red velvet. It was a handsome present and she was thrilled with it.

She touched it with her fingers as her mother said goodnight to her, and murmured how much she liked it. Tomorrow, Doreen decided, she would have Rosemary write a careful thank-you note to Anthea Webb-Goring – and then, with any luck, Rosemary would get an invitation to a party at Languard House some day.

Doreen left her excited and very tired daughter and went downstairs as her mind spun through one of her familiar fantasies. A boy like James as a husband for Rosemary . . . a huge top-hat-and-tails wedding with simply hundreds of people . . . surely it would be the culmination of all her hopes and dreams. Doreen's whole world revolved around Rosemary, like the spindle upon which the tiny dancer bobbed in the white box – and the dancer would dance for ever when the lid was open, unless the spindle ever got broken. . . .

Rosemary went to Guides for the first time a week after her birthday. She looked very smart in her new Girl Guide uniform, and paraded herself obediently before her mother before she went. Suddenly she was growing up, Doreen thought, and was so proud of her. Nevertheless she petted and fussed, as the doe-like Rosemary obediently accepted the attention, as was her lot in life.

'Now remember,' Doreen said, 'you leave immediately it's over and go straight to the bus stop, and you're to get off at the top of Recreation Ground Road, cross over and walk home without stopping. And you don't talk to anybody on the bus, all right?'

Rosemary nodded and watched her mother press her lips together thoughtfully. Then came what she had expected.

'Oh I don't know, I think perhaps I ought to ask Daddy to come and collect you, I do really.'

'Oh no, please!' Rosemary cried. 'Let me come home on the bus, Mummy. I'll be good, I promise I will.'

Doreen mused as Rosemary waited desperately, then relented.

'Oh, all right,' she agreed. 'We'll see how long it takes this first time, but if I'm not happy with it you'll have to agree to Daddy picking you up – or you won't be allowed to go until the light evenings come.'

Rosemary went off to Guides full of excitement.

Dorothea sat curled up in one of the two armchairs in front of Aunty's tiled fireplace and thought with a faint envy of her friend. Guides sounded so much more sophisticated than Brownies, and

Brownies wasn't going to be so much fun now, either, with Rosemary gone, but she wouldn't be able to go until after the summer, and she had to put up with it.

Supper and homework out of the way, she and Aunty listened to an episode of *The Clitheroe Kid* on the radio, then Aunty read to her from a lovely, fat book of stories which had once been James's, and which he had lovingly given her. After that they had a mug of cocoa each, and Dorothea, yawning widely, trailed away to bed. She was often tired by the end of a day at school, but even if she wasn't she never minded going to bed, for she still revelled in a bedroom of her own. Okay, it might not always have been terribly warm, but it was dry and cosy and most of all, it was hers.

At the orphanage she had shared a dormitory with twenty-nine other girls; a huge attic room with a great arched ceiling and windows so high up in the walls that seeing anything other than a patch of sky through them was impossible. In the months before that, trying to sleep at all had been a nightmare. Living with her desperately sick father in a room with water running down walls and stinking black patches of damp, bedclothes at best musty, at worst, sopping . . . it was hard to even think about that room. But she did think about it often, usually as she waited for Aunty to come up and kiss her goodnight and she snuggled down in her little bed, enveloped in safety.

Rosemary was just getting on the bus to come home as Dorothea went upstairs. She had had a splendid time at Guides; had been complimented by her leader on her appearance and her enthusiasm, and couldn't wait to get home to tell her parents. Arthur had got on the bus about three stops before, cold and weary from a hard day's work, and was astonished to see her waiting in the queue. His heart lurched uncomfortably in his chest as he watched her, and he turned in his seat as she climbed on, raising his hand so that she should see him.

'Here, dear,' he called, 'there's a seat beside me.'

Rosemary was horrified, but she was much too young to know how to deal with such a situation, and politely sat beside him, trying hard to appear friendly. At once he was aware of her long white socks and smooth, firm legs, then of her almond eyes and her rich, dark hair. The bus smelled of stale cigarettes, but she was fresh, sitting in the seat beside him, and he longed to touch her.

'Did you have a good time at Guides, then?' he asked, and watched as she handed over her bus fare to the conductress.

'It was lovely, thanks,' she replied enthusiastically. 'I can't wait for next week.'

Arthur nodded. On the floor between his feet was his sample case and suddenly he leaned forwards, snapped it open and took out a tube of mixed-fruit Spangles. Spangles cost more than most of the local children could afford with their tuppence or three-pence pocket-money, so they were a treat, and much appreciated.

'Sweetie, dear,' he said, offering them to her, and when they had both taken one, he cheerfully dropped the packet into her lap. 'There, you have them,' he said with a smile. 'Take them to school with you tomorrow and share them with your friends.'

Rosemary gulped and felt her face flood with colour.

'Oh, I shouldn't, Mr Johnson. . .' she began, but he waved aside her protests.

'Nonsense,' he replied, 'your mummy won't mind you taking a packet of sweets from me.' He chuckled. 'It isn't as if we're strangers, now is it? And talking of strangers, where do you plan to get off the bus?' Reluctantly she told him and he nodded. 'Then I'll get off there with you,' he announced. 'See you home safely. Well I'm sure you wouldn't want to run into someone like that drunken old tramp again, would you?'

Surprised, she turned her head and blinked at him, and Arthur realized he'd made a mistake. He thought the girls had seen him on Boxing Day; he was certain little Dorothea Sprake had, but obviously Rosemary hadn't and now he'd frightened her, which was the last thing he'd wanted to do. With a calculated air of absence he put his hand on her knee and patted it.

'Oh he's long gone,' he assured her, smiling. 'Long gone, I promise you. The only reason I know he frightened you was because I happened to be walking down the lane beside the allot-ments that day, and I saw him shouting at you. I'd have driven him off, but you and Dorothea had already scarpered by the time I got there. Anyway, I followed him and told him that if he didn't sling his hook I'd report him to the police. He'd gone within a few days.'

Rosemary looked down at his hand, still resting lightly on her knee. She did vaguely wonder why on earth he should have been on the path between the rec and the allotments on Boxing Day, but she wouldn't have dreamed of asking, and she submitted to his arm across her shoulder as he walked her down Recreation Ground Road twenty minutes later because she had no idea how *not* to. He gave her a little squeeze as he said goodbye and she hated it, but it served to seal her mouth shut, because it stopped her telling Tim and Doreen anything about his being on the bus with her. And she definitely didn't mention the Spangles.

Arthur didn't tell Edith about Rosemary, either. She was sitting in their tiny front room knitting a red jumper for one of the girls when he came in, and as she looked up her never terribly animated face seemed even blanker than usual.

'I kept your dinner warm,' she said. 'It's in the oven.'

He thanked her and went obediently into their sterile kitchen, and suddenly life seemed to stretch out in front of him like an empty corridor. He watched her as she served his dinner, and listened to her dreary conversation as he ate, and suddenly his heart cried out for freedom . . . or perhaps not freedom so much as a chance to go back and do things differently. He wished desperately for his life to change. And that night in bed he gave free rein to his fantasies, sneaking off to the bathroom to finish them by himself. He dreamed of Rosemary in his sleep, dreamed of her almond-shaped eyes gazing at him with confident assurance; and in his dreams he hugged her close. . . .

The following morning at break-time, Rosemary and Dorothea collected their bottles of milk from the milk-monitor and went away into a corner of the playground together, where Rosemary took the packet of Spangles from her coat pocket.

'Oo, where d'you get them?' Dorothea asked, gratefully accepting one.

Rosemary pressed her lips together and glancing around her as if she thought they might be overheard, she fingered the tube of sweets uncomfortably.

'Mr Johnson gave them me,' she murmured eventually, and told Dorothea the story.

It was February and the day was cold, the sky above them was grey and school lunch today was mince, mash and cabbage. The two little girls gazed at each other and then leaned against the school wall and watched their fellow pupils doing all the different things they did in the grey playground. But they saw nothing except the spectre of Arthur in their minds.

'Aunty says I'm not to take sweets from Mr Johnson any more, even if he is Shirley's father,' Dorothea said at length. 'I don't think she likes him . . . and neither do me and James much. I wouldn't've come home on the bus with him, if I was you.'

Rosemary shrugged her shoulders in defeat.

'Well I couldn't help it, could I,' she answered. 'I didn't see him till I was already on; and anyway, I wouldn't have dared get off to wait for the next one, Mummy would have been furious if I'd been twenty minutes late.' She stopped, and for some moments they sucked at their milk through paper straws, aware of the strange mixture of milk and orange sweets in their mouths. Then Rosemary glanced at her friend and her beautiful eyes were troubled. 'I don't like him, Dorothea,' she whispered, 'I don't like the way he looks at me, and he's always touching me – like – well – like putting his hand on my shoulder, or on my knee. I feel really mean, because he's Shirley's father, but I hate it when I see him in the shop or anything, because I know he'll put his arm round me, and I don't want him to.'

'Should I tell Aunty?' Dorothea asked, but Rosemary shook her head.

'No!' she said firmly, and then added quietly: 'Well, it's silly, isn't it, and anyway if Aunty says anything to Mummy, I'll only be allowed to go to Guides when Daddy can drive me.'

The bell for the end of break sounded and Rosemary broke the packet of Spangles in two and gave half to Dorothea, then they put their empty milk bottles into the crate by the door and went back to lessons.

But it was a dilemma, and they knew it wouldn't go away.

Chapter 5

There was a bitter cold snap at the end of February, which disrupted the Guides meeting on the fourth occasion Rosemary went because the heaters were faulty in the hall, and by six-thirty it was much too cold to go on. The meeting was abandoned, and Rosemary went out to the bus stop muffled in hat, coat, gloves and scarf, to catch an earlier bus. She wore long, thick, navy stockings and held her scarf across her mouth, and she was pleased because catching the earlier bus would mean Arthur wouldn't be on it. Or so she thought.

Arthur had thought he wouldn't see her that evening, either. In fact he'd even contemplated getting off the early bus and waiting for the next one so as to be sure he didn't miss her, but in the end he hadn't, and his heart lurched with excitement when she was waiting at the stop.

Arthur had left work earlier than usual because the buyer at the shop he always visited last on his list was away with the flu. Coming out into the cold, dark, early evening he had felt angry. No sale, no comfortable sojourn to the pub when it was signed and sealed, and no chance of seeing Rosemary either. Now his spirits lifted, but as he was on the top deck of the bus he couldn't signal to her as he normally did, and he obviously couldn't go running down to find her.

He sat still in his seat as the bus pulled away. She didn't come upstairs, but then he hadn't expected her to and he knew he could catch up with her when they both got off. But she was there, below him, and as the bus lurched along in the darkness he began to form a faint idea in his head. They were early, so the Archers wouldn't be expecting her yet awhile, and he still had the scarf and gloves he had bought in Bentalls. The scarf and gloves he had bought for her. Perhaps she could be persuaded to go with him so that he could give them to her. It wouldn't take more than a few moments, and he wanted her to know so badly how much he thought of her.

Rosemary sat on the downstairs deck of the bus, close to a window, and felt her chest begin to tighten against the cold and the unhealthy fug of the inside of the bus, the cigarette smoke and crowds of people. This wretched asthma; if she had an attack as soon as she arrived home, then her mother would make all sorts of fuss about her going to Guides again and she was desperate to avoid that, so she struggled to keep herself calm. She would walk briskly home once she got off, keeping her scarf tight against her mouth, and with any luck there wouldn't be any trouble.

As she stepped down from the bus and then watched its lighted windows lurch away, she was aware of the black, velvet darkness of the allotments on her right, and was anxious to cross the road and get under the streetlamps. She was nervous anyway, so when a gentle hand suddenly closed over her shoulder from behind, she uttered a squeal of fright and jumped galvanically.

'It's only me, dear,' Arthur said, feeling the shudder of her body beneath his fingers . . . and liking it. 'Sorry, I didn't mean to frighten you. I didn't realize you was on the bus . . .' He was lying now. 'Guides finish early this evening did it?'

Rosemary coughed and tapped her chest. Once her surprise at his appearing out of nowhere had subsided she tried to examine what she felt, and mainly it was weariness at another walk down Recreation Ground Road with his arm unwelcome across her shoulders. She didn't wonder why he had crept so quietly off the bus, or, apparently, had hidden in the shadows until it pulled away, but then Rosemary was eleven years old; her mind was innocent of those sorts of thoughts as yet.

'You made me jump, Mr Johnson,' she whispered unsteadily. 'Gosh, you give me such a fright. I've got to get home, 'cos . . . my asthma's bothering me this evening.'

Arthur thought she was trying to get away from him and suffered a sudden paranoid fear that she didn't like him. She had to like him. He thought the world of her. Standing there before her in the gloom, with his long raincoat tightly belted at the waist, his huge sample-case in his hand and his hat pulled down over his brow, it never occurred to him that he might be a menacing figure to her; he was just desperate to ingratiate himself. Smiling, he put his arm about her shoulders.

'You know, being this bit early is quite fortuitous actually,' he told her, leaning down to whisper in her ear. 'Because, as it happens, I've got a little surprise for you. I bought you a present when I was in Bentalls last.'

Rosemary glanced up at him uncomfortably; his face was very close.

'Yes, I know,' she replied, 'A post-office set.'

Arthur chuckled.

'No, not that,' he replied. 'I bought you something else, something that would look a real treat with that lovely red coat of yours, and as we've got this bit of time to spare we could pop and get it without worrying anybody about you being late. When your mummy sees it she'll be delighted.'

Rosemary felt faintly nervous and glanced down the road towards her home.

'Mummy said that I wasn't to . . .' she began and felt his fingers tighten on her shoulder.

'Oh come on,' he urged. 'We'll only be a minute or two, and I promise you your mummy will love your present. We don't have to go right up to Cheddar Close, you know, I've got a sort of little office by the allotments, and no one's going to be worrying about you for a while yet, are they?' He tugged her towards him. 'Come on, be a brave girl, I don't bite!'

She went with him extremely reluctantly, but it didn't seem to her that she had an option. He walked close, and when they turned off Cavendish Road, into the allotments, it was very dark. Much to her surprise he had a torch in his pocket, and as he led her between the winter-dead vegetable and flower-beds towards the path that went to the scrubby copse he chatted to her all the time.

Above them the freezing night was clear and brightly studded with stars. As they came on to the little path there were soft rustlings of small, nocturnal animals in the undergrowth around them. Rosemary picked her way carefully, always aware of Arthur's proximity. When he stopped and pushed aside some brushwood, to expose the hole in the fence, she raised her eyes to his face in astonishment.

'The water board buildings?' she said in surprise.

Arthur laughed and though he was much too frightened to admit it to himself, the idea of having her this close to his secret place was making him tremble slightly.

'Well, they belong to the water board, but they don't use them, so I rent one from them,' he lied. 'For store deliveries and such-like. Well, I haven't got a garage and with my three girls there's no space at home.'

The mention of his daughters brought him up short, but he thrust them fiercely out of his mind. He couldn't think about his little girls at the moment, the conflict of emotions was too painful and cut across him with awful guilt. He knew that what he was doing was wrong, and he knew that if Rosemary had known how he felt about her she would have run screaming in panic, but he wasn't going to hurt her. He only wanted to give her a scarf and a pair of gloves.

He unlocked the little brick hut, and pulled the door open. Cold seeped out, along an with an earthy smell. Rosemary stood in the doorway feeling extremely uncomfortable and she watched him strike a match and light some candles. The hut was bare brick with a line of thick, opaque glass windows near the roof, and if this was where he kept his deliveries, well there weren't any there at the moment, that was for sure. There was nothing in the hut at all but two old deckchairs and a table upon which stood a big wooden box, plus four empty bottles containing candle-stubs.

To her amazement, he took a small parcel from the box done up in a Bentalls bag, and held it towards her reverently.

'Here you are, my dear,' he said. 'A little present I bought especially for you.'

For reasons that she couldn't properly understand she was suddenly extremely frightened. She took a couple of steps backwards in an effort to escape. Something wasn't right about all this and she wanted to run home as fast as she could. She groped for the door, and immediately Arthur neatly side-stepped her and closed it behind him, so that they were shut in together.

'I'm not going to hurt you, Rosemary,' he murmured, coming close to her. 'I just wanted to tell you what a lovely girl I think you are, I find you very beautiful, you know. Here,' he pushed the bag towards her, 'please open your present.'

She took the bag with trembling fingers and found inside it the red-and-white scarf and gloves that James and Dorothea had seen him buying in Bentalls at the beginning of January. She was bewildered, for she was much too young to know how to react in a situation like this, and as her throat became dry she licked her lips nervously, watching him with terrified eyes in the flickering candlelight.

'They're very nice, Mr Johnson,' she murmured at last. She could smell him because he was so close, could smell stale cigarette smoke and hair that needed washing. 'Very nice. Thank you . . .'

There were beads of sweat on his upper lip as his face came closer and closer, and he was suddenly extremely menacing.

'I knew you'd like them,' he said very softly. 'I said so, when I first saw them. So how about giving me a little kiss then, to show me how grateful you are?'

As she instinctively backed away he put his hands on her shoulders to stop her, and panic overtook Rosemary like a giant runner coming from behind.

She screamed in terror, throwing out her arms to escape from him.

She howled: 'No! I want to go home!' and made a panic-stricken bolt for the door, but it was closed and she couldn't get her fingers to work properly, to get it open. Then he grabbed her as she screamed again, dragging her backwards, the noise seeming to bounce off the walls in the tiny hut, and they were grappling: he rough with fright and she drowning in a maelstrom of terror and claustrophia, but Arthur was much stronger than she was; she didn't stand a chance.

Terrified that someone would hear her and desperate to make her be quiet so that he could explain that he didn't want to hurt her, he wrapped his arms tightly around her and clamped his hand across her mouth.

Rosemary fought and wriggled as a massive asthma attack clutched at her bronchial tubes with an iron fist. His hand across her mouth was tight and allowed no space for breath and she couldn't breathe through her nose. Her heart began to thunder in her chest as her fists clenched and she twisted her head desperately, mad for air. Then the light from the candles began to thread out and blackness washed down across her vision. She fought to the bitter end with every last ounce of her strength. Even as unconsciousness closed over her she still struggled weakly and because of it Arthur went on holding her when she was still. She was warm and heavy, and he shushed her softly.

In the end, and after a very long time, he moved his hand cautiously and her head lolled sideways. She had become like a dead weight in his arms and he realized she had fainted.

'Come on, dear,' he whispered, bending his head close to her face. 'I'm not going to hurt you, but you really mustn't scream like that. Promise me you won't scream again and I'll let you go, and then you can put on your scarf and gloves and go home. I only wanted a little kiss, you know.'

He loosened his grip slightly and her knees buckled, obliging him to grab her quickly before she crumpled to the floor. Her head fell backwards, her eyes were half-open. In the semi-darkness Arthur patted her cheeks to rouse her.

'Rosemary,' he said urgently. 'Come on, there's a good girl, wake up.'

She remained limp and unresisting in his arms and he held her, gazing down into her face. But as the seconds ticked by and became minutes, and the hut was silently full of deep, flickering

71

shadows, the fear scratching at the back of his brain became a horrified understanding that gripped his heart with numbing disbelief.

Rosemary hadn't fainted . . . *She was dead.*

Desperately he lowered her into the deckchair which the tramp had left behind after Christmas. He knelt beside her, struggling to jolt some life back into her, but Arthur knew nothing about artificial respiration and as each moment passed, Rosemary's heart and lungs became less and less able to remember what it was they were supposed to do. She was dead and he could not bring her back to life. He had killed her. It might have been an accident, but she was still dead, and there wasn't a thing he could do about it.

He fell back on to his haunches and gaped at her in the flickering candlelight as a jolt of revulsion made his stomach heave and brought bile into his mouth. He thought of Edith and of his children, of what would happen to him when the truth came out, and instinctively he knew that he mustn't panic, that he must plan his next move very carefully.

He stood up, finding his legs extremely shaky, and carefully blew out the candles. Then he went out into the freezing air and securely locked the hut, leaning for a moment or two against the wall, breathing deeply to steady himself. He would go home and eat his dinner as if nothing had happened, and then he would give himself a chance to plan what he would do with the body. He didn't actually think about the promising life he had just snuffed out, because panic, and his conscience, wouldn't let him; and self-preservation was closing out all other thoughts very quickly.

He walked quite briskly up Acacia Road towards Cheddar Close, thinking only about himself. He did not cross the road to walk past Rosemary's house, and it never crossed his mind to consider what Tim and Doreen Archer were going to suffer.

By nine o'clock it was freezing hard and there was no sign of Rosemary. Doreen was beginning to succumb to the fear that gripped her imagination and would not be quieted.

'I'll drive to the hall,' Tim said. 'See if for any reason they've stayed late, or she's missed the bus.'

His wife's eyes bulged and her hands trembled uncontrollably.

'The bus!' she retorted. 'Five buses at least! I want to come with you, Tim.'

He shook his head.

'No, dear,' he replied, trying to keep calm. 'You can't leave the house empty. What if she was to come home and find nobody here? No, I'll be as quick as I can, and I bet by the time I return she's either here, or I've found her.'

The streets were bleak and cold, there was little traffic around. Anyone with any sense was in for the night, trying to keep warm against the ever-dropping temperature. When Tim arrived at the hall where the Guides met, he found it locked and in darkness. There was no one standing at the bus stop, either. Since he had faithfully followed her route, if for any reason Rosemary had been walking he would have passed her, which he hadn't.

He went straight home, and the sight of Doreen standing on the doorstep wringing her hands told him long before he asked her that his daughter was still missing.

'I'm going round to Edna Buddry's!' Doreen declared. 'Dorothea is Rosemary's closest friend at school. If anyone knows where she is it'll be Dorothea.'

Tim couldn't find any reason to quarrel with that and when, a few moments later, Edna Buddry got up from her armchair by the fire to see who was so urgently hammering on her front door, she found herself confronted by the usually so neat and careful Doreen wearing no coat, and her bedroom slippers with Tim hovering behind her.

Doreen was unable to keep her voice down, such was her terror, and upstairs in her darkened bedroom Dorothea heard the three voices, mingled together in the tiny hallway, Doreen's loud and frantic and full of fear. She slid from her bed and opened the door, then she crept forward and sat on the top stair, gazing down.

'Doreen, calm down,' Aunty was saying, touching Rosemary's mother with a gentle hand. 'I'm sure she'm all right, but we'll ask

Dorothea if she knows anything first, and then, if she doesn't, well, we'll call the police.'

She glanced up the stairs and saw Dorothea hunched on the top step, her face white against the dimness of the hall light. Another woman might have spoken sharply, but Edna was never sharp with Dorothea, for she was never able to quite forget the state the child had been in when they had first met.

'Come down, sweetheart,' she said, holding out her hand. 'Don't be frightened, everything's all right. It's just that Mr and Mrs Archer can't find Rosemary, and they thought you might know something.'

'I don't know nothing . . .' Dorothea replied in a tiny, frightened voice as she saw the wildness in Doreen's eyes, the sharp terror on her pale face.

'You do!' Doreen cried. 'You must do! Where is she? Where's Rosemary? If she's told anybody it'll be you.'

Dorothea shrank into herself, blinking in fright, but Edna shushed Doreen sharply. She climbed the stairs, held out her hand to the little girl and gently led her down into the sitting-room. With four of them in there, three of them adults, it seemed very full and Dorothea stood close to Aunty, sensing the fear in the room and finding her heart thudding in her chest.

'Rosemary didn't come home from Guides, my lovey,' Aunty said quietly, gazing down into the child's scared face. 'Now what we needs to know is if she might've said anything to you at school, you know, that she was going to a friend's or something? Maybe someone new, p'raps? You don't have to be afraid to tell us, you won't get in any trouble, and neither will Rosemary, but as you can see, Mrs Archer is very upset, same as I would be if you didn't come home when you said you would.'

Dorothea bit her lip as she thought of Rosemary. Almost unwillingly she remembered the conversation they had shared at school break-time a couple of weeks ago. She thought of James, too, and the more she thought about it, the more Arthur crept, uninvited, into her fears. There wasn't any real reason for her to think of him, only the idea seemed to go hand in hand with Rosemary coming

74

home from Guides on the bus. She moved uncomfortably from foot to foot; she knew she must say something, because there wasn't time to leave it and speak to James about it first.

'She didn't tell me about any new friends,' she whispered at last, 'but she did tell me that . . .'

She stopped. Doreen Archer stared at her with burning eyes.

'She told you what? *What?*' she shouted.

Aunty put a loving hand on Dorothea's head.

'Doreen,' she said firmly, 'if you don't stop shouting at the child I shall turn you out. Dorothea ent done nothing, and I'd like you to remember that.'

Actually Dorothea felt sorry for Doreen, for even at only ten she recognized the agony in the woman's eyes, but she thought she might have been extremely frightened if she hadn't had Aunty to cling to, and surreptitiously she tightened her grip.

'So, poppet,' Aunty murmured, gazing down at her, 'what did Rosemary tell you?'

To Dorothea it felt as if she was betraying a confidence, and yet there was no reason to feel like that; she owed Arthur no loyalty. It was just, she supposed, that the conversations about him which she had shared with Rosemary and James had always been whispered, and it made her feel guilty. She had got as far as the tube of Spangles, and was beginning to feel less uncertain of herself, when Doreen abruptly stopped listening. She spun on her heels, fighting to get past Tim and out of the house in her panic, her arms flailing, her body rigid and quaking.

'He's got my daughter!' she screamed. 'Johnson, he's got my daughter!'

'Doreen . . .' said Tim, but she shoved past him, almost falling over the doorstep into Aunty's tiny front garden. Desperately he stared at Edna.

'Well don't let 'er go runnin' up there on her own, Tim,' she murmured. 'That won't do anyone any good.'

Tim turned and hurried after his wife, and in the blast of cold air that seemed to rush in through the open front door, Dorothea began to cry.

'Is there something else you didn't tell us?' Aunty asked softly, going to close the front door. 'I know Doreen weren't listening, but I am, so tell me, sweetheart. It might be important.'

Dorothea wiped her nose on the sleeve of her nightdress and went to stand by the fire. She was shivering and wretched, and the idea that Rosemary had disappeared was dreadful. Rosemary had befriended her on her very first day at Franklin Road Juniors. Skinny Dorothea, bewildered by her life in Manchester and still a bit nervous with Aunty, had been shown such kindness by Rosemary, who was so different and so beautiful.

'Me and James,' she began, 'saw Mr Johnson buying a red scarf and gloves in Bentalls . . .' She stumbled through the story as the tears trickled down her cheeks and the idea of Rosemary's being missing grew ever more terrible in her mind.

Edna gathered her up, holding her tightly as she sifted through what she had heard. She comforted the child and promised confidently that they would soon find Rosemary, but the more she thought about it the more she was haunted by extremely bad feelings. Dorothea hadn't actually accused Arthur of anything – and yet – they didn't like him, the children. With child's logic, they didn't like him, and they didn't trust him either. When she eventually took Dorothea back upstairs she put her into her own bed, because she suddenly had a passionate, overwhelming need to keep her safe.

Tim managed to persuade Doreen that it was far more sensible to go up to Cheddar Close in the car, than to run screaming up Acacia Avenue. When they were in the car he begged her to be careful what she said when they got there, but he knew he was wasting his breath.

Doreen was still wearing her slippers as she tumbled out into the freezing night air in Cheddar Close and as Edith Johnson opened her front door in answer to what could only be described as pounding, she was extremely surprised to be confronted by the wild-eyed, wild-haired Doreen in her bedroom slippers, because everyone in the area knew Doreen Archer's views on etiquette.

'Where's my daughter!' Doreen shouted. 'Rosemary. Where's Rosemary?'

Edith Johnson's bland face took on an expression of faint amazement, but underlying that there was more than a hint of resentment. Edith didn't care for Doreen, because Doreen had made it abundantly clear that she considered herself to be socially well above the Johnsons.

So, the perfect Rosemary was missing? Gone to a friend's house and forgotten to tell her mummy, perhaps. It was nice to know that under the white socks and perfect manners she was as human as any other child.

'I'm very sorry,' she said quietly, 'but I have no idea where Rosemary is. She isn't here, nor has she been here. She's not a close friend of Shirley's, you know, even if she did invite Shirley to her birthday. Perhaps you should ask Edna Buddry.'

Tim Archer put out a warning hand towards his wife, but Doreen shook him off violently, and as she spoke her tongue was scathing.

'Oh, believe me, I've already talked to Edna Buddry,' she retorted, 'and to little Dorothea as well, that's why I'm here! Your husband has been interfering with my daughter, and now she's missing, and if I don't get a satisfactory answer within the next two minutes, I'm going to the police!'

Edith Johnson felt her heart lurch in her breast as the other woman's words struck fear into her very soul, but even as she stood on the doorstep looking uncertain, Arthur hove into view behind her. He put his hands on her shoulders in a sort of restraining gesture and looked across her at Tim and Doreen indignantly.

'I heard that last remark, Mrs Archer,' he exclaimed in a tone of injured astonishment, 'and I can't believe it! Dorothea Sprake says I have been *interfering* with Rosemary? I never heard anything so preposterous. Well, you can take my word for it that I have never interfered – as you put it – with your child, or anybody else's, in my life. Yes, I asked her and the Sprake child to see Shirley across the road to school of a morning, but that's hardly interfering! Good Lord, I have three daughters of my own, I don't interfere with children!'

'Doreen . . .' Tim said, but Doreen was bursting with rage.

'She told Dorothea that you came home from Guides with her on the bus each week, and that you gave her sweets, and put your arms round her,' she snarled at Arthur furiously, her lips curled with anger, 'and in my book that's interfering, Mr Johnson, especially as she claimed not to like it!'

Arthur felt sick as he tried to thrust the picture of the dead Rosemary out of his mind, but he still managed to twist his face into an expression of surprised sadness, and shook his head, as if he couldn't quite believe what he was hearing.

'All right,' he admitted, 'I *do* see her on the bus on her way home from Guides most weeks, and I do walk down Recreation Ground Road with her, because it's late and it's dark. I admit I gave her a packet of sweets, too, because I had them in my bag and thought she might like them; but for the rest of it, if I've ever put my arm about her it was only as a protective gesture, I can assure you. If you want my honest opinion, Mrs Archer, I don't think you should be letting her walk home from the bus stop alone of an evening.' He carefully drew Edith back into the hall with him. Tim and Doreen saw him put his hand on the door, and knew he was about to close it. 'Tonight, however, Rosemary and I were not on the same bus, I'm afraid, and I haven't seen her. So, if that's all, I should like to get back to my work.'

Doreen's eyes abruptly flooded with tears as her anguish spilled over into panic and thrust her slippered foot into the doorway, so that the only way Arthur could have closed the door would have been to slam it painfully against her foot.

'I'm going to the police, Mr Johnson!' she sobbed. 'I'm going right now, and I'm going to tell them precisely what Dorothea Sprake told me!'

Arthur shrugged.

'And I shall tell them what I've just told you,' he replied. 'Mrs Archer, I feel for you, truly I do. I should be beside myself if Shirley were missing, but I haven't seen Rosemary this evening. She wasn't on the bus.'

It couldn't go on, Tim knew that, and he actually hauled Doreen backwards so that Arthur could close the front door. Doreen turned on him, sobbing hysterically, and fought him in her suffering, but he held her tightly, doing his best to quieten her.

'Doreen, there's no point in this,' he said firmly. 'We haven't any proof that Arthur Johnson has done anything to her. Now please, come on. Get in the car and we'll go to the police station. You must!'

Slowly they went back on to the pavement together. Tim handed her into the passenger seat of the car as Edith Johnson watched them from behind her net curtains. Her heart thumped in her chest and a sensation of nausea seemed to close her throat as unspoken fears thrust themselves up in her troubled mind. She knew how Arthur felt about Rosemary Archer, she'd seen him looking at her, and recognized the indecent longing in his eyes. She knew about the arrangement he had made with her and her quaint little friend Dorothea, to walk Shirley along Franklin Road each morning. But it was impossible to believe that he had hurt her in any way. Arthur might lust after girls who were too young, but he didn't hurt them.

Tim's car pulled away and Edith turned and went into the kitchen where Arthur was sitting at the table balancing his books. He looked up at her, but she didn't speak, she just put the kettle on to make some tea. Suddenly the heavy weight of unspoken questions and answers that hung between them was familiarly claustrophobic.

Chapter 6

Edna took one look at Dorothea's haunted little face the next morning and decided to take her to Languard House instead of sending her to school. The village was already full of policemen – and full of speculation and gossip – and Edna wanted the child as far away as possible.

When they got to Hampton Court, James was at the front door to meet them, and Edna and Anthea watched in sympathetic silence as he took Dorothea by the hand and led her away upstairs.

'It was good of you to keep him off school for the day to keep her company,' Edna said. 'And good of you to have her to stay for the weekend, too. I don't believe she slept a wink last night. Tossing and turning all night and clinging like a limpet, she was.'

'Heavens, it's the least I can do, Mrs B,' Anthea retorted, frowning up towards the bend in the stairs, where they had last seen the little pair. 'I remember just what it was like when Peachy disappeared . . . the *agony* of those parents. Poor things, they must be frantic.'

'Doreen's half out of her mind,' Edna said quietly, 'and not for *one moment* do I think the news is going to be good. Little Rosemary's a lovely girl, she wouldn't never put her parents through suffering like this. She hasn't run off, and she hasn't stayed over with no friend and forgotten to let Tim and Doreen know, neither. The kiddie met with someone who didn't ought to've been on that bus last night, and my gut feeling is well . . .' she tailed off into silence for a moment, then added very quietly, 'not good . . .'

Anthea winced.

'You really think she's dead?' she whispered.

Edna pressed her lips together grimly.

'Well it had to be a fair bit below freezing last night didn't it,' she replied, 'so if they don't find her in anyone's house – which they won't – then her chances wouldn't have been good, would they? I don't want it to be true, I really don't. I want more than anything for her to be eating breakfast at someone's kitchen table at this very moment, only it's about as likely as Dorothea wandering off and forgetting to tell anyone.'

They turned and went away together to the kitchen to have a cup of coffee, where they encountered Mrs Minns who stared at Edna with haunted eyes. She was laying cups and saucers on the table and on the kitchen range the kettle belched forth steam. In a moment she would fill the coffee pot and they would all sit down together, but nobody bothered with biscuits this morning. Nobody felt remotely hungry.

Edna knew that, even as they sat there, dozens of policemen were combing the village, searching the allotments and the recreation ground, knocking on doors, taking statements, hunting through outbuildings and gardens; and deep in her heart she also knew they weren't going to find Rosemary alive.

Arthur waited until the police had left the recreation ground before he went back to the hut, and it was a long, sickening wait. The police had scoured the allotments, the little copse, the trees behind the huts and finally the area with the water board buildings. That was the bit Arthur had waited for in terror, and watched from his hiding place as a young policeman climbed over the locked gate and made his way to the buildings.

An old pumping station and the tool shed: they'd been around these buildings only a matter of weeks ago, when some tramp had been reported to be making a nuisance of himself in the area, and they'd found nothing. The pumping station had a metal door, but on the door of the hut hung a stout brass padlock, firmly locked. The policeman gave it a sharp rattle and then abandoned the area, heading back to the gate.

'No one's been in here,' Arthur heard him shout. 'All firmly locked.'

'Nothing, then,' came an answer, 'we can mark this area off as searched!'

They began to move slowly away towards their next area and the recreation ground became silent and empty. Arthur stood in his hiding place, aware that his hands were freezing cold and gripped in such tight fists that it hurt to open his fingers. He winced as he flexed them to get the circulation going again, and finally he came out of hiding, took a very long circle round to come upon the buildings from the opposite direction and, feeling satisfied that there was no one else around, slipped through the hole in the hedge. He went towards the hut.

He fumbled in his pocket for the key and found his hands shaking as he fitted it into the padlock. Oh God, wouldn't it be wonderful if Rosemary was sitting in the deckchair awake, and nothing more than cold and hungry . . . or perhaps unconscious but alive, so that he could move her and leave her where she would quickly be found. In an agony of prayer he struggled to get the padlock out of the staple, and then lever open the hasp. The wooden door swung slowly open.

Rosemary lay exactly where he had left her, in the deckchair. Her head was turned to one side, with her hair dark against her cheek, and her face waxy in death. She was icy cold and rigid . . . like a beautiful doll, he thought, feeling dreadfully sick. Clutched in one of her hands were the red-and-white gloves. The scarf was on the floor.

It took Arthur the strength of pure fear to get the gloves; she didn't want to let them go although they would never warm her hands again. Only her hair moved freely as he struggled to wrest them from her grasp, the rest of her body jerked stiffly in the deckchair but didn't yield. In the end he was obliged to break the rigor in three of her fingers, and by that time he was trembling violently and ready to vomit. He stuffed the gloves into the green-and-white Bentalls bag along with the scarf, then rammed the whole lot into his coat pocket and stood, wiping cold sweat from his brow, staring at what he had done.

He had hoped it would be different in the cold light of day, and it was. It was a hundred times worse.

There was nothing he could do with the body like this, but he remembered he had read somewhere that rigor mortis passed away after a while, and bodies became flexible again. He would have to move her eventually he realized, but not for a while. Perhaps he could leave her until everyone had stopped looking for her, and then, maybe, he could think of a way. In the meantime, however, the only thing to link him to her was the scarf and gloves so they must be disposed of immediately.

For one more moment he stared at her and his heart ached in his chest. He remembered reading in the newspapers once that many murderers got pleasure from what they had done and liked to look at the bodies, as if they were trophies. Arthur felt a great many emotions as he stood and stared at the beautiful dead child, but certainly, as yet, none of them was pleasure.

The weekend crawled by for everybody, but particularly for Doreen and Tim. Doreen did no more than doze occasionally as she sat rigid, listening all the time for the door, repeating over and over again 'She'll be home in the minute, listen, I think I can hear her . . .' until Tim dreaded being in the room with her. Both his mother and hers did their best to keep some semblance of life moving in the pristine house that spoke of Rosemary at every turn, but for Doreen time had stopped.

On Monday morning Edna arrived at Franklin Road Juniors, clutching tightly to Dorothea's hand. She was not unduly surprised to find that pretty well every child in the school was accompanied by an adult; no one wanted their child out of sight.

She leaned down to kiss Dorothea, hugging her close as she did so.

'And you wait for me right here after school,' she said. 'Mrs Webb-Goring is letting me leave early for the time being, so don't you set foot out of this playground 'til I gets here, all right?

Dorothea nodded and cast a frightened glance towards the big, grey school building.

'I don't want to, Aunty,' she whispered as tears sprang into her eyes. 'I don't want to, not without Rosemary.'

Edna led her into school and spoke first to the headmaster and then to Dorothea's form mistress, so that by the time Dorothea came to take her place in class she found herself sitting next to somebody else on the opposite side of the room from Rosemary's empty desk. It didn't make it any easier to bear though, it was still a horrible, miserable day.

At three o'clock she waited obediently at the school gates and felt her spirits lift a little as she saw Aunty coming along Franklin Road to meet her. Behind Aunty was Mrs Johnson . . . and to everybody's horror, behind Edith was Doreen Archer.

Edna spotted her first and moved swiftly to head her off as most of the waiting parents shuffled and turned their backs, frightened because they had no idea what to say.

Edna grasped her shoulders gently and held her.

'Doreen, lovey, you shouldn't be here,' she whispered. 'C'mon, we should go home.'

Doreen's eyes were bulging, her appearance unkempt. She struggled to escape from Edna, wildly searching for a sign of Rosemary.

'No! She'll be here, she'll be here!' she cried and fought to escape. 'She *must* be here, she's *got* to be!'

Edna turned her head slightly and to her dismay she saw a tiny sneer touch Edith Johnson's lips. She had not even glanced at Doreen, and whilst everyone else around them was visibly touched with pity, Edith marched in through the school gates without slowing her pace. Edna felt a surge of annoyance and at the same moment saw Tim Archer running down the road towards her.

'Doreen!' he cried and abruptly Doreen's face crumpled in agony as a fresh flood of tears streamed down her face. Her body seemed to wilt and she collapsed against Edna in terrible defeat. Tim took her into his arms with great love and care.

He looked dreadful. He was white-faced and dark-eyed and his hair seemed to be standing on end. Edna felt a fierce rush of pity for him, and at the same time an almost hysterical need to keep Dorothea safe. She pulled the child against her, holding her as if she feared she might suddenly just disappear into nothing, and the hands that clutched at the tiny thin shoulders shook with a mixture of fear and despair.

'Thanks, Mrs B,' he murmured, rocking the sobbing Doreen in his arms like a child. 'We didn't realize she'd gone out . . . er . . .'

He tailed off and Edna recognized that in his pain he had allowed himself to hope, almost as much as his wife that their daughter would be in school the same as usual.

'Let me bring round something for you to eat, Tim,' she offered, but he shook his head, forcing a smile that was almost unbearable to look at.

'Our mothers are both here at the moment, Mrs B,' he replied, 'and we're sinking under uneaten food . . .' His eyes filled with tears and he swallowed back a sob, 'but thanks, anyway. Thanks very much. You're very kind.'

The flood of tears spilled down his cheeks and he didn't even try to wipe them away, because he knew they wouldn't stop. He turned and led his wife away. Edna took Dorothea into Gregson's to buy some tomato soup because she felt helpless and frightened and wanted, absurdly, to fill the child with gallons of tomato soup so that whatever happened she would be safe and secure.

The mountainous Mrs Gregson stood behind her counter with her hands on her vast hips; her very familiarity oddly comforting in a way. She and Edna began at once to talk about the missing Rosemary, and immediately Mrs Gregson came up with her theory. Everyone had a theory. Only Edna had a suspicion which she greatly feared was grounded in truth, and about that she said nothing to anyone.

'You don't think it could've had anything t'do with that tramp, do yer?' Mrs Gregson demanded. 'You know, the one what scared little Dorothea in here? I didn't like the look of him, I'm telling you. I s'pose the p'lice have looked into *his* goings on?'

Edna shook her head.

'He's been gone ages,' she replied. 'Weren't nothing to do with him, I'm sure. I fancy we have to look closer to home, frankly.'

Mrs Gregson frowned. She was really quite frightening when she did that, for she had a ferocious face. She had a ferocious nature, too, with people she didn't like, but she was at heart a very caring woman. Mrs Gregson knew the movements of her regulars inside out and backwards, and no newspapers or milk-bottles were ever allowed to build up on an old person's doorstep without her demanding someone should look into it.

She picked up a penny bar of chocolate, unwrapped it and handed it to Dorothea.

'You got suspicions, Edna?' she asked.

Edna shrugged. She was not keen on its becoming common knowledge that Doreen had been screaming on the Johnsons' doorstep on Thursday night.

'Not to point a finger at, you understand?' she replied carefully. 'I simply meant that Rosemary wouldn't've gone near that tramp, she was as scared of him as Dorothea was. If she was taken by someone, then it has to be someone she weren't initially afraid of, else she'd've screamed her head off.'

Mrs Gregson nodded sagely and was about to say something when the shop door opened and Edith Johnson came in with her three children. Shirley ran straight up to Dorothea, her golden ringlets bouncing prettily about her face, and Dorothea broke off a piece of her chocolate bar and offered it to her. The two little girls blinked at each other in the subdued light of the shop.

'Always smells of cheese in here,' Shirley said quietly, glancing about her as if she would get into trouble for saying so.

Dorothea nodded.

'It's a nice smell though,' she replied. They watched as Edith picked up a loaf of bread, came to the counter, asked for two tins of oxtail soup and reached for her purse to pay. The coolness between her and Edna was screamingly obvious – as obvious to the children as it was to Mrs Gregson.

Eventually Edna drew a deep breath and faced the other woman squarely.

'I saw how you looked at Doreen just now, Edith, and a little compassion wouldn't go amiss,' she observed quietly, keeping her voice steady. 'Tim and Doreen only have Rosemary and she's their whole life. Dorothea wasn't lying, you know, when she told them Rosemary had complained about Arthur's attentions. It may very well be that he *was* only being kind, but Rosemary was nervous of him.'

Edith sniffed and her expression was unforgiving.

'Arthur has three daughter of his own,' she pointed out coldly, 'and he likes children, likes to keep an eye out for them. He's just a friendly man, that's all, and concerned about the children round here. If he's been walking Rosemary home from the bus of a Thursday evening, it's because he doesn't think she should be out there on her own after dark. He wouldn't let Shirley, I can assure you.'

Edna was aware that Mrs Gregson was absorbing the conversation greedily, and realized that there wasn't any point in being careful what she said any longer, because Edith was happily spilling it out without a thought.

'Edith,' she said firmly, 'Shirley is only eight. Of course Arthur wouldn't let her out on her own after dark. Rosemary's eleven and going to Guides. Now please, if Arthur knows anything at all, if he seen her at the bus stop, or outside the hall – *anything* he *will* tell the police, won't he?'

Edith Johnson pushed her shopping down into her bag and grasped hold of Shirley so abruptly that she almost pulled the child off her feet.

'Thanks to Doreen Archer,' she snapped, 'we've not had a moment's peace from the wretched police this weekend. And I can assure you Arthur's told them everything he knows!'

She spun on her heals and marched herself and her children out of the shop, leaving only the sound of the jangling bell fading into silence behind them.

'*Arthur Johnson!*' Mrs Gregson whispered with a kind of thrill in her voice. 'Not really, Edna?'

Edna sighed and gathered Dorothea against her, finding her

need to keep the child safe was becoming almost paranoid.

'I don't say Arthur's done anything,' she replied, 'but there is no doubt the local children don't like him much. He spends far too much of his time standing around up at them swings, smoking and watching the girls, and if he had Shirley there with him – well – but he don't. And that's all I'm saying. And I'll be the first to apologize to him if I have to.'

Outside, as they walked around the crescent together, Dorothea held tightly to Aunty's hand. The weather was icy, the sky iron grey, and Dorothea longed to get inside, to give Blackie a kiss and rub her face against his fur, then run down the garden and give her beautiful Charlie and his hens some scraps. Edna was grim-faced and walking quickly, obliging the child to trot from time to time, and she seemed lost in her thoughts.

At last, as if for something to say rather than for any other reason, Dorothea asked:

'Do you really think Mr Johnson took Rosemary, Aunty?' To her enormous surprise, Aunty turned on her furiously.

'You got big ears, my girl!' she snapped. 'And you shouldn't be listening to grown-ups' conversations. Just you remember what I told you, eavesdroppers never hear good of themselves, so you just watch it!'

Dorothea fell silent immediately, and it took Edna all of five minutes to admit to herself what she'd done and say sorry, but in the warm darkness of her bed that night Dorothea realized that, from the exchange, she had learned something valuable, and very frightening. Aunty did think Mr Johnson had taken Rosemary . . . and she was frightened.

On the following Thursday, exactly a week after Rosemary's disappearance, Edna's careful plans for collecting Dorothea from school went awry. Along the Hampton Court Road an accident had caused a long hold-up in the traffic, and although she got off the bus and began to walk immediately, there wasn't a hope that she could reach the school before all the children had gone.

It had been a dreadful week. It seemed as if the whole village had become gripped by suspicion and fear. No children went to play on the swings and none was seen seen playing out after school. Doreen and Tim Archer had shut themselves away by Tuesday, and no one saw them at all except for the policemen who went in and out of their home. There was no news of Rosemary.

Everywhere had been searched and re-searched: bomb-sites, allotment sheds, the river right down to Teddington Lock and beyond, anywhere that might conceivably hide a body; but nothing had been found . . . and Arthur went quietly on with his daily routine, the only person party to the deadly secret in the water board hut.

He had been back three times. Rigor had passed off and Rosemary was limp now, but her skin had lost the sheen of the living and was pasty and grey. She had been dead so long that drastic changes were taking place within her; it began to seem to Arthur that she had perhaps never lived, that she had always been a colourless rag-doll lying in his deckchair.

He didn't know how many more times he would come back, for he realized that the only reason she wasn't stinking yet was because the temperature outside was so cold. He had already half made up his mind to leave her lying there until she was skeletonized before he buried her, because by then she would be much easier to move, but just at the moment the thought of her – his secret – lured him back. And as the shock of accidentally killing her had begun to fade he was finding that he could be callously indifferent to the suffering he had caused her parents.

If he'd killed her on purpose, he reasoned, then he would deserve to be punished, but he hadn't, so it was only right that he should put himself and his family first . . . because after all, nothing was going to bring Rosemary back; was it.

So on Thursday afternoon, as the weather began to warm up and a wind was rising, promising a wet and windy night, Dorothea stood in the playground waiting for Aunty as all the other children left with their parents, and by half past three she was all alone; only the teachers were left now in the school, and none of them was watching from the windows as they went about their end-of-day routines.

She leaned against the railings by the gate, swinging from side to side as she waited. It would be getting dark quite soon, because grey clouds were rolling in from the west; and almost certainly she was going to get wet if she waited much longer. So, she reasoned, if she went home on her own, surely that would be better than standing here in the dark, getting wet through to the skin? After all, she could still make it in the daylight if she hurried.

Having made up her mind, she poked her head out through the gate and glanced up and down the road in both directions. To her horror she saw, coming around the corner into Franklin Road, the bully-boys who had tormented her so cruelly when she had first come here to live. What she did after that was instinctive.

Harvey, the ring-leader, had never forgiven James for bloodying his nose in front of his gang, and as far as he was concerned the fault was Dorothea's. A frightened, skinny orphan, she should have been a push-over, and so should the stuck-up kid as well. How was Harvey supposed to have known that James had learned the art of self-defence quite early in life?

Now as Dorothea saw him swaggering along with his hands in his pockets she didn't wait for him to see her, for there was no Aunty and no James, and she was easy prey to a boy itching to get his own back. Grabbing her school satchel she ran as hard as she could in the opposite direction, and then scooted in through the bottom gate on to the rec, her heart hammering with fright in her chest.

She heard Harvey and his mates pounding along the pavement outside and knew that they had seen her. If they came into the rec behind her she hadn't got a prayer unless she had a good head-start, so she ran like the wind across the grass towards the swings and the allotments. Once she turned back, fearfully, but there was no one behind her; nevertheless she still continued towards the top gate, for she was far too scared to go back. If she came out of there, she thought, crossed the road and ran down to Gregson's on the corner she'd be safe. Mrs Gregson hated Harvey with a vengeance, and no one stood up to Mrs Gregson.

The swings behind their chicken-wire fence moved gently in the rising wind. Dorothea shivered and glanced across at the trees from which the tramp had lurched on Boxing Day, noticing how dark it already was beneath them. She hurried on towards the little path, thinking of Rosemary and James. She remembered how many happy times they had shared up here and an idea struck her.

Just supposing something had happened to Rosemary to frighten her, and she was hiding in the summer camp in the copse? No one would have found her because no one but she, Dorothea and James knew about it. She might be crouched there, cold and scared, and just waiting for someone to come.

Disastrously Dorothea turned away from the gate and began to pick her way along the path. Not for a moment did it occur to her that Rosemary couldn't possibly have been hiding in the bushes for a week, because she was not quite old enough to reason that cleverly.

And the first angry spits of rain began falling from the sky.

The copse was cold and extremely scrubby and unattractive in the winter. Bare trees rose above sad, lank undergrowth and damp dead leaves, and there was a rank, earthy smell. If Dorothea hadn't been so familiar with it she might have been frightened to go poking about on her own; as it was it might have been a neglected corner to most people, but to her, James, Rosemary and a few other carefully selected friends, it was a place of endless games and boundless imagination.

It wasn't difficult to find the camp. Round the first bend and then sharp left into the bushes, the path was well worn from their feet in the summer. Dorothea crouched down to crawl through the entrance they had carefully made, and found herself in the familiar hiding-place where they had shared sweets and comics or played games on warm early summer evenings. Last summer they had collected some long grass and laid it on the earth floor, and during the summer it had dried and become really quite fragrant. Also in the summer, with the foliage on the bushes, this secret place was snug and completely private, but now she found she could see out to the path.

There was no sign of Rosemary and Dorothea was disappointed. She hunkered down in the den, gazing about her at the bareness of winter, and it was some seconds before she became aware that someone had disturbed the floor. The grass, now virtually disintegrated, had been scraped out of the way, and the earth beneath it was loose. As if someone had been digging there recently.

Dorothea began to scrape it away with her fingers. She didn't have to go down very far, for what had been buried was only just beneath the surface. A torn, wet, green-and-white paper bag, the word 'Bentalls' still just legible . . . and inside it, filthy and covered with earth stains, a red-and-white woollen scarf and a pair of matching gloves.

The little girl felt her heart lurch with fear and almost gave in to her instinct to run for it, but she was a plucky child when it was needed, and she knew she mustn't leave her find behind. She eased it out of the ground, trying to avoid tearing the bag any further, and then wrapped the whole lot carefully into a bundle and crawled out into the gathering gloom of the late afternoon, where the rain had begun to fall quite hard.

She trotted back along the path towards the gate hurriedly now, for it was spooky in the wood; the rain sounding like thousands of tiny, running feet as it pattered on dead leaves. Clutching her prize in her hand she hurried past the water board buildings keeping her head down against the worst of the rain, and all the time thinking of Aunty. She had no idea anyone was on the path ahead of her for she wasn't paying attention, and when she abruptly stumbled into somebody she fell back, uttering a nightmarish little noise in her throat.

For a second nothing moved as fear held her in its grip. Then she looked up. . . .

Edna ran as fast as her age and weight would allow her across the empty school playground, shouting for Dorothea at the top of her voice, but everywhere was locked and dark. The school was empty, and Dorothea had gone.

With tears streaming down her face Edna rattled the doors and pounded with her fists, as her heart hammered in her chest and nausea closed her throat. She had been to Boxgrove Crescent first, expecting the child would have taken herself off home when it started to rain – and, of course, she wouldn't have been remotely cross. Surely Dorothea understood that? I mean it wasn't written in stone that she couldn't walk home on her own, not whilst it was still light . . . not written in *stone*. . . .

Oh please God! she prayed. Please, *please* God . . . and the rain grew heavier, plastering her untidy grey hair about her face. . . .

Dorothea and Arthur stared at each other for some seconds on the muddy little path, as both ran through a succession of wild emotions. He saw what she carried in her hand, and had he not been so guilty and so frightened he would have ignored it, admonished her for being up there on her own, and walked her back to the gate. It would have been the intelligent thing to do. As it was a wave of panic washed over him and he acted purely out of instinct.

She fell back from him as his expression hardened with fury, obliging him to grab her arm before she started to run. As he yanked her upwards his fingers bit into her flesh. In his hand she trembled; she was small and vulnerable and completely helpless, but any shred of pity he might have experienced was drowned in the knowledge of his terrible secret.

'Dorothea Sprake,' he muttered dangerously softly. 'What a pity you couldn't have minded your own business, you nosy little *brat*! Well, now, you've got yourself into all sorts of trouble, haven't you?'

Dorothea gazed up at him like a mesmerized rabbit. She didn't struggle, she hardly even breathed, she just stared as terror took a series of razor-sharp bites out of her insides and the world seemed to wobble unsteadily before her eyes.

'I won't tell. . .' she squeaked at last. 'I won't tell, Mr Johnson, I promise . . .' and suddenly her knees buckled so that she hung by her full weight from his fist.

'You're so right you won't tell,' he retorted, dragging her back towards the water board buildings and then kicking open the carefully hidden hole in the hedge. 'In fact I give you my *word* you won't tell!'

She was dirty and grazed when they reached the hut, and he forced her to her knees at his feet before he struggled to undo the padlock. He needn't have bothered; she was much too frightened to have tried to run from him. His fingers were clumsy with his fear and it seemed to take an unconscionably long time, but eventually he clawed open the hasp, and allowed the door to swing open.

Inside it was extremely dark, but as a glimmer more of daylight crept in, Dorothea saw the old deckchair and its contents. For one, glorious moment her heart lifted with relief . . . then to her horror she realized what she was looking at, and the world seemed to tip upside down.

Dorothea had seen death once already in her short life, and knew it when she saw it. She had sat for hours beside her dead father, and he had been newly dead. Rosemary's face was collapsing, the skin slipping and beginning to discolour. Rosemary, she realized, had been dead for a long time and with a wail of terror she fled from the deckchair into the far corner of the hut, sliding down on to her haunches and crouching like a animal.

Unfortunately for her the thick, opaque windows in the hut let in just a minimum of cold, grey light where dark might now have been better. There was enough light in the room to make Arthur a black, nightmare figure, standing before her, staring down, and she cowered in terror.

'And now, you wretched little nuisance, you're going to stay here for the night,' he said slowly. 'Stay in the dark with your little dead friend and think about what you've done, because you do need to think about it, you really do. And if you're really good and don't make a sound, well then I might let you go back to Aunty tomorrow. But you got to prove to me that you can be trusted, and this is the only way.'

Dorothea crouched against the cold, brick wall and stared up at him in mute terror. He was huge and nightmarish above her, his face deeply shadowed now by the brim of his hat.

'I promise,' she croaked at last. 'I promise!'

Arthur reached down to touch her face with his fingers.

'Then sleep on it,' he said softly, and went out of the hut locking the door behind him.

Chapter 7

The Webb-Gorings had been enjoying a comfortable evening together in front of the fire when the phone sounded in the hall. An evening alone together was a rare treat in their normally hectic social life, and particularly enjoyable this evening, because the rising wind was beating a loud tattoo of raindrops against the french windows and it was very pleasant not to be out in it, dashing about trying to keep dry.

Anthea went to take the call and James, upstairs in his room doing his homework, set about listening with only half an ear, because although he never missed an opportunity to be nosy, in the main his parents' telephone conversations were extremely boring.

When he heard his mother replace the receiver, however, he was alert and his heart was thumping in his chest. He'd only heard his mother's side of the conversation, but he knew it had been Aunty at the other end. He knew something dreadful had happened, and he was creeping downstairs to listen at the door even as Anthea went back into the drawing-room.

Charles Webb-Goring's jaw dropped when he saw his wife's face, for she was white to the lips. He rose swiftly from his chair taking a couple of steps towards her, and she waved her hands helplessly, as tears of panic welled up in her eyes.

'Dorothea's disappeared,' she whispered at last through trembling lips. 'She's gone, Charles. Mrs B went to collect her from school, and she wasn't there . . .'

She tailed into silence as a vicious gust of wind punched the glass doors at the far end of the room, rippling the curtains.

Memories came flooding in like the enemy. Dreadful, dark memories that were horribly familiar.

'Oh, God . . .' he murmured, and they both knew what the other was thinking. Both recognized their emotions and remembered them in familiar dread.

Charles helped his wife to a chair and then leaned over her gently.

'Tell me, darling,' he said and she did, spilling out Edna's terror to mingle with her own. When she had finished he straightened up and glanced at the clock on the mantelpiece. 'We must go,' he declared. 'We'll leave a note for James, in case he wakes up and finds us gone, but we *can't* leave Mrs B there on her own, it's not human!'

Anthea shook her head as a stream of tears coursed down her cheeks, and sobs shook her body.

'She doesn't want us there, Charles,' she wept. 'She said we were to stay here with James, and that under no circumstances were we to leave him alone, or tell him. She said he simply mustn't know, not for the time being—'

'Which is too late, I'm afraid,' James interrupted fearfully, pushing open the door and walking into the room. 'Mummy . . . ?'

Anthea hugged her son as they cried together, but James knew the horror that gripped his parents, he could see it in their eyes. Peachy had disappeared one day, years ago before the war; and no one had ever seen or heard of him again. Well, he couldn't relate to Peachy; he knew him only as a photograph but he could relate to Dorothea, and over his dead body was Dorothea going to disappear without trace!

'I want to go and look for her, Mummy!' he declared, stumbling to his feet and standing there, a vulnerable little figure in his pyjamas. 'I want to go *now*!'

Charles put a hand on his son's shoulder and squeezed it gently. He was proud of James, he was a gutsy little boy – and at the same time he was suddenly appalled, for he was forced to confront his emotions. If James ever vanished, he thought, he'd never survive it!

'Not tonight, old boy,' he murmured fondly. 'There truly isn't any point in the dark, we wouldn't know where to begin. Besides, the police are out already. What you need to do, if you want to be really helpful, is think through everywhere you've ever been with Dorothea, everyone you've ever met, and everything she might have said to you about anyone. Would you do that?'

James nodded and after a while he began to talk. His parents listened, at the same time listening for the phone; but it didn't ring again, and outside the wind grew ever stronger.

Edna had searched everywhere she could think of for Dorothea as wet darkness had closed around her hours earlier, and as Thelma Gregson telephoned the police, she had circled the village yet again, calling into the darkness, over and over, until her voice was hoarse.

Eventually, back home in Boxgrove Crescent, she had run down the path in her tiny back garden to see if by any wonderful chance the chicken shed had been locked up . . . which of course it hadn't, and then there hadn't been anywhere else to look. By then she had been dirty and bedraggled with her grey hair plastered to her face and her feet squelching in her shoes, but oddly she hadn't been cold. Now, with the police gone, she sat in her dressing-gown in front of the fire which she had lovingly built and lit, and was now allowing to quietly die. She shivered uncontrollably as piece by terrible piece her world fell apart around her.

She'd told the Webb-Gorings she didn't want them there, and she'd told Thelma Gregson the same thing, for even the *thought* of people in her tiny front room seemed to threaten her sanity, but no matter how hard she tried she couldn't keep her memories away. They came like a flood, bursting through her weak resolve, and as she stared at a black-and-white photograph of the smiling Dorothea on her mantelpiece, it felt as if she would drown in a flood of despair.

Dear little Dorothea, tanned and grinning, holding up a great length of seaweed on the beach at Pengloss last summer. Aunty's little blessing; her gift from God, to whom for every day of their three years together Edna had never failed to say thank you.

And suddenly she was gone!

Coal shifted in the small grate, sending an army of sparks marching up the back wall of the chimney. Edna hugged Blackie in her lap as she closed her eyes, reluctantly letting in her memories of the orphanage.

What a God-forsaken place *that* had been. A municipal building of the worst kind, standing upon the brow of a hill and weeping black tears of industrial waste in the rain as huddled amongst its colonnades and carved façade, bedraggled pigeons struggled to find a little shelter. A Dickensian edifice of monstrous proportions, designed to freeze the heart and squash the spirit even before one set foot in the place.

She remembered the thin, mealy-mouthed woman who had called herself governess and who had clearly never loved anything in her life, let alone an orphaned child. Particularly she remembered the avaricious gleam in the woman's eyes when they had lit upon Anthea Webb-Goring, followed by the 'of course you do understand . . . necessary costs . . . for all my other *dear* children . . .' as the cheque book came out.

Effectively they had had to pay for Dorothea: buy her from this woman. Then, to add insult to injury, they had been required to return her clothes, once new ones had been obtained for her! Well Anthea had got her own back there, she'd left the orphanage clothes in a brown-paper bag, placed on the doorstep, in the rain.

Oh, but that first night, in a tiny women-only hotel in Manchester, sitting beside the bed as her vulnerable, underfed, *beautiful* niece had finally allowed herself to sleep, accepting that she was safe. Oh the love, the catching of her heart, the silent promise to her that she would never, *never* be hurt or abandoned again, and all the time the rain had spattered relentlessly against the windows. . . .

The rain . . . the rain . . . the rain. A spiteful gust of wind suddenly blew down the chimney and sent a cloud of smoke billowing out into the little room, dragging Edna rudely back to the present. Blackie, warm on her knees, jumped galvanically and leapt down in disgust . . . and suddenly the place he had occupied on her lap was cold and bare.

Dorothea's place.

It was the last straw. Edna cried out in despair, put her face in her hands and dissolved into an agony of tears that threatened never, ever to stop.

Dorothea crouched unmoving against the wall in the little brick hut as the night wore on. Outside the wind howled through the branches of the horse-chestnut trees, roaring with a monstrous, deafening voice. Cold had seeped through her clothes and was sending shivers up and down her spine, she could feel neither her hands nor her feet and in the velvet darkness of this terrible prison one thing was uppermost in her mind, that no more than a couple of feet away, Rosemary lay dead in an old deckchair.

She tried to remember whether it had been like this sitting with her dead father, but of course it hadn't, because it hadn't been so dark. The dark now seemed to fill her nose and mouth and threaten to suffocate her. Sobbing softly to herself she thought of Aunty in their cosy little room, with Blackie washing himself on the window-sill and the wireless playing in the corner.

Strangely she didn't think of Arthur at all, for he had told her he wasn't coming back until the morning, so the idea that he might return and kill her in the dark didn't occur to her. All she thought about was her horror of Rosemary and her longing for Boxgrove Crescent; time passed dreadfully slowly. She eventually drifted in and out of a light doze at about two in the morning, but the cold woke her regularly, and she still had a very long time to wait before it began to get light.

James was walked gently up to bed by his mother at midnight, after he had been asleep for an hour or more on the sofa. Not awake enough to talk he willingly slithered into bed and welcomed her light goodnight kiss, but the sheets were chilly, and long before he was able to go back to sleep the memories of Dorothea crept back to haunt him.

Hour after hour the gale blasted on furiously and he tossed and turned, finding himself frightened, angry, desperate and miserable, but *never* tired. Then, at around half past four, the wind at last began to drop and he became even more wide-awake.

By half past five he had made up his mind. He had to go and look for Dorothea, there was no other way. If anyone was going to know where to look it was him, and he must go now, because if she had been out all night, then she needed him to find her quickly. He dressed in the denim jeans and smart green 'wind-cheater' that his uncle had brought him back from America some months ago, found his trusty torch, crept downstairs and let himself out into the wind-weary morning. Crossing the Hampton Court Road he set off towards the village. It was going to be a very long walk.

It took him the better part of an hour and a half to reach the rec, and by the time he got there it was light – or as light as it was likely to get that morning. He passed the water board buildings without a glance as he headed for the camp where Dorothea had gone the previous afternoon, and successfully muddied his jeans as he crawled through the sad and dripping undergrowth to reach it. But that very undergrowth had sheltered it from the worst of the storm, and James could see immediately that someone had been there.

Scraping about, as she had done, he found three slivers of wet paper-bag. White and green ... like a Bentalls bag. For a few seconds he sat back on his haunches as he tried to think through his find, and then he was off, back towards the swings, scouring every inch of the muddy little path, searching desperately for more clues.

As he hunted he thought that this detecting game might be quite fun if only he wasn't hunting for his beloved Dorothea; briefly he wondered whether it would be fun to be a policeman. Then he dragged his concentration back firmly to continue with his search. Five minutes later he was rewarded. He found a hole in the hedge leading into the water board buildings, a hole that someone had apparently tried to hide, and when he pushed his head through it he saw something that made his heart lurch.

Half-submerged, in a muddy puddle, was a red knitted glove with a white flower on it! Mr Johnson's scarf and gloves – so Dorothea was here somewhere? It was completely illogical, but as far as James was concerned it was a firm pointer, and he followed it.

He circled the two buildings with great care, looking for a way in. There was none into the pumping-station, that was certain. It had a huge, metal door which quite obviously would have required a special key, but the little brick hut, that was different. The hut had a green wooden door and a big padlock.

Tentatively he banged on it with his fists.

'Dorothea!' he called out, alarmed by the sudden loudness of his own voice. 'Dorothea! Are you in there?'

Dorothea was still crouched against the wall, and so cold and stiff that any idea of moving was out of the question. She was light-headed and confused, and though enough daylight filtered in through the thick glass windows above her head to show her Rosemary still lying in the deckchair; amazingly, she thought she could hear James's voice calling her name.

She closed her eyes and thought about him. James. It gave her a warm feeling. It was nice to think she could hear him calling her name.

He called again and hammered with more force on the door, abruptly jolting Dorothea into the real world; it *was* James. He was outside the door! She wriggled slightly and tried to call out, but nothing came from her throat, so she struggled harder to move and that brought forth a howl of agony as her joints screamed in protest.

Desperately she hauled herself to her feet and began to lurch across the hut, terrified that he would go away and not find her. In a weak, croaky voice she muttered, 'James . . . James . . .' and knocked into the deckchair in her hurry, but even as she landed against the inside of the door she knew he had heard and relief flooded through her small, freezing body.

Then Rosemary toppled sideways and landed on her back, half

in and half out of the chair, and Dorothea screamed at the top of her voice.

Galvanized into action by the sound of her terror, James hunted around inside the fenced site for something to use to open the door, and was delighted to find the remains of a rusty old spade lying in the grass.

He shouted to Dorothea what he was going to do, and crashed the spade repeadedly against the padlock, until the hasp, rather than the padlock, finally gave up the unequal struggle. It had been there a good many years longer, and the screws that held it were pretty rusty. One finally broke and fell out, whilst the other bent forwards, and James smashed it off with the spade. He was in.

As the door swung open Dorothea fairly shot out into his arms, dirty, tear-stained and weeping with terror, and as he hugged her his heart seemed to burst with relief. He had found her. His beloved Dorothea. He had found her.

'Who was it done this to you?' he demanded indignantly, as she sobbed in his arms and it began to lash with rain again. 'Was it Mr Johnson, was it?'

Dorothea's pale face crumpled and she cast a terrified glance towards the hut. She whispered: 'Rosemary . . .' and James followed the line of her eyes. Abruptly the joy of rescued and rescuer was gone and they were frightened children standing in the pouring rain, faced with the end of their innocence, staring at death in bewilderment.

Unlike Dorothea, James had never seen death before. Rosemary was lying with her mouth open and her limbs twisted. His resolve almost crumbled as he stared at her, for terror bit viciously into his psyche.

'Oh, crikey . . .' he whispered. 'Oh . . . crikey . . .' and he had never wanted to run from anything so much in his life.

He didn't know what he might have done at that moment if Dorothea hadn't suddenly clutched at his arm. He thought afterwards that he would almost certainly have been sick, and he was so grateful to her for needing him, for ultimately ensuring that he clawed his courage back and acted like a man. For they were not yet safe, the two of them, in fact they were about to be in mortal danger.

Edith Johnson had been very angry and extremely rude when the police had fetched up on her doorstep the evening before. She had muttered about persecution and harassment and pointedly refused to offer cups of tea to the officers; but dread had kept her rigidly still beside her husband in bed when they were at last alone in the night.

Dorothea Sprake! The idea was terrifying. That quaint little orphan so beloved of Edna Buddry, and so gentle and kind to others. Their Shirley admired Dorothea enormously because she was always sweet to her. And Edith liked her, too, much better than she liked Rosemary Archer. Not that she didn't like Rosemary, it was Rosemary's mother she objected to – but Edna: no one could object to Edna, she was a lovely woman.

As the night had roared angrily and busily on, Edith had been quite well aware of the fact that Arthur wasn't asleep beside her, despite the fact that he was so still. In fact it had probably been his stillness that had alerted her, and to relax enough to sleep had very quickly become an impossibility. He had climbed quietly out of bed at two o'clock and gone downstairs to have a cigarette, and she knew perfectly well that he had something serious on his mind. But not Dorothea, she pleaded with her God, *please*, not little Dorothea.

Arthur had gone over and over it in his head, desperate to find a way out of his dilemma other than the obvious one. If for one moment he had believed that he could sufficiently frighten the child into keeping quiet he would gladly have let her go; he had no desire to hurt her at all. He'd killed Rosemary by accident, for God's sake! But there was no way Dorothea was going to go back to Edna Buddry and not say anything. In no time at all the place would be crawling with police, and she would be bound to tell in the end.

There really was no choice other than to kill her, and that, of course, would leave him with two bodies to dispose of.

He washed and dressed early for work, barely speaking to Edith or any of his girls. They played nosily on the landing, as children will, and it was as much as he could do to stop himself from yelling at them to be quiet. Then, when Edith came up from the kitchen with her expressionless eyes and told him his bacon and eggs were on the table, he retched in the toilet.

He answered that he was in a hurry and didn't have time for breakfast. He glanced out into his tiny garden as he drank some tea, and noticed that the gale had ripped the corrugated-iron roof off the coal-shed in the night. He said, vaguely, that it might be time to build a new one, then he found himself wondering whether, when the next school holidays came and he could pack Edith and the girls off somewhere for a few days, he could build a nice new coal-shed and secretly bury Rosemary and Dorothea beneath it. The main problem would be getting the bodies up to Cheddar Close from the rec . . . but there'd be a way, he decided, with careful planning.

Distracted and obviously nervous he left the house, clutching his sample-case. He disappeared along the close towards Acacia Road, and knew, as he went, that Edith was watching him from the front-room window.

By the time he reached the recreation ground he had made up his mind what he was going to do. He couldn't possibly kill the child as she stood and looked at him, so he would tell her she could go, and make her promise not to tell. That would be easy enough; after a night locked in that hut with Rosemary's body Dorothea would be willing to promise anything, he knew. Then as she was going out of the door he would hit her from behind with one of the empty wine-bottles the tramp had left after Christmas. He hoped that one blow would kill her, but if it didn't she would almost certainly be unconscious and it wouldn't be so difficult to kill her after that. He just knew he didn't dare look into her eyes.

He saw them as he came to the hole in the fence. They were standing by the gaping door of the hut, hugging each other in the pouring rain and panic robbed him of rationality as bile rose in his throat and his heart began to pound with terror. God, it couldn't be true, he thought wildly, as he ran towards them. As he might have expected, they tried to flee.

Arthur lurched at Dorothea with the idea that if he could subdue her, he might be able to control the boy. She squealed in fright, dodging out of his way and James yelled at her to run.

Dorothea obeyed, almost throwing herself at the fence in her need to escape, but Arthur was on her and grabbed her by one arm, swinging her round so that she fell heavily, knocking the breath out of herself. She lay beneath him, staring up, her eyes frozen with fear, and as he bent to haul her up he was stupid enough to forget about James for a few seconds. It was a few seconds too long. James had just tripped on a large knobbly branch which had come down in the gale and was lying in the grass. With a strength born of rage and fear he snatched it up and swung it like a cricket-bat.

It hit Arthur squarely in the temple, bowling him over into the mud. Blood began to dribble from his head as he lay stunned, and James hit him again for good measure.

'You're going to get hung for what you've done!' he screeched as he dragged Dorothea to her feet. 'You're going to get hung, because you're a wicked man, and my daddy says wicked men deserve to get hung!'

Throwing aside the branch he scooted Dorothea through the hedge, scrambled after her and then grabbed her hand and ran with her like the wind.

Anthea Webb-Goring had found James missing from his bedroom at just before eight o'clock. He had very thoughtfully left his mother and father a note saying simply: *Gone to find Dorothea*, and by twenty-five past eight they were screeching round to Boxgrove Crescent in Charles's car.

They had been in Edna's tiny council house for less than five minutes when James hammered on the door; there'd been barely enough time to notice that the room was cold and cheerless and that Edna looked to have aged twenty years in one night, let alone make any plans for a search.

106

They were just standing there, completely at a loss to know what to do next. When the children came tumbling in it seemed for a second that it must be some sort of wild, wishful dream. Then Dorothea threw herself into Aunty's arms, sobbing hysterically, and James stood between his mother and father looking frightened. He fully expected a telling-off, but he had to get his bit in first, he decided firmly!

'It was *him*, Daddy,' he announced, trying to sound brave and determined. 'It was Mr Johnson, an' I hit him with a tree branch . . . He – he's killed . . . Rosemary.'

Anthea's eyes opened wide in horror and she stared at her son incredulously.

'James . . .' she whispered as unspeakable images flashed into her mind, 'you know you mustn't say things like that if you can't substantiate them, don't you?'

James's eyes suddenly became dark with his memories and his lip trembled.

'I saw her, Mummy . . .' he whispered. Anthea snatched him into her arms.

Charles went for the police and a doctor whilst Edna banked up the fire and put on milk for cocoa. Anthea, who took on the task of divesting the children of their wet, muddy clothes, was painfully aware of Dorothea's chalk white face, but as she struggled to remove her school jumper she noticed that the little girl was favouring her arm.

Delicately she explored and saw the child wince with pain. Looking up she found herself staring directly into Edna's eyes.

'The man's broken her arm, Mrs B,' she murmured as a thousand unspoken fears seeped into her mind. 'How do you suppose he managed to do that?'

'He knocked her down,' James announced. 'Mr Johnson did. He was trying to catch her, an' that was when I hit him with the tree branch . . .' Suddenly his mouth twisted as he struggled with his emotions. 'Rosemary was all sprawled in a deckchair . . .' he whispered, 'and she fell over when . . .'

Anthea held him tightly as she felt at once both relief and

horror, but though she held him, she was careful not to smother him like a child. He *was* a child, of course, but he was struggling desperately to be a grown-up, and it was not his mother's place to spoil it for him. For a couple of moments there was an uncomfortable silence in the room as the adults tried to work out what to do next, then Edna had a brain-wave. She clapped her hands together.

'Right then,' she declared. 'I'm going t'get the bath in here soon as I've heated enough water; and you two're going to get warm and clean. First things first, I think, don't you?'

James's eyes abruptly glowed with delight.

'Oh hurrah!' he cried. 'Now then, Mummy, now you're going to see what fun it is taking a bath at Aunty's!'

It was an excellent idea, but it had a more serious purpose than just bathing and warming the children; one look at Dorothea's skinny, naked body told Edna's fairly practised eye that whatever else had been done to her, she had evidently not been interfered with. That, at least, was a blessed relief . . . only she did wonder what might have been done to Rosemary . . . and tried to push the idea from her mind swiftly for it was calmness and efficiency that was wanted at this moment.

And so it was on to a strangely domestic little scene that Detective Inspector Maltby, a local CID officer, and his DC came a short time later. In a tiny front parlour he found two naked children being bathed in a huge tin bath in front of a roaring fire.

The local police station was not large and all the bobbies were familiar figures around the village. Station-Sergeant Wicks had given him all the background he needed to know about the orphaned little Dorothea, and the rich James who loved Edna Buddry so much and he thus sized the two children up shrewdly as Edna and Anthea went quietly on with bathing them. Five minutes later the doctor arrived and the room was so full it was shortly going to require a shoe-horn to move anyone, but Maltby was pleased to see how calm everyone was.

James's father had gone to Hampton Court to get clean clothes for his son, and in the meantime the little boy submitted to a lady's dressing gown without any fuss. He was remarkably contained for an eleven year old, the Inspector thought, and found he liked the boy immediately. With any luck he was going to be fortunate with these two.

Dorothea sat on Aunty's knee when she was clean and dry, but to the trained eye of the policeman her growing shock was obvious. Edna kept kissing her to reassure her, but during the telling of the morning's activities she said nothing. She nodded now and then in agreement with James, but she actually offered nothing of her own at all. Still, he thought, there was time enough for that later, when she was feeling better.

He was highly impressed with James. He had half expected the boy to start crowing with success and stealing all the glory, but he didn't do anything like that at all. He simply repeated, as succinctly as he could, precisely what he had done.

'And why,' Maltby asked him, when he had gone through his story minute by minute, 'did you think to go looking for Dorothea in the water board buildings?'

'Oh I didn't,' James replied truthfully, 'I went looking for her in the den.'

It seemed to fall into place then and Edna suddenly realised, with a sickening jolt, that but for James neither Dorothea nor Rosemary would ever have been seen again. That copse, such as it was, had already been searched once. The police would have been most unlikely to go back again, and even if they had done so, slivers of an old paper-bag would have meant nothing to them. James, with the childish conviction that Dorothea would have gone to 'their place' if she had needed a refuge, had simply followed his child's logic, and for the better part of an hour he talked honestly about his actions and feelings.

Then the doctor politely invaded the conversation and announced that it was time Dorothea went to the hospital.

Maltby was faintly reluctant, because so far Dorothea had offered nothing at all; but the sight of her grey, haunted face and small body hunched over her injured arm allowed him to give in. He was to regret it later, but now he was much more conscious of the importance of keeping the adults on his side and saving the children any further pain, so he smiled and glanced warmly at James.

'And how do you feel?' he asked.

James shrugged.

'I'm fine, thanks,' he answered. 'But ... then ... I didn't get hurt, did I?'

The policeman nodded.

'Then do you think you might feel up to coming to the police station with me and making a statement?' he enquired, keeping it as gentle as he could. 'It's nothing to worry about; I shall just ask you to describe again what happened and then sign the paper after someone's written it down. Your mother and father can come with you, of course.'

He had seen the awful mixture of pain and relief in Anthea's eyes as she kept glancing at her son and had felt a lurch in his heart, for there would be no relief, later, on the faces of Tim and Doreen Archer.

Angrily he looked at the two children and felt sickened. What damage had been done to them, for heaven's sake? The little girl was white and silent, and the boy, brave as he was, was never far from tears and would have to close his eyes to sleep at some point, and then the memory of what he had seen would flood back.

Would it keep on and on flooding back until their lives had been destroyed by it, he wondered, or was there really any truth in the resilience of childhood?

Suddenly James looked him full in the face, and Maltby saw his uncertainty wavering in his eyes.

'Will you make it all right, Inspector?' he asked.

Maltby touched his shoulder gently.

'I can't bring Rosemary back to life, James,' he replied truthfully. 'But I can punish the man who killed her – and with your help I will. I promise.'

Chapter 8

In the plaster room of the local cottage hospital, Dorothea's arm was X-rayed and fitted with a cast. It took some time and all through the process she seemed to grow visibly weaker until, without warning, she vomited everywhere and fainted. After that it was evident that she needed to be admitted, and she was carried up to a ward where in her bemused, fragile state she allowed Aunty to undress her and put her into bed without protest.

Almost immediately she fell into a deep, dreamless sleep.

When she awoke darkness was creeping across the windows, and she realized that the whole day had gone by. She was in a ward of nine beds, all of them except hers occupied by extremely old ladies. As she lay watching what was going on she was aware that her broken arm ached spitefully – and she was still a prisoner.

She desperately wanted to go home to Aunty.

At six o'clock some food came round on a trolley, and suddenly the ward smelled of boiled cabbage, along with all its other not so pleasant smells. She ate, because she was hungry, but when they tried to settle her back to sleep again afterwards, her eyes filled with tears. She didn't want to go back to sleep, she'd been asleep all day.

'Oh never mind, sweetheart,' said one of the nurses fondly. 'I'm sure we can find something to cheer you up.'

She actually found a teddy-bear and an Enid Blyton *Famous Five* book, and Dorothea took both items gratefully; but all around her the old ladies were making awful noises, shouting and moaning, and it seemed that she wasn't supposed to notice.

The old lady in the bed next to her was lying flat on her back with her mouth hanging open. She had skin the colour that Rosemary's had been in the hut, and her mouth had collapsed around her gums so that for all the world she looked as if she was dead. She filled Dorothea with terror with her lacklustre skin and her half-open eyes . . . like Rosemary . . . in death. . . .

Looking up into the face of the nurse who was plumping her pillows she whispered:

'Rosemary . . . I want to talk about . . .' She was instantly patted on the head.

'No, sweetheart,' replied the well-meaning lady softly. 'You don't have to worry about it any more. It's all over now, and you're safe. So come on, read your book and take your mind off it, like a good girl.'

But Dorothea didn't want to take her mind off it. She wanted to talk about Rosemary, to ask about what she had seen. She wanted to be certain that Rosemary's body had been found and she wanted, desperately, to know about Arthur. She began to cry quietly, as the realization that she would never meet Rosemary again at the corner of Acacia Avenue sank in and became real; that now they wouldn't go into the grammar school together on their first day . . . that they would never ride their bikes again. She wept as if her heart would break, as she silently begged for someone to listen. But nobody seemed to have time to hear what she needed to say.

Time crawled by and the day-shift gave way to the night-shift. They told her she must go back to sleep now and took her book away, then the lights were dimmed and the night yawned ahead.

Yawned. As the night before in the brick hut had yawned.

An old lady in the corner vomited repeatedly, moaning and bleating as the nurses attended her, and then calling out immediately they left her bedside. Another continually wailed: 'Alf! . . . Alf!' until she was sharply told to be quiet and dissolved into low, sobbing moans. Dorothea clung to the teddy she had been given, but she wanted Aunty, and couldn't quell the agony inside her. She was lonely without anyone she knew to comfort her ... and Rosemary's dead face kept swimming up in her mind ... Rosemary's ... and his ... dark and angry and ... *huge.*

When at last the old lady drifted into a noisy sleep, the two night nurses did a swift round of each bed and fearing she would get into trouble, Dorothea pretended to be asleep. She felt them deftly straightening her top sheet and tucking her in, then she almost jumped when she felt soft fingers briefly against her cheek.

'Poor little mite,' one of the nurses observed quietly, 'it doesn't bear *thinking* about, what she went through last night, does it? What a bastard, to do that to a little girl, I hope they catch him, and string him up!'

The other nurse clicked her tongue sympathetically.

'And it was her best friend, too,' she replied seriously. 'I can't think of anything more awful! Well at least she's as safe as houses in here. Bless her. And God rot him wherever he is, I say.'

It was careless talk at best and entirely incorrect, but for Dorothea it was the most damaging thing anyone could have said at that moment. So, Arthur was still out there somewhere, and trying to get at her. She felt physically stabbed with terror, and as the two nurses moved away from her bed she thought she had never been so alone in the whole of her life!

She was without help, and he was coming to get her. At considerable cost to her aching arm she turned over and lay perfectly still, trying to make herself so small that no one would see her, all the while fixing her gaze on the ward door. She began to think that if she could stay alert all night she might be safe, but it was dark and there was nothing to hold her attention. Inevitably she began to feel heavy-eyed again.

God rot him wherever he is ... echoed the nurse's voice in her head, as her terror of Arthur made her fight to stay awake ... *but she's as safe as houses in here ... in here ... in here ...*

Dorothea's eyes flew open suddenly. To her horror she realized she must have eventually fallen asleep, but she had no idea for how long. It was still pitch dark and the ward was very quiet, in fact abnormally quiet. Silent. Neither of the nurses was at her station and the ward door was propped open, with a weakish light from the corridor filtering in. As her heart pounded in her chest she watched, straining her ears for any noise, and she thought she heard him just before she saw him, though she couldn't be sure. She knew he was coming though.

He was tall, silhouetted in the doorway, his raincoat belted at the waist and his hat pulled down to hide his face. He carried his enormous samples case and he came straight towards her bed. He knew where she was. Exactly where she was.

Dorothea turned and pulled her knees up to her chest in an agony of terror, staring desperately at the next bed in the faint hope that the old lady with no teeth might suddenly be awake. She was not only not awake, she wasn't there. Rosemary lay in the bed in precisely the same position; on her back with her mouth open, and Dorothea began to whimper in panic.

Arthur bent his head so that his face was frighteningly close, and in the semi-darkness his eyes were shadowed, his face cruel and mean.

'If you tell,' he whispered, 'I'll take James and Aunty away from you, Dorothea Sprake. But if you promise that you won't breathe a word, not *one word* to anybody, then just maybe they'll be safe. And I'll be watching you, you wretched brat, I'll know immediately if you open your mouth, I'll be watching you all the time . . .'

Dorothea shot upright in bed screaming at the top of her voice, and it was not Arthur who stood before her, but the two nurses. They shushed gently, promising her that she was safe and had only had a nightmare, but it had been far too real to be a nightmare . . . surely? Frantically she searched for Arthur, but there was no sign of him and eventually, wretched with her own torment, she allowed them to comfort her.

They cuddled her until she had calmed down, then gave her a nice hot drink, but they didn't ask her any questions, so they apparently didn't notice that she wasn't speaking any more. Neither of them noted it in the book, anyway, and by the time she next awoke the shifts had changed again and the ward was busy with its morning routine.

She sat up quickly again, but this time found herself blinking in the daylight. Within seconds it became obvious to the ward staff that something was very wrong, for whatever had happened during the night had turned her into a silent, haunted little girl. They fetched the hospital matron, and then a doctor came to see her, but it wasn't that she didn't want to speak to them, she simply couldn't. She sat in bed, bewildered and frightened, and around her everyone talked to everyone else.

Unfortunately no one thought to tell her that Arthur had been arrested not long after she had been admitted the day before, and by the time anyone did it was much too late. Dorothea had taken herself into a place of sanctuary inside herself, and firmly closed the door behind her.

Arthur had lain on the ground, stunned and bleeding, for some time after James and Dorothea had made their escape. James might only have been eleven, but he was a strong boy and he had known exactly how to swing that branch. Rainwater stained pink with Arthur's blood dripped from his head as he tried to collect himself, and by the time he lurched to his feet he knew there was no point in chasing them, they were long gone.

So the game was up, then?

He stumbled towards the hut door and stood for a moment, mopping his forehead with his handkerchief and gazing at the bent and twisted hasp hanging from the padlock. Even if he'd had the necessary items in his bag he doubted he could have repaired it, it would have needed holes re-drilling in the wood and something to straighten out the hasp. And there certainly wasn't time for that.

Then he raised his eyes and unwillingly looked in through the door and to his horror he saw Rosemary's body sprawled untidily about the deckchair like a grotesque rag-doll. It made his stomach

115

heave in protest. Unable to leave her like that he eventually gripped his courage in both hands and lifted her to put her back into the deckchair, but it wasn't easy. Her skin was beginning to slip now, and touching her was nightmarish, but his conscience forced him on with the task, though it was sometime before at last he succeeded in getting her to stay reasonably upright again. Then, feeling thoroughly queasy, he wiped his hands on his mac, left the hut, pushed the door shut, gathered up his samples-case, crawled through the hole in the hedge and began to walk slowly away.

His first thought was to give himself up, to beg them to believe that Rosemary's death had been a terrible accident. But then what was his excuse for his treatment of Dorothea Sprake? So, abandoning that idea and making himself walk slowly so as not to attract attention, he began to make alternative plans. If he kept his cool there was still a chance, he thought . . . still a chance. . . .

The rain was pouring down relentlessly, and in no time at all he was soaked through to the skin. He didn't mind that though, because it was a logical reason for his being so generally unkempt, and it was washing away some of the mud from his mac. It was also keeping most people off the streets.

He must go home. He must get in before Edith returned from taking the girls to school, get the other key and dispose of them both, as well as the red scarf and gloves. Slowly he put his hand into his mac pocket and felt his heart tweak with fear.

Scarf and one glove.

Well, there wasn't any point in going back to search for the other one, even if the children hadn't found it first; the place would be crawling with police any moment, so the best he could do was dump what he'd got.

In his neat little house, which smelled of cooked breakfast and seemed to mock him in its normality, he ran upstairs for the other key. Then he went out into the garden and putting the keys, the scarf, the glove and a large stone into a canvas moneybag, he knotted the end tightly and heaved the lot over the chicken-wire fence on to the railway embankment. It bounced once and then tumbled away. Arthur prayed it would disappear into a thicket of bushes, never to be seen again.

He was upstairs in the bathroom putting antiseptic on his wounds when he heard Edith come in. She must have seen his case by the door, because she immediately came thumping up the stairs, and stared at him in horror through the open bathroom door.

'I was going to tell you that Dorothea Sprake didn't come to school this morning,' she exclaimed, 'but what on earth happened to you? Did you have an accident on your way to work, or something?'

Arthur's temple was swollen and bruised, his eye showed signs of blackening. James's second blow had caught him across the back of the head and the blood had dribbled down from it all over his shirt collar. He winced as he touched the open wounds with TCP, and watched his wife in the bathroom mirror.

'I was attacked,' he told her flatly, 'by Dorothea Sprake and that posh little boyfriend of hers. They were playing on the water board property, and when I went to see what they were doing, the boy started hitting me with a tree-branch.'

Edith's eyes grew wide with incredulity as she stared at him, enraged.

'I don't believe it!' she cried. 'What were they doing, for God's sake?'

Arthur shushed her softly, still dabbing at his wounds and uttering painful gasps.

'They'd just found Rosemary Archer's body, Edith,' he murmured. 'In that brick shed on the land. I can't blame them for being frightened when they saw me, but I wasn't expecting the boy to be quite so vicious!'

Edith Johnson suddenly felt a lurch of fear. She stared at her husband, pressing her lips together as her mind skipped frantically through what he had just said.

'Rosemary Archer?' she whispered. '*Dead*! Arthur, promise me . . .'

Arthur turned towards her. He looked awful, filthy and bleeding; but his eyes were not angry, just terribly sad.

'Promise you what, Edith?' he murmured. 'That it wasn't me? I freely admit I liked little Rosemary, I thought she was charming, and yes, I did travel home with her on the same bus on a Thursday evening – but kill her? Do you really believe I'd do a thing like that? Really?'

Edith lowered her eyes as she struggled to silence the voice in her soul which immediately shouted *yes*! But that made her feel guilty, and disloyal, and suddenly she hated herself.

'Of course I don't, Arthur,' she replied firmly. 'I'm sorry, that wasn't really ... Look, do you want me to go to the phone-box and call the police whilst you put on some dry clothes? Someone should report it, surely?'

He smiled crookedly at her naïvety.

'I think you're a bit late for that, my dear,' he said quietly. 'Now, I'd better go and change.'

Inspector Maltby arrived in Cheddar Close whilst Arthur was still upstairs in the bedroom. He had his DC with him and Edith gave them a hostile reception, but she felt sick at her own chaotic thoughts. She watched Arthur come downstairs and heard Maltby politely asking him to accompany them to the police station, and allowed her husband to squeeze her arm reassuringly and then gently kiss her as he prepared to go.

She wanted to shout her anger, protest his innocence, accuse the police of not doing their job properly . . . and not a word actually found its way out of her mouth as the three men stepped over the doorstep and went down the tiny pathway to the road.

The house was silent as the front door closed, and she watched the car depart from the front-room window. She wanted so much to believe what Arthur had told her, because if he was lying her whole world had suddenly been plunged into a nightmare from which they would never recover. But however hard she tried she could not silence the alarm bells that rang in her ears and almost deafened her!

Anthea, Edna and James arrived at ten o'clock in the morning to collect Dorothea from the hospital. James had had a rotten night and was more subdued than Anthea had ever seen him but, like all the other adults around her, she tried to chivvy him along instead of letting him talk – and all he wanted was answers to some of his haunting questions.

He fetched up short when he saw Dorothea, for her face echoed his agony as loudly as if it was shouted at him. Then the ward sister intercepted the adults and he went alone to her bed.

She stared at him in silent suffering, and he put his arms around her protectively.

'It's going to be all right, you know,' he told her doubtfully. 'Daddy and Mummy and me were at the police station yesterday when they brought in Mr Johnson, and they're not going to let him go, I promise. Daddy said, and so did 'Spector Maltby.'

He could see that she was unconvinced, and was far too young to know what to say next, but thankfully he didn't have to try because Anthea and Edna were approaching the bed. Dorothea flung herself at Aunty hugging her fiercely with her one good arm and bursting into noisy tears.

Edna held her tight, folding her in safe and trusted arms.

'It's all right, it's all right,' she promised soothingly. 'You're safe, sweet'eart, and you know I would *never* let any harm come to you. So please, talk to me, there's a good girl.'

Dorothea gazed into the face she loved so much and immediately Arthur's voice whispered: *If you tell, I'll take Aunty and James from you* . . . At once, and without any conscious decision on her part, her speech mechanism closed down, and she faced the fact that it wasn't that she didn't *want* to speak, she *couldn't*. Desperately she made a strange little noise in her throat and then buried her face in Edna's coat. Edna, deciding not to push it, exchanged glances with Anthea, and gave Dorothea gently into James's care. Hand in hand they went out into the fresh air together, towards the car.

'We're going back to Languard House,' James told her as they slid into the back seat and sat like two little refugees, hunched together on the leather upholstery. 'You and Aunty are going to be staying with us for now, 'cos Mummy thinks it's best.'

Dorothea stared out of the car window and thought of not going home to Aunty's little house . . . not seeing Charlie . . . and suddenly it seemed to her that her world was falling to pieces about her. Where were the constants, the things that had become so important in the last three years? It had all been so certain . . . and now it was gone.

I want to talk about Rosemary! her heart cried out in pain, but James, sitting beside her, was saying nothing, and in the front seats Anthea and Edna were talking about something else. Dorothea felt trapped inside her suffering, trapped and isolated.

So home was to be Languard House in future then? Without Blackie and without Charlie? Dorothea felt weary and bewildered, but as Anthea turned off the main road into the slip road that led to Languard House all at once her problems multiplied, for suddenly a sea of men in raincoats and hats, popping flashbulbs in their faces and all talking at once, surged around the car. Hands hammered on the bodywork and sounded sharply in the car, raised voices seemed to fill the small space within from corner to corner and Dorothea shrank in terror. Squeaking in fright she flung herself at James, and the two of them fought to get out of the way.

Slamming her foot furiously on the accelerator Anthea shot the car up the drive with a squeal of tyres, then, shielding the children as best they could, she and Edna shepherded them into the house.

'For God's *sake*!' she exclaimed as she slammed the front door in the faces of the surging throng. 'What the hell do they think they're doing? These are frightened children they're preying on. Have they no scruples?'

It appeared not. Charles found himself just as beleaguered when he arrived home from work that evening, and already by then it had become necessary to keep the drawing-room curtains drawn.

So Languard House was not going to be a place of refuge after all, and two days later, when Inspector Maltby called, Anthea complained bitterly to him.

'Oh I know you can't *order* them to go away,' she explained, 'because they're clever enough to stay just off our land, but there's always someone out there: press or sightseers. God, I really think people are taking day-trips out of London to come and gawp at us. One wonders if they then go on to the village. I do *hope* not!'

Maltby sighed heavily.

'Well, I'm afraid they do,' he replied. 'They're making the Archers' lives a misery, and they're tormenting Mrs Johnson cruelly.'

He saw Anthea's stylish blond head come up quickly, then he saw the sharp intelligence in her eyes which immediately stopped her speaking. At once they acknowledged each other as allies, sharing and understanding the deeper suffering of this dreadful thing.

'I'm so sorry,' she muttered, 'I was about to be rude, and I have no right to be, have I. Little Mrs Johnson hasn't done anything, and she deserves no condemnation from me. There but for the grace of God go all of us, right?'

Maltby, who was a battle-hardened policeman and had faced the worst of humankind over and over again in his long career, suddenly found his cynical nature deeply touched. She was a remarkable woman, this one, he thought; he knew he met her kind very rarely.

'Mrs Webb-Goring,' he said, 'I'm going to level with you. Arthur Johnson has been formally charged with Rosemary Archer's murder, and will appear before the magistrates tomorrow morning – but without Dorothea's evidence, it could be harder than you think to convict him. I need to have her speaking again.'

Anthea frowned and he watched her thinking it through.

'You mean James can only tell you so much?' she asked.

He nodded.

'Johnson admits he was on the water board property that

morning, but claims it was because he saw James and Dorothea playing there, and went to shoo them away. He says that of course his fingerprints are all over the inside of the hut, because he went in and found Rosemary's body. He is happy to agree that he travelled home with the child on the bus of a Thursday evening, but maintains he was on a different bus that particular Thursday, and we can find no one who saw them together.'

'And the gloves and scarf?' Anthea asked.

He chuckled mirthlessly.

'Anyone could have bought them,' he replied. 'It was sale-time, and the lady on the counter has no idea who she sold them to. He simply says it wasn't him and he knows nothing whatever about them . . . and if James and Dorothea think they saw him in Bentalls that afternoon – well, they're wrong.'

Anthea drew a deep breath, staring bleakly about her as frustrated anger tightened her mouth.

'And so who,' she demanded, 'does he maintain imprisoned little Dorothea?'

'A tramp,' the policeman answered, 'who we know was in the area and who terrified the life out of Rosemary and Dorothea on Boxing Day. He's got his story off pat. The only weak part is that this tramp is missing, and has been missing for ages as far as anyone can tell. Only Johnson claims to have seen him recently and we can't find him. Johnson will be remanded in custody tomorrow, because our case against him is good and strong, but when it comes to court we'll need Dorothea.'

He paused for a moment, and then turned his eyes to look at Anthea, who, he suspected, was a little ahead of him.

'Am I right,' he asked, 'in thinking that you have a sister in Cornwall with a nice, private hide-away that both children know and love?'

Anthea smiled.

'Bella, you mean,' she replied. 'How did you know about her . . . ?' she paused and then grinned. 'Oh, James, of course,' she said. 'You got him talking about batty Aunt Bella, no doubt. He's a naughty boy, she's not nearly as batty as he says . . . not any more, anyway. Ah well, at least he was talking about something else, I suppose. We've been trying to chivvy them up, talk about other things to take their minds off the horror of that brick hut. I suppose he told you about Peachy, whilst you were at it?'

Maltby chuckled.

'He asked me if I thought I could solve the mystery,' he replied, 'so I told him to have a go at solving it himself, and said he could have the job of my second-in-command if he did.'

Anthea laughed at him warmly.

'Well, you'd better watch it!' she exclaimed. 'Because he'll keep you to that if he does. I'll phone Bella now, and we'll get Mrs B home to pack, then we'll creep away like thieves in the night and bury ourselves at Pengloss for a bit. Bella'll be delighted, she adores having the children there.'

Maltby was hugely impressed. He knew this woman was a busy socialite, and that she probably had any number of appointments in her diary, but she hadn't given them a thought. Her priority had immediately been the welfare of the children.

So at least, he thought these two would be safe; and he remembered, with a painful stab, the agony in Tim and Doreen Archer's eyes when he had been obliged to tell them about the brutal and wretched end of their beautiful little daughter.

Anthea drove Edna to Boxgrove Crescent where she packed all her and Dorothea's belongings, and organized the care of the chickens by the neighbours. She lingered over her job for ages, because she knew that one task she had so far balked at had now to be undertaken, and she must force herself to go. She could not leave without seeing Tim and Doreen.

Tim opened the front door to her knock, and Edna thought he looked as if he had aged fifty years. It had fallen to him to formally identify Rosemary, so she had heard, and she knew from what James had said that it hadn't been a pretty sight. Just over two weeks. Was that really all it was since life in this little corner of the village had been comfortable, ordered and safe? It seemed like years.

How did you ever move on from anything like that? Edna wondered as she gazed into his empty, lifeless eyes. How did you lose the picture from your mind and remember instead the beautiful daughter that terrible vision had once been? Surely the answer was that you didn't.

'Mrs B,' he said with a pitiful bleakness in his voice. 'It's good of you to call. Doreen's in the lounge if you'd like to come in.'

Edna would have loved to have said no, that she was too busy and had only called for a few seconds, but she knew she couldn't do that.

She went with him into the predominantly rose-coloured lounge, with its television set and its discreet pile of Vogue magazine. Once Doreen, perfectly coiffed, elegantly dressed and subtly made up, would have greeted her like royalty. Doreen, whom everyone laughed at behind her back for her airs and graces. Now the woman she saw was almost unrecognizable: thin, haunted and unkempt, and spreading her suffering about her like a flood.

Edna sat down beside her on the sofa and took her hands, holding them warmly in her own.

'I'm so sorry, Doreen,' she whispered. 'So dreadfully sorry.'

Doreen snatched her hands away and her eyes were both agonized and hostile.

'So you should be,' she snorted. 'You got Dorothea back . . .'

Tim reached for her sharply, but his hands shook uncontrollably as he did so.

'That's enough, Doreen,' he said. 'Mrs B's come here to offer us her support, not to be bullied. She didn't have to come, remember.'

Doreen began to wail; it was an unearthly sound, like a suffering animal screaming for death. She rocked backwards and forwards, stuffing her fists into her mouth, and a flood of tears coursed down her puffy, swollen face. Almost immediately her mother came quietly into the room and Tim and Edna went out into the hall where Edna hugged him close to her, sharing his dreadful pain.

'Tim I . . . I can't come to the funeral,' she whispered eventually. 'I'm so sorry. I would've, you know I would, only I got to take

Dorothea away from here as quick as I can. She's stopped talking, won't say a word to anyone; and her nightmares, well . . .'

'Oh God, I understand,' Tim whispered, as a stream of tears began to course down his cheeks and he could do nothing whatever to stop them. 'No one wants to go to a child's funeral, do they? Children shouldn't die. Not beautiful children full of promise like our Rosemary . . .' Abruptly he broke into low sobs, wiping his hands furiously across his face to try and stem the tears. 'What did he think, when he was killing her, do you imagine? Do you think she knew she was going to die? Did she beg him for her life . . . ?'

Edna shushed him softly, recognizing that his pain longed to explode from him and spill out with the fury of a mad dog. He wanted to hurt someone to soothe his rage, and there was no one he could hurt. Given a gun and a moment alone with Arthur he would have pulled the trigger without hesitation, she thought.

'Tim,' she murmured, holding him in her arms like a little boy. 'You won't get any . . . silly ideas, will you, my love? And you won't let Doreen, neither. Promise me?' He frowned at her and she went on: 'Edith Johnson and those little girls, they ent to blame for Rosemary, don't forget that, will you?'

Tim understood and a look of ineffable pain crossed his face.

'It's hard, Mrs B,' he whispered. 'I want to go up there and throw bricks through the windows. In my bleakest moments I want to take one of their children and . . . but it won't come to that, I promise. I think in a little while we'll put the house up for sale, I'll apply for a transfer and we'll go somewhere right away from here. Start again. If that's possible.'

'Could you have any more children?' Edna asked.

With a bitter twist of his mouth, he shook his head.

'No, Rosemary was our only chance,' he replied flatly. 'Our little miracle, if you like. He stole our miracle from us without a second thought . . . and why did he want our child, he's already got three of his own. Maybe children aren't miracles when you can have as many of them as you like!'

Edna took her leave of him and then went across the road

125

towards the little corner shop. It was a sunny day, wrong for the deep pain they were all suffering, she thought. There would be hardly anyone in the village who hadn't known Rosemary Archer, by sight if nothing else. And equally there would be hardly anyone in the village who didn't know Arthur Johnson. It was all so bitterly close and personal.

Thelma Gregson was familiarly huge behind her polished wooden counter, but unfamiliarly grey and haunted. She greeted Edna warmly, they had been friends for many years, and expressed her relief at the news that she and Dorothea were off to Cornwall, but twice during their conversation she rubbed her hands across her face, and Edna knew that she was deeply troubled.

'Edith Johnson?' she asked eventually, and Thelma nodded.

'She's behaving as if nothin's happened,' she replied. 'Would you believe she sent them kiddies to school as usual? Headmistress had to get her to come and fetch 'em home, 'cos the other kids in the playground was throwing stones at 'em. And they're prisoners up there now. There's MURDERER sloshed across the front door in red paint, and I can't *tell* you what people's bin throwin' in their front garden, but she still walks down here every day with the girls, comes in the shop and buys food, and people spits at them out on the pavement, Edna! It's bloody awful!'

Edna pressed her lips together, appalled at the thought.

'Can't you deliver, Thelma?' she asked and the huge shopkeeper spread her hands in despair.

' 'Course I could,' she retorted, 'but she won't let me! She says he ain't done nothin', and that when it's proved all these people'll 'ave to say sorry to them. But he's guilty, Edna, and we know he is. Dorothea don't make mistakes; she's much too bright for that, and she knows him far too well to've mistook him for someone else.'

The two women stared at each other in silence for a moment as Edna found herself haunted to the point of breakdown, and was obliged to yank herself up and pull herself together with extreme effort.

'Take care of them, Thelma,' she whispered eventually. 'There's only you respected enough in this village to stop the worst of it, so do what you can, won't you.'

'Oh I intend to,' the other woman snarled fiercely, 'you can be sure of it. Only . . .' suddenly her eyes were desperately bleak. 'They're going to 'ang him in the end, Edna, and what future is there in that? Three little girls with their lives permanently blighted, one little girl dead, and one haunted for ever. Is that the answer, is it? Why do I think it ain't?'

Chapter 9

On the morning that Anthea, Edna and the children left Hampton Court, the police moved in to the house in Cheddar Close in force, and began taking the place apart.

Edith and her three little girls were like victims of a storm, clinging to the wreckage as policemen in great boots tramped all over their lives; but pathetically Edith stayed just inside rudeness, and even made them all tea. She was bewildered and frightened, Maltby could see that, and forced by circumstances to be belligerently loyal to her husband. How he would have loved, he thought sadly, to know what she *really* thought.

Anthea and James said goodbye to Charles very early in the morning, quite some time before it was light, and Charles prepared himself for some lonely times ahead. But Charles was a resourceful man, and as concerned as his wife for the welfare of the children. Besides, Mrs Minns was getting ready to do battle with the reporters camped on the doorstep, and Anthea privately thought she would probably feed Charles to death in self-defence in the following weeks!

'I'll miss you,' he said as he kissed her goodbye. 'And as for you, James, you behave yourself, all right. Your job is to look after Dorothea and be nice to Aunt Bella – and that isn't asking a great deal, so you be sure you do it to the best of your ability!'

James smiled at his father rather wanly. This ought to have been a fabulous adventure, sneaking off to Pengloss at six in the morning, and during term-time as well. What was more, they wouldn't be going to school when they got there either; his mother had arranged for Miss Forrester, a retired headmistress who lived in the village, to come up to the manor each day and give them lessons.

So, there would be lessons in Uncle David's old schoolroom, the ruined chapel to play in whenever they liked and the delights of Pengloss available for the foreseeable future. It would all have been quite perfect if it hadn't been for Rosemary, he thought . . . but he couldn't close his eyes without the sight of her, sprawled on the floor of the hut, and he was getting so tired of his questions being side-stepped.

Nobody would talk to him. Dorothea patently obviously couldn't, and everyone else kept being nice, but evasive. 'Go and play with your trains, darling . . . have a walk, blow some fresh air into the pair of you . . .' It was as if Rosemary had just sort of crept into the ether, leaving behind only the nightmares. And he wasn't sure which was most frightening, his own dreams, or Dorothea's screams when she awoke from hers.

Their journey to Cornwall was a long one, and it being February it wasn't possible to have the windows open much, which meant that Blackie made his presence known somewhat forcefully in the car. What with that and the brooding silence in the back seat, when usually there was giggling, game-playing and general uproar, it seemed to Anthea and Edna that it took for ever, and when eventually they turned off the village road to take the winding drive to the house it was dark again and the sight of warm lights glowing from the windows was an overwhelming relief.

Pengloss was a small manor, long and low and extremely old in places. Somewhere about the time of the Middle Ages there had been a priory standing on the site, and remains of the priory walls still existed, having been incorporated into the house. David Rosenthal, whose parents had bought Pengloss when it was almost derelict and then lovingly restored it, had grown up with wonderful stories about grey ladies, and ghostly monks, and it had been these which had excited his interest in the old ruined chapel that was so beloved of James and Dorothea.

The library had a number of books on the subject, detailing its building and the supposed holy well which it protected, but no well of any sort had ever been located – not by anyone living, anyway – and it seemed that for more years than anyone could remember the little ruined chapel had simply been a playground for the manor's children. Tomorrow with any luck, Anthea thought as she slid the car to a standstill outside the front door, James and Dorothea would go there to play – and start the long, long process of healing.

Molly Newby, Bella's housekeeper, let them into the house and greeted them in her usual friendly way, taking their coats and promising that her husband, Judd, would bring in the cases.

'Got a nice big chicken stew for you all,' she said, 'after you seen Mrs Bella. She's proper excited about you coming.'

Judd and Molly Newby had grown up on the Pengloss estate, and had played with Edna when they were all children together. Now they, and their son Seth and his family, were the only resident estate workers left, living their lives in two of the tied cottages close to the home farm. They were fiercely loyal to Bella, and had protected her with great compassion ever since Peachy had disappeared and David failed to return from the war; from Anthea and Edna's point of view, Judd Newby was a star.

Judd had a way with children; he was like a sort of pied piper. He had worshipped the sunny little Peachy; it had broken his heart when the child had so mysteriously vanished. At the time he had spent four days without sleep searching for him, risking his neck clambering on the cliffs and tearing his face and hands crawling through tangled undergrowth; and forever afterwards had blamed himself for the tragedy – although no one else ever had.

Now he looked upon James and Dorothea as his second chance, and at any given time was always to be found working close to where they happened to be playing. Well, tomorrow, Anthea thought desperately, he can start working his magic on them in force. And if anybody's going to do it, it's going to be Judd!

So with the smell of Molly's chicken stew exciting their senses, they went into the drawing-room to say hello to Bella. They were greeted at the door by her two border collies, Cyrus and Juno, who leapt at them in delight.

The drawing-room was large and beautiful. It covered the length of the house from front to back, sported big french windows that looked out across the cliffs towards the sea, and was filled with enormous, comfortable furniture. At this time of year it was subtly lit by soft lamps, warmed by a blazing fire, and rich velvet curtains hung over the windows, keeping out the chilly night, but for all its space it was a busy room.

Everywhere, on every flat surface, there stood framed photographs of Peachy. Photos of him on his own, with his parents, laughing, pensive and even sleeping. Amid all these reminders of her vanished child, Bella came forward to meet them, holding out her hands in welcome.

Her long, dark hair, which was flecked with grey nowadays, had been gathered up that morning into a large clip at the back of her head, and was now carelessly falling down, framing her beautiful face. Her clothes were, as always, mismatched and flowing, but there was an aura of gentleness about Bella that could not fail to touch those around her. Of course James and Dorothea had never seen her during any of her bad times because Anthea had made sure they didn't, but in her good times she was the perfect foil for her busy, efficient younger sister. Placid and peaceful.

She greeted the children first, placing a hand on each of their shoulders.

'James,' she said softly, bending to kiss him and enveloping him in a haze of her familiar perfume. 'My hero nephew. What a super chap you are, aren't you, but it's only what I would have expected of you, of course.'

James gave her his non-committal look.

'Thank you, Aunt Bella,' be replied politely.

Then Bella turned her attention to Dorothea. Unlike James, who even when he was feeling as uncertain as he did now didn't really care for hugs and kisses, Dorothea returned the hug she received fiercely, because she felt warm and safe, and she wanted so badly to be safe.

'Poor lamb,' Bella murmured. 'You're having a pretty awful time of it at the moment, aren't you. Never mind, you'll get your voice back, sweetheart, I promise you will.' She cupped Dorothea's face in her hands and gazed down at her lovingly. 'And in the meantime,' she said, 'you're in the safest place possible. No one will be allowed to hurt you at Pengloss, I give you my word.'

Dorothea found herself inclined to believe that – well, she had always been safe at Pengloss in the past, and it was just possible, she thought, that Mr Johnson wouldn't be able to find her here. She hugged Bella, squeezing her eyes tight shut, and just for a moment – no, a second – she found herself able to forget. But it was only for a second. Still, she thought hopefully, there might be more seconds in the days to come.

After dinner she and James were allowed to root out all the toys and games that had been packed away at the end of last summer and could be heard, for a while, having a busy time upstairs. Edna took the chance to sit before the kitchen range and catch up on the news with Molly, and Anthea sat in front of the drawing-room fire with her sister, opening her heart at length. At last she could really talk about it.

Bella listened without comment for a while; then, finding herself faintly alarmed, she asked:

'Anthea you have sat down and talked it through with James, haven't you?'

Anthea stared at her sister in blank astonishment, annoyed that she had so obviously missed the point.

'For God's sake, Bella'' she retorted. 'That's exactly what we *don't* want to do; talk about it with them. We want the children to forget it, not keep dragging it up.'

Bella Rosenthal stared into the dancing fire for a moment, then she inclined her head slightly.

'Well, I'm sorry,' she observed, 'but *you* obviously want to talk about it, so what makes you think they don't? If you persistently refuse how do you know what they're really thinking? There might be questions they need to ask, but never get the chance to.'

Furiously Anthea turned on her. The past week had been

exhausting and she, Charles and Edna had spent lots of it agreeing details of procedure. This she didn't need, not at the moment, she was stressed enough as it was.

'Well, persistently talking about it never did you much good, did it?' she snorted unkindly; then, blushing to the roots of her hair she put her hand out quickly. 'I'm so sorry,' she murmured, 'I really didn't mean to say that, it was unforgivably cruel. Bella, please, we've discussed it non-stop since it happened and Mrs B and I really do think it's best not to keep bringing little Rosemary into the conversation. So leave it be, I beg of you, just let us do it our way, will you?'

Bella shrugged and put her head back against the chair, staring at the ceiling.

'All right,' she agreed eventually. 'I'll do it your way. But if James asks me anything, then I have no intention of fobbing him off; I shall tell him what he wants to know. All right?'

Only James wouldn't ask Bella, because he had always been encouraged to be very conscious of Bella's great loss, and it would never have occurred to him that of all the adults in his life, his Aunt Bella might be likely to be the one to be truly sympathetic to his needs. And if Bella wanted proof that her way might be the right way, she certainly got it that night. Despite being miles away from the horror, and despite being allowed to share a room, James and Dorothea had definitely brought their nightmares with them, in force.

Come breakfast-time the next morning everybody was white with tiredness, and then, to cap it all, as James and Dorothea were being encouraged to go out to play, they suddenly found that rules were to be imposed. There had never been rules at Pengloss before. Normally they could go where they liked, out on to the cliffs, down to the bay, into the village, now it was all forbidden.

'We can't go off the estate?' James cried, staring indignantly at his mother. 'What, not even to the sweet-shop? Why not, I don't understand!'

Anthea and Edna exchanged uncomfortable glances. In a few days Rosemary Archer would be buried, and unless Anthea was much mistaken the village would be crawling with pressmen. Besides, the sweet-shop sold newspapers, and she didn't want them to see any which hadn't been vetted first.

'I'll take you to the shop if you wants to go,' Edna offered, throwing James one of her baleful stares. 'Us'll have a walk after lunch together if you like, the three of us, and you can have a penn'orth a sweets each – but *only* if you do as you'm told, all right?'

James nodded sourly, genuinely aggrieved by what felt very much like a punishment to him and then, as if on cue, the back kitchen door opened and Judd Newby came in.

Judd had a brown, wrinkled face and twinkling eyes; he smelled of earth and strong tobacco. His hands were calloused and nicotine-stained, he was barely literate and extremely slow of speech, but there was nothing he didn't know about the world of mother nature, and the children loved him dearly.

He took in their pale faces and tired eyes without comment, then he sat himself comfortably down at the kitchen table, between them.

'Hullo,' he said in his long, slow, deep voice, as his wife put a cup of tea down in front of him. 'I'd heard you was here, and I see I's not wrong. That's good, 'cos happens I'm be needing a bit of help around the place at the moment. Thought us'd go to the chapel first, check on the snowdrops and daffs, and then there's eggs to collect in the barn, and the milking parlour needs a good scrub down. You up for it?'

'Oh indeed we are!' James exclaimed. 'Well we're banned from going anywhere else. You coming, Dorothea?'

To Edna's and Anthea's delight they saw a small smile touch the white faced Dorothea's lips and she obediently went to fetch her coat and boots.

'She'll be right,' Judd promised when she'd gone. 'She'll be right. You'll see.'

Five minutes later he went out with them and a blast of cold air blew through the kitchen as the door closed behind them.

Much later in the morning, when Anthea was helping to chop

vegetables for lunch, she glanced out of the window and saw them again, walking in the kitchen garden together. James and Dorothea stood one either side of Judd as he held them in conversation. James was listening avidly, whilst Dorothea clutched the old man's hand, and Anthea smiled happily.

'Thank God for Judd,' she murmured. 'He's a miracle worker, your husband, Molly. If anyone's going to calm them enough to sleep, it'll be him.'

And Edna, who remembered how as a child he had always had any number of wild animals as pets, and been so gentle with them, continued to chop vegetables and felt herself relax for the first time in days. Suddenly the horror of it all was beginning to recede.

In a couple of weeks, Anthea thought, she'd arrange for them to begin lessons, but for now the time they spent collecting eggs in the barn, watching proceedings in the milking shed and taking pony-and-trap rides with Judd would do them more good than anything.

Pretty, charming Rosemary Archer was far from the first child to be snuffed out by a man who should not have felt about her in the way he did, and she would not be the last, but her death had captured the imagination of the entire country – largely because of Dorothea's and James's part in it. Her funeral became a focus of a great deal of public emotion and anger.

People lined the streets to the cemetery and the hearse was laden with flowers, as with pops and flashes, press photographers starkly captured her mother's and father's grief on camera. Doreen collapsed at the graveside, as above them a sun-drenched, china-blue sky seemed incongruously out of place on such an occasion, and as Tim lifted her to her feet she fell against him, sobbing in agony.

Rosemary's coffin was small and white, with a simple engraved plaque on it. The hole into which it was lowered was small, too, and dreadfully deep. The roses her distraught family threw down upon it, to be suffocated under tons of earth just as she had been suffocated under Arthur Johnson's hands, were pink.

As they drove away in the funeral car, Tim looked at Doreen in despair. It was over, Rosemary was dead and buried and nothing could bring her back. The only option open to them now was to move on and try and piece their lives back together, but he could quite clearly see that it would never happen. Doreen was never going to be able to let go of the pain. Even if Arthur Johnson was hanged, which seemed likely, there would never be justice for Doreen.

Later that afternoon, Edith Johnson was cut by flying glass when someone threw a brick through her front window. After that a uniformed constable was put on guard at her front door.

It was starkly evident that her neighbours no longer wished to speak to her, and after the public outpouring of anger and grief at the funeral there wasn't anyone in the village prepared to go anywhere near her if they could help it, except Thelma Gregson. Mrs Gregson, the ferocious female from the little corner shop, of whom most people in the village were at least somewhat wary if not downright frightened, didn't forget what Edna Buddry had asked of her. She became like a vast guardian angel, taking the beleaguered little family food from the shop, purchasing items for them from the other shops in the village, and daring anybody from the neighbourhood to criticize her.

Edith knew it couldn't go on, it wasn't fair on any of them, but her alternatives were horribly limited, and she went on putting them off for as long as she dared.

James and Dorothea never saw the newspapers covering Rosemary's funeral, but they knew the day on which it was held because Bella (whether Anthea like it or not) insisted on prayers being said for her.

In the village – which had long been extremely grateful to the Rosenthal family for the prosperity they had brought with them when they had come to Pengloss – everybody quietly but firmly closed ranks.

The hungry swarm of pressmen who descended looking for James and Dorothea were met by a wall of silence. They tried asking questions to no avail; they tried finding accommodation also to no avail but rather more frustratingly they discovered that they couldn't even get a drink in the local pub. When it turned out that they couldn't find the entrance to Pengloss either, for it wasn't easy at the best of times and Judd had taken down the sign, most of them drifted disconsolately away, and within a few days everything had gone back to normal.

But it didn't change the fact that Rosemary was dead and buried, and the fact that James and Dorothea were safe and so carefully watched over at Pengloss was no comfort at all to Doreen and Tim.

It was an encounter with Doreen, some days later, which finally decided Edith Johnson she must leave, for it was painful and humiliating. She and her three little girls, all of whom were still turned out with their mother's usual loving care, even though they were excluded from school, had ventured out early of an afternoon to walk down to the shop. Edith simply could not keep them cooped up indefinitely, and rightly she resented the fact that they had done nothing and yet were tormented and pilloried.

The walk down Acacia Road passed without incident and Thelma greeted them warmly in the shop, giving each child a penny bar of chocolate. Then, as they stepped out to go home, they came face to face with Doreen, and Edith was trapped. There was no escape.

Doreen was walking unsteadily across the road, and she looked unspeakably dreadful. She had lost so much weight that she was almost skeletally thin, and her once beautiful hair seemed not to have been brushed or combed for weeks. There were deep hollows in her face and terrible suffering in her eyes and as she suddenly fetched up in front of Edith her lips seemed almost to peel back from her teeth in a savage sneer. Appalled, Edith shrank from her, but there was nowhere to go.

'You *bitch*!' Doreen snarled, as spittle flew from the corners of her mouth in fury. 'What're you doing parading your children in front of me! *How dare you!*'

Edith tried to step backwards, but there wasn't room for them all to get in through the shop door, and anyway as she searched frantically behind her she couldn't find the handle. Then Doreen grabbed Shirley, dragging her away from her mother. As the child wailed in panic, she began to yank her golden curls, as if she would tear them out.

'How would you like it if I smothered the life out of her?' she shrieked, shaking the sobbing Shirley as Edith grappled to free her. 'Think it would be fair, do you? Kill her, shall I? Like your *filthy* husband killed my Rosemary!'

Abruptly the shop door flew open behind Edith, and Thelma Gregson darted out with remarkable speed for a woman of her size. The twins, who were howling with fright, and clinging to their mother as she and Doreen scuffled, found themselves removed and pushed inside the shop. Then Thelma prised Doreen and Edith apart, and thrust Doreen backwards, getting firmly between her and her quarry. At that moment Tim Archer came running across the road towards them.

Little Shirley was sobbing piteously as she clung to her mother, and Edith was white-faced with shock, staring at Doreen open-mouthed.

'Tim,' Thelma said sharply, 'take 'er 'ome. Now!'

Tim began to gabble an apology, but Doreen, wild-eyed and screeching with rage, fought to get back at the objects of her hatred, her arms flailing and her nails sharp.

'I'll kill them!' she screamed. 'Kill them, like he killed Rosemary!'

Thelma held her firmly, forcing her arms down to avoid the clawing nails.

'Enough!' she barked loudly. 'Stop it, Doreen. *Now!*'

Doreen abruptly dissolved into tearing sobs that seemed wrenched from her very soul. Tim wrapped her in his arms and led her away across the road.

Thelma turned quietly to Edith and Shirley and edged them back into the shop, then closed the door behind them and turned the sign to read CLOSED.

'Oh Lord,' she said softly, 'I'm so sorry for that. You better come through the back and have a cup of tea; you looks like you needs one. And we better talk about your future an'all, I'm afraid, 'cos I really don't think you can stay here any longer, do you?'

Edith Johnson felt her heart sink as misery engulfed her.

'But I haven't *done* anything,' she cried bitterly, and for an instant Thelma held her in a sympathetic hug.

'I know you haven't dear,' she replied sadly, 'but you just seen for yourself what you're up against, and you can't expect Tim and Doreen to move away to suit you. Rightly or wrongly they're the injured party. Besides, it's time them kiddies of yours went back to school and tried to live a normal life. You has to see that. I know you said you didn't fancy going to yer sister's, but I really think you ain't got a choice no more, so you best phone her from here, eh? When you've had your tea. What d'you say?'

'I say it's not fair!' Edith retorted on the edge of tears. 'It's just not fair!'

But fair or not it was the only option open to her, and the following day, with the assistance of Thelma's grown-up son who had a small van, Edith, Shirley and the twins left Cheddar Close with a few of their possessions and were driven to Balham, to Edith's sister Phyllis.

It might have been a place of sanctuary, if Phyllis Brown and her husband had been good people, but they weren't. Phyllis was jealous of Edith because she had never been able to have any children of her own. Phyllis's husband Reg was – of all inappropriate things – a prison officer, and both of them had always mistrusted and despised Arthur.

So poor Edith found herself allotted a cramped, back bedroom in a grimy, terraced house in Balham, in which she and her children were expected to make their home, with one small double bed and one camp-bed between them. Beyond Phyllis's dispirited square of back garden the trains ran, but unlike at Cheddar Close there was no steep embankment to muffle some of the noise and the whole house seemed to shake at the foundations when an express thundered through.

The house rules were many and inflexible. Reg Brown worked

shifts, so every couple of weeks he was sleeping during the day and at those times even a squeak out of place from the girls caused trouble. Treats – such as a couple of bits of broken biscuit from the tin in the pantry – were handed out as rewards, but the rule was that if one child erred, none of them received a biscuit, and so very quickly there were no treats. Dinner was at six-thirty in the evening, and immediately afterwards they were expected to take themselves off to their one room, whilst Reg and Phyllis watched the television together in the parlour. There, in the tiny cramped bedroom, the pretty children and their mother, who had done no wrong to anybody, grew pale and silent in their suffering.

They went to school one single time and were so badly bullied that Edith never sent them again. After that they spent their days in a scrubby little park half a mile away from the house in Balham, and there they either played, or sat beside their mother on a bench seat and shivered. The park, had swings and a slide, and they became the highlight of the little girls' lives – ironically, considering how often, without them, their father had stood beside another playground and lusted after someone else's little girl.

So in this miserable state of limbo, as Edith made fortnightly visits to see Arthur and life for herself and her three little girls was unspeakably awful, winter passed and spring began to make an appearance. The park became warmer, warm enough even to give them lessons outside sometimes, and daffodils bloomed in the council flower-beds. Arthur would stand trial in July, she was told, and after that, she confidently assured the girls, they would all be going home to Cheddar Close to pick up where they had left off.

But in her heart she very much doubted it. Cheddar Close was becoming like a dream. A place where they had been so happy once, but must have somehow not paid enough attention, for now with each passing day it slipped further and further into a world of unreality.

With the coming of spring to Pengloss, life had settled into a routine for James and Dorothea; a routine so different from the life they had lived before that memories of that dreadful, wind-weary morning in February seemed sometimes almost like a glimpse into a dream that hadn't actually been theirs.

No one talked about Rosemary or Mr Johnson – none of the adults did, anyway. James talked about them, when he and Dorothea were alone. He wondered aloud what it would be like to be dead – and sometimes what it would be like to be hanged. He even made a gallows out of sticks, and hanged an old china doll he found upstairs in a deserted bedroom; but when he pulled the string tight her head came off, and fell to the ground. It landed face up, and lay in the dust with its mouth open . . . and it looked so much like Rosemary for a moment that he began to cry.

Dorothea would have comforted him had she known how to, but unbeknown to anyone at all she was floundering about in a different horror now – and its incipience had been sadly missed by those around her, because her initial reactions had been written off as something else.

She had been given a warning and it had sealed her mouth shut even tighter than before. Now she knew she would never speak again, and it didn't matter how much Aunty begged her or cuddled her; or how much everyone else at Pengloss assured her she was quite safe to talk to them. She knew she wasn't, she had been warned.

The shock had happened on her birthday, a warm, April day when she had been made a huge fuss of, received presents, had a little party, worn her best dress and eaten quantities of gorgeous cake. It had been a perfect day, the nearest she had come to speaking and when she and James had gone to curl up beside Bella on the sofa after supper as usual, she had almost spoken out loud, because she had felt so happy and contented.

And then Mr Johnson had handed out his warning.

On her birthday. Just so that she wouldn't forget!

Bella had been reading to the children for an hour every evening ever since their arrival at Pengloss, and since she had an endless supply of books at her disposal in the library, it was a routine that could have gone on for years, had they so desired it.

James and Dorothea chose the books in turn, and already it had become a sort of competition; each child trying to outdo the other's previous choice. That night James's choice of *King Soloman's Mines* was finished, and as Bella closed the book in her lap, Dorothea uncurled herself from the sofa, cast James a significant glance, and headed off to the library to make a selection. She was wearing her maroon-and-white frock, the one Anthea had bought her for Rosemary's party, and she felt good. She would take her time, and this time, she promised herself, she would come up with a real winner!

She had been happily perusing the shelves for ten minutes when she came upon *Moonfleet* by J. Meade Falkner. Just the name seemed romantic and it caught her imagination at once, but like most of the books in the library it was old and valuable, and she knew she must handle it with great care. It was on a shelf just above her head, but reachable if she stood on tiptoe, so keeping her fingers well away from the spine in case she damaged it she tipped it carefully backwards towards her . . . and another book, a paperback which had been carelessly tossed on top of it, tumbled down and landed at her feet.

This was a cheap paperback crime novel which Anthea had purchased from the bookstall at the village fête the summer before, and read whilst sunning herself in the cove. Having finished it she had simply chucked it on to a shelf at random, and because it wasn't the sort of thing Bella would ever read, it had lain there ever since.

It was called *This Man is Death*, but that, in itself, was not the problem. On the cover, which was orange and white, was a thick, black line-drawing of a man. He was leaning his back against a streetlamp, the light from which cast dark shadows across him, so that the hat pulled down over his eyes completely shaded his face. There was a cigarette in his hand, with a little black thread of smoke curling upwards, and his raincoat was tightly belted at the waist. At his feet was a small, square suitcase.

Dorothea stared at the book as her heart seemed to freeze in her chest . . . and Arthur, faceless but there, stared back at her.

'. . . *I'll be watching you,*' his voice hissed, leaping out of the

142

depth of her fear like a monster rising from a lake. *'If you tell, I'll take Aunty and James away from you'* . . . So he *had* been at the hospital that night, and he *was* able to be in two places at once?

She picked up the book and held it in trembling hands. She remembered the smell in the little brick hut and her terrible fear of the dark, and of the death hidden within it. Then she remembered the smell of age and disinfectant in the hospital ward, and the door propped open in the weak light as he came . . . closer and closer . . . and no one was there to stop him. . . .

She put the book back, sliding it on to the shelf as if it was likely to explode, grabbed *Moonfleet* and ran from the library as if the hounds of hell were after her, bursting into the drawing-room.

'Oh about time!' James exclaimed, as she stumbled in. 'We thought you were never going to choose . . .' and broke off in mid sentence as he saw her face.

Bella saw it too and held out her arms.

'Sweetheart?' she whispered.

Dorothea threw herself into the embrace, shivering and clinging as her breath came in frightened little gasps, and the horror of it all closed in around her again.

It was a big set-back. The nightmares raged for ten nights in a row until everyone became hollow-eyed from lack of sleep. In the end, in a desperate attempt to help herself, Dorothea wrote a story in which appeared the words: *He is in the libery*, and at Miss Forrester's suggestion that it might be a cry for help, Bella, Anthea and Edna searched the library from top to bottom. But they didn't know what they were looking for: they found *This Man is Death* but ignored it.

'Honestly, Anthea, the tripe you read!' Bella said disgustedly, and tossed it carelessly back on to a shelf.

Dorothea found it again when she was alone and moved it to a place where she could keep a close eye on it. And she checked on it every single day. It was her only defence. If he was watching her, then she must constantly keep a watch on him too.

So the pain dulled again, at least to an acceptable level, and she stopped screaming in the night. The adults put it down to its having been her birthday; dredging up the memories of Rosemary's birthday, and the dress was put away right out of sight.

But it wasn't the dress, it wasn't the dress at all . . . only how could she tell them?

Chapter 10

In the middle of June there was a sudden, typically British heat wave: hot and oppressive; Edith found travelling across London to visit Arthur a thoroughly distasteful experience. She found sitting across from him in the prison visiting-room unpleasant, too, for there were big, wet patches in the armpits of his shirt and his hair smelled stale and unwashed. He was pasty-faced, discontented and sorry for himself and didn't seem remotely interested in anything but his own discomfort.

It pulled her up short, because as they exchanged their familiar, banal conversation she found that she wanted more than anything to walk away from him. Edith knew in her heart that he had killed Rosemary – although she felt certain it had been an accident because Arthur would certainly never have set out to do such a thing – but it didn't alter the fact that he had three beautiful little girls of his own, and yet he had yearned so much for a different one that he had put himself in the way of killing her!

In a way, she thought, she was jealous. What had Rosemary Archer ever had that their girls had lacked, to make their father so indifferent to them? And how was it fair that he was now causing them so much suffering, when clearly he had failed in his love for them in the first place?

Suddenly she knew he no longer deserved to be shielded from the suffering of his family and, harshly, without pity, she proceeded to tell him the truth. As flies buzzed sleepily against the barred windows of the smelly room, and the heat made her stick to the chair, she explained in graphic detail why the girls didn't go to school any longer, and how they were bullied and ill-treated at Reg and Phyllis's. Once she had begun it all seemed to pour out of her in an unstoppable stream, and she did her best to hurt him as she told him that they weren't even properly clean any more, let alone pretty; that they didn't have a single friend between them and were trapped in a dreadful kind of limbo which was all of his making.

In the end she reduced him to tears, which she found strangely satisfying, and had to steel herself to remain still when he clutched her hands and promised her it was all going to come out right eventually.

'We *are* going home to Cheddar Close, Edith,' he promised earnestly as tears trickled down his sweaty face. 'I promise you we are, and I'll make it up to you, as God is my witness I will.'

She nodded.

'A jury will definitely find you not guilty then?' she asked. 'I mean there is no evidence against you, right? Inspector Maltby has got the wrong man and the jury will see that; is that what you're saying?'

She saw his eyes flicker and she knew the look so well – she'd seen it so many times before, when he had told her he'd been working and clearly he hadn't.

'I didn't do anything,' he answered earnestly, leaning towards her so that the smell of his hair was worse and made her jerk her head back. 'I saw Dorothea Sprake and her little boy-friend playing on water board property and went in there to stop them. And whatever she thinks, I didn't shut her up all night in that hut. My God, if only she could speak we could talk to her and make her see that she's mistaken.'

Lies, all lies! Unless Edith was much mistaken he was *banking* on the fact that Dorothea couldn't speak, and if he was as guilty as she suspected he was, then God wasn't going to do *anything* to help. She was going to have to find a way out of this by herself. But it was to be a particularly bad day for Edith, this unbearably hot, oppressive summer's day, for when she got back to Balham, dusty and sweating and longing for a bath, she found her little girls in floods of tears.

Phyllis Brown had taken it upon herself to give them a haircut. Each child had been thrust on to a kitchen chair, had a pudding-basin pushed down over her head and been shorn of her fine curls. And they looked awful, for the job had been done without the slightest care and with blunt, kitchen scissors.

'You had no right!' Edith screamed at her sister as the three little girls sobbed in their mother's arms. 'Who do you think you are, to treat us like this?'

Phyllis sneered in disgust.

'I had every right,' she retorted. 'You live in *my* house, you abide by *my* rules. For God's sake, Edith, all that bloody nonsense of dressing them all the same and doing their hair in curls, it's all gone! Can't you see that? Them kids've got to toughen up, my girl, because they've got a hard road in front of them, and the first thing they've got t'get used to is being like other kids. Grey socks, plimsolls and short hair! Besides, it's costing us a fortune you always wanting to bath them and wash their hair, and Reg is sick of great long hairs blocking up the plug-hole.'

That was a cruel slander, for Edith never left any hairs in the plug-hole or anywhere else, in fact it was only since her arrival in Balham that Phyllis and Reg had had the luxury of a clean bathroom, because beforehand it hadn't been something Phyllis bothered with much.

Now Edith gathered her weeping children around her and took them upstairs, where in direct defiance of her sister they all had a bath and washed their hair. Sitting in their cramped back bedroom she made an effort to style the butchered locks as best she could, telling herself firmly that in time it would grow again; but as, in the heat and misery of the day, life seemed to be more and more an endless downward spiral of pain, she found that there was a clarification of her emotions taking place within her, which would not be silenced.

Even if by an outside chance Arthur was innocent she still hated him for what he had done to them. In fact she hated him for everything; for all the years of loveless marriage and deep-seated doubt which had culminated in this humiliation, and left her with three

147

beautiful, vulnerable children and not a friend in the world. Whatever happened in the end, she decided, he would *never* get his children back! Only until July did they have to stay here; then, once the trial was over, she would take her girls and start a new life somewhere else. Change their names perhaps and begin again. One thing was for certain, they would not stay in Balham, and in the unlikely event that Arthur was freed, they would not live with him again either!

She began to think about what she could sell to raise a bit of money, and what she could do to earn some, as well. She was good with a sewing-machine and kept a meticulously clean and tidy home; there must be somebody who could use her services, she thought. Somebody, somewhere, who wouldn't condemn her out of hand because she was who she was.

But Edith was on a slippery slope and sinking into depression. She saw a doctor because she couldn't sleep and he made placatory noises and gave her sleeping-pills: they were not what she needed. She didn't take them anyway, simply put the bottle away in her handbag but had the prescription renewed a month later. And as the weeks dragged by to the trial, she and the children became ever more isolated from everyone else around them.

At Pengloss life for James and Dorothea was vastly different from that of Shirley and her sisters, but whilst the adults didn't really give the Johnson children more than the occasional passing thought, Dorothea made a point of *not* thinking about Shirley – as hard as she could. For to think about Shirley was to think about Arthur . . . and that would make her heart beat painfully in her chest as her fears crowded in on her.

She kept a close eye on the book in the library: in fact she carefully moved it on a regular basis, so that at any given point she knew where it was. At least that way she felt marginally less agitated.

The June heat wave brought a change in their routine, for David Rosenthal's old schoolroom was a stuffy place, and Miss Forrester decided on lessons out of doors. However, studying maths to the accompanying sounds of the sea slapping lazily against the cliffs in the distance and herring-gulls calling mournfully overhead did nothing to improve James's concentration, for sure, though Miss Forrester had long since realized that actually teaching these children anything during this difficult, fragmented time, was of secondary importance. Simply keeping them occupied and giving them some order in their lives was what mattered, and there were no hard-and-fast rules.

During break-time on the first morning of their outdoor lessons, the children showed her the ruined chapel, their special place, and James enthusiastically told her its story.

The chapel, set as it was on the edge of a romantic little copse, was so perfectly picturesque with its ivy-covered, crumbling walls and empty, arched windows, that Miss Forrester felt faintly suspicious that it was a folly, and if that was the case, then the holy well it was supposed to shelter was unlikely to have existed at all. But it made a good story.

Over the years bushes had grown up inside and outside the walls, and in one corner a huge Albertine rose wound its way around two of the empty windows, filling them with bobbing pink roses on summer days. Inside there was nothing but a stone altar and a profusion of self-seeded weeds and flowers, plus a vast collection of 'treasures' which James and Dorothea had brought up from the beach in their summers together.

It was their place of sanctuary; Miss Forrester recognized that, and later in the day she did a bit of research in the library. After that she abandoned school-work, concentrating instead on the story of the estate, and for the next four days the children had the most splendid history lesson of their lives, finishing on Friday afternoon – as the heat wave was showing the first signs of its typically English end – with instructions to write about it for their weekend homework.

For Dorothea all the talk and study of Pengloss in the past had brought Peachy to the forefront of her thoughts; evidently the same had happened to James, too, because much to her astonishment, and to his aunt's great gratification, he chose *Alice in*

Wonderland as the new book for Bella to read to them that evening. So, as the wet and extremely noisy end to the heat wave began to get under way with a vengeance, James and Dorothea snuggled up against Bella on the sofa watching her finger the copy of *Alice in Wonderland* in her lap.

The room was darkening, lit by soft lamps, the dogs were close together on the hearth-rug, the decorative clock on the mantelpiece ticked cheerfully and James felt an unusual sense of peace. Pengloss made him feel safe. He didn't like thunderstorms, although he never admitted as much, and he would have hated a huge storm like this at Hampton Court, worrying dreadfully in case the power lines came down. Now he didn't care if the lights went out. It couldn't have mattered less.

'You do know, don't you,' Bella asked as she opened the book to chapter one and prepared to start reading, 'that this was Peachy's book? It was his favourite story in the world, *Alice in Wonderland*, and we gave him this edition for his fifth birthday.'

James nodded. Thinking hard about his vanished cousin he inspected a hand-tinted photograph of Peachy close by him, seeing it abruptly spring to life as a flash of lightning brilliantly illuminated the room.

'I *wish* I'd known him, you know,' he murmured as the thunder began to grumble and Juno and Cyrus put their ears back uncomfortably. 'I really wish I had.'

'Yes,' Bella agreed softly. 'I wish you'd known him, too. You'd have liked him; both of you would. He would have helped you; he was so good like that.'

Another enormous flash illuminated the room, and outside fat raindrops began a steady, but increasing drumming, until there was nothing to see beyond the french windows but a sheet of water.

James studied his aunt thoughtfully. In the months they had been here at Pengloss his perceptions of her had changed out of all recognition, and he no longer thought of her as batty Aunt Bella at all, in fact he would have been extremely indignant if anyone had called her that any more. He was almost certain he could talk to her much more honestly than he could talk to his mother, but he hadn't quite found the courage yet.

Another eye-popping flash was immediately followed by a bang that made the house shake. Juno slithered forwards on her belly and placed her head miserably in Dorothea's lap.

With the artlessness of childhood James turned to look fully at his aunt.

'Aunt Bella,' he asked, in that way children have of directly cutting through to the truth without being offensive, 'do you *really* still believe Peachy's going to come back one day? I mean, do you really, honestly think he's still alive somewhere, truly?'

Bella blinked in surprise for a second, then she looked steadily back at him as for the first time for weeks she allowed herself closely to examine her feelings. Immediately she knew that left to themselves for the first time for years, they had changed. Her perpetual agony over Peachy was becoming dulled around the edges . . . and falling into perspective. Her son, the thirties, her husband, the war, they were the past. They were gone and finished, and this was now.

Another violent flash of lightning lit the room and Cyrus crept forward to join Juno, gazing at Dorothea in abject misery. Dorothea hugged the dogs to comfort them, and Bella hugged her nephew . . . as, abruptly, the lights went out.

'No, James,' she replied into the semi-darkness. 'I don't think so, not really. How could he be? He'd be grown-up by now, and he'd have come looking for me if he was, wouldn't he? I just . . . wish I knew what had happened to him, that's all.'

The dim, grey room was awash with noise; rain and thunder vying for attention in the heavens, and James was remembering that February morning and the little brick hut.

Suddenly he looked at Bella and his eyes were haunted.

'Aunt Bella,' he said anxiously, 'where do people go, when they're dead? Do you know? I mean can you tell me – for certain?'

Bella smiled.

'Some people say they go to heaven,' she replied and felt him move sharply beside her.

'Yes, but *when* do they go?' he demanded. 'I mean Rosemary . . .

was she in heaven, when we . . . ? She looked so strange, not like Rosemary at all . . . and dead. Dead is such a horrid word because I don't understand what it means. Why wasn't she able to somehow tell someone where she was . . . like why hasn't Peachy ever . . .'

Bella instantly dismissed her sister's warnings from her mind as she put her arms around both the children and drew them into her lap.

'You want to talk about it, don't you,' she asked softly. 'There are things you want to ask. Well, you ask, and I'll do my best to tell you the truth. But first of all you must never be *frightened* of Rosemary. What you saw in that hut is something quite different from the person you knew as the 'real' Rosemary, and she had long gone.'

So James asked, and was told. He talked about his fear of death, and his aunt tried as best she could to explain it to him. Sadly for Dorothea, however, even though she thought she trusted Bella every bit as much as she trusted Aunty, no words would come from her lips, and she was not able to voice her fears. Had she been able to she could have fetched the dreadful book and told of the agony and fear in her heart, even told of the horror of her night in hospital, but she couldn't.

That night James went to bed feeling much more settled about the fears in his mind, but Dorothea still lay in the grip of hers, and every day the trial grew nearer. The moment when she would have to stand face to face with Mr Johnson and . . . *what* . . . ?

At the end of June Miss Forrester announced her intention to close lessons. Arthur Johnson's trial was scheduled to begin on 20 July, and James and Dorothea would have to go back to Hampton Court to prepare for it.

They were to be taken to the Old Bailey a few days before the trial, to be shown how it looked, where James would stand to give his evidence, where Arthur would be, and so on, and then, with any luck, everything would run to schedule and be all over inside a fortnight. After that, they had been promised, they were coming straight back to Pengloss, and after that, too, decisions as yet only skirted around would have to be made. Some semblance of normal life had to be returned to eventually, it was just in what form, the adults wondered. Particularly, they wondered, in Dorothea's case, for as yet she showed not the slightest sign of wanting to talk.

Inspector Maltby had been on the telephone numerous times, hoping for good news about her, but it was seeming more and more likely that she would never give evidence, and the nearer the trial came, the more confident Arthur Johnson appeared to be growing. It could only be to his advantage if she never spoke again, he knew, and as his confidence grew, Maltby longed, almost spitefully, to spoil it for him. Maltby wanted justice for Rosemary, and from his very soul he knew he would fight to get it, but it would have been so much easier if it had been simply cut and dried.

A few days before Miss Forrester's decision to put a stop to regular lessons, Charles Webb-Goring had arrived at Pengloss for a short visit, carrying in his car two boxes; one contained Dorothea's beloved Charlie cockerel, and the other one of his hens with eleven adorable golden chicks. Judd and Seth had immediately build a good, stout chicken-ark in the kitchen-garden for the new arrivals, and they had become James and Dorothea's project.

Every morning they let them out of the little hutch to run about in the sunshine, fed and watered them and gave them fresh straw; and every evening they carefully put them away again. Every day, too, Blackie, who over the weeks had begun to get rather bored with spitting at Juno and Cyrus, sunned himself on the kitchen window-sill and watched the chicks with sly interest. But as far as James and Dorothea were concerned Blackie was guarding their babies – and as far as the grown-ups were concerned this naïvety was a welcome sign that even though the wretched Arthur had dragged them so rudely into the real world, their world of childhood had not been completely destroyed.

'Let them rear their chicks and play their knights and princesses game in the chapel,' Miss Forrester said as she enjoyed a cup of tea with Bella, Anthea and Edna on her last afternoon. 'It will do them a great deal more good than trying to study maths and French.'

'I think you'll find it's Dan Dare that they mostly play,' Anthea retorted caustically, as from the window of the drawing-room the adults watched James and Dorothea running across the lawn towards the chapel. 'James thinks he *is* her knight in shining armour, but he would never admit it, he'd think that was "soppy". Poor little Dorothea has simply gone along with it over the years – and she reads his *Eagle* comic avidly every week, so at least she knows what is expected of her.'

Edna chuckled softly. Suddenly all four of the adults present were pulled up short when they saw Dorothea reach the Albertine rose and cup one of the blossoms in her hands very gently, bending to smell it with obvious pleasure.

'Look at that,' Bella murmured slowly, gazing at the little girl. 'How touching. How very beautiful. She's such a lovely child, and when you think of everything she's been through. You should be very proud of her, Mrs B, very proud indeed.'

'Oh I am,' Edna assured her. 'She'm my whole life, that little girl, and I'd give everything I had to spare her what's coming. Spare James, an' all, 'cos it isn't fair. But if I know James, he wants justice for Rosemary, same as he would for Dorothea, bless him.'

Bella went on gazing at the chapel wall and the rose, even as Dorothea disappeared inside behind James, and Anthea saw her frown in deep concentration. She seemed lost in her thoughts and, slightly wearily, Anthea thought she was probably digging up memories of Peachy again and wished like mad that she wouldn't. But she wasn't. Bella had moved into the real world now, and her thoughts were for James and Dorothea, not for Peachy any more.

She looked at the three other ladies in the room and tipped her head slightly to one side, tapping on the window softly with her finger as she did so.

'I've just had an idea,' she said softly, 'the *perfect* way those two can fill the next three weeks, with lots of attention from Judd and Seth; have something to comfort them whilst they're away, and then to come back to when it's all over. I'm going to give them a memorial garden for Rosemary. I'll get Judd and Seth to clear the chapel back to the floor – if there is a floor, and then they can turn it into a garden. They can design it however they want, I'll organize a plaque, like the ones in that beautiful little garden of remembrance Judd built for David and Peachy, and we can take them to buy plants . . . lots of rosemary bushes and things. Then Rosemary's garden will always be here for them, their special place to remember their little friend. What do you think?'

For some seconds there was complete silence in the huge drawing-room, as Anthea, Edna and Miss Forrester stared at Bella in amazement. This woman who had spent the past twenty years drowning in self-pity had apparently, in the last four months, taken a gigantic leap into life. Her idea was wonderful, and as far as Anthea was concerned, a remarkable sign of healing; for David Rosenthal had loved the old chapel and Bella had preserved it almost like an unhealthy shrine, after his death. Cleared of its rubbish and given to the children it would still be a shrine, if that was what Bella wanted, but a realistic one, beautiful and on-going and not simply static in time.

Congratulating her on the plan, they finished their tea, and Miss Forrester prepared to leave. Anthea went with her to the front door and as it opened on to the drive the smell of summer drifted in to them deliciously.

For a few seconds they stood in silence, gazing at the sun-drenched world beyond as a bumble-bee careered drunkenly past, then Miss Forrester turned to Anthea and decided that now was the moment to say what was on her mind, for time had run out for her, and she needed to plant her seeds of doubt, even if it wasn't strictly her business.

With a polite, but headmistress-like smile which rather pulled Anthea up short, she suddenly said:

'Mrs Webb-Goring, since I've now finished my time here, I'm going to ask you a rather personal question, if you don't mind. When all this is over, the trial and so forth, what do you intend should happen next? I mean, is it your hope that everyone will simply return to their old lives and pick up where they left off?'

It was not a question Anthea had expected, and she was much taken aback. She stared at the elderly headmistress in surprise.

'Pick up where we left off . . . ?' She mumbled, and shrugged, finding herself suddenly uncomfortable at the abrupt voicing of fears that she had been chewing over in secret for sometime. Licking her lips she said: 'Well . . . James is off to Marlborough in September, of course, and there's no doubt that Dorothea was on track for Hampton Grammar before all this happened. Hopefully once the man Johnson is hanged – *if* he's hanged of course – she will start talking again and everything will be back to normal.'

Miss Forrester pursed her lips for a moment, then she shook her head firmly.

'I'm afraid I very much doubt it,' she observed. 'In fact, I'm sorry, but I *very* much doubt it, indeed.'

Anthea blinked at her and actually found herself blushing slightly, for it felt, in some undefined way, as if she was being severely criticized.

'Well so do I, if you must know,' she said slightly acidly, 'but what else can we do, Miss Forrester? We came here to get the children away from the horror of what had happened, but we can't simply stay here for ever; we have lives to pick up else-where.'

The tall, thin, white-haired Miss Forrester, whom Anthea had often thought must have been very beautiful in her youth, and who must have greatly loved her life as a teacher to give up the oppor-tunities of a husband and children of her own, suddenly smiled. It was a simple, genuine smile, followed by a starkly simple question.

'Why can't you stay here for ever?' she enquired, and Anthea's eyes shot open in astonishment.

For some seconds they gaped at each other, then Anthea's face creased indignantly and she snatched her gaze away.

'Miss Forrester,' she replied shortly, 'my husband has been living all by himself in Hampton Court since the third week of February. He would like his family back, and this part of his family would very much like to go back. Pengloss drives me nuts, if you must know; the Christmas carol service, the summer fête, and nothing in between. Frankly, it may be very selfish, but I'm going barking mad here!'

Without warning Miss Forrester suddenly broke into a hearty chuckle, and with an uncharacteristic plunge into intimacy she put her hand on Anthea's arm.

'My dear, forgive me,' she begged. 'I've offended you and I wouldn't have done that for the world. I'm quite sure Pengloss does drive you up the wall, and I can very well see why, but let me go back a bit, if you would. James is rather frightened of going away to school and he's been saying so for weeks, in different ways – although not to you, I suspect. The point is that once upon a time I would have said let him get on with it, it'll be the making of him, only I'm afraid I don't think so any more. After what he's been through, and still has to go through in July, I really, truly don't think making him start afresh with strange people in a strange place is going to be what he needs.'

Anthea put her hands up to her face and rubbed her forehead with her fingers wearily. In her heart she had been through all this time and time again, and listening to her fears being voiced was not a comfortable experience.

'But Charles so wanted his son to follow in his footsteps,' she murmured. 'And not just his, but his own father's as well. The Webb-Gorings have been attending Marlborough for four generations.'

Miss Forrester nodded.

'Only not following a trauma in their lives the likes of which James has suffered,' she said quietly. 'At least, not in the modern way of thinking. And as for Dorothea, do you really think she should go back to Mrs Buddry's little house in the village and pick up from where she left off? Go to the grammar school in September without her best friend? Keep being reminded of all the things she would have done with Rosemary, if her last sight of Rosemary hadn't been a week-old corpse?' She paused, and in the silence a thrush sang loudly and brilliantly into the summer's day beyond. 'You know,' she continued eventually, 'there's an excellent grammar school not five miles away from here, and both James and Dorothea are quite bright enough to attend it, and do very well.'

This time Anthea pressed her fingers to her eyes and held her breath sharply. It was too much, just too much!

'I can't!' she burst out. 'I'm sorry, but I don't want to live apart from Charles and have a marriage of the odd weekend together now and then. I'm sure it's selfish, and I'm sure it singles me out as a wicked, self-centred mother, but I am not geared up for spending the rest of my life buried in the damn country, and that's all there is to it!'

Miss Forrester nodded her head in agreement.

'Of course you're not,' she replied cheerfully, 'but Mrs Buddry is. She was born here and she is a countrywoman to her soul. On your own admission James would no longer have been a daily part of your life come September, he would have been away at school. So supposing he and Dorothea were to stay here with Mrs Buddry instead? And let's face it, they're enormously fond of Mrs Rosenthal, and she of them, so I can't see any problem there. What would you say to that? I mean I know it's not the public school education you'd planned for James, but it's not a bad compromise, you know, if you think hard about it.'

Anthea stared in silence as she digested the woman's words, and to her astonishment she felt a sudden rush of relief. It was as if something she had never dared actually put into words had suddenly been voiced . . . and the sky hadn't fallen in. Everything was just the same. It would be possible for the children to stay at Pengloss, of course it would. Possible for them to start completely afresh . . . and then maybe, when they grew up, all the horror of what had passed between them could be properly pigeon-holed into well-ordered, adult lives and not left, for ever, as ragged stumps to haunt them.

She offered the charming ex-headmistress a genuine smile of gratitude.

'Thank you, Miss Forrester,' she said, 'thank you so very much; you can't begin to understand how much of a help you've just been.'

And Miss Forrester, who had stepped out into the sunshine on to the drive, pressed Anthea's hand swiftly and prepared to leave.

'My pleasure, my dear,' she replied, and walked away feeling satisfactorily confident that she would be seeing much more of James and Dorothea in the near future.

Chapter 11

James and Dorothea were enormously touched when Bella asked them whether they would like a garden of remembrance for Rosemary. To Dorothea, who still sloshed about in the mire of her fear, it seemed to represent a shaft of sunlight, penetrating a black prison. Rosemary could find a place in their garden, be a part of their beloved little chapel . . . she would have somewhere to go . . . as would Dorothea herself, if she made sure she never, ever told.

Bella took them to a stone-mason, where they chose a plaque of polished slate upon which would be written, in gold, *Rosemary's Garden*, with, beneath it, simply her name and her dates. They began to draw pictures of where they would like the plaque to hang and where to plant some rosemary bushes in remembrance; then they waited eagerly for Judd and Seth to bring up the farm equipment required to clear the chapel floor.

Seth made them wait outside as, with a vicious-looking piece of equipment on the back of his tractor, he began the business of grinding up the impacted surface of the chapel floor. It would be a long job, because the accumulated rubbish of hundreds of years had been flattened down over time, along with a surprising amount of sand and earth, all of which was heavily tangled with brambles and general undergrowth. Moving it was a long job and it was a couple of days later when at last, on the very bottom, they came upon the remains of the roof.

So there had been a roof, then; it had been a place of worship? Bella and Anthea wondered suddenly whether the story of the holy well might not be a fable after all.

On the evening of the third day of the clearing operation, Judd suddenly began walking up and down the stone floor which they had uncovered, tapping on it with the handle of a rake. All that was left now were the last few feet beyond the altar, and as Seth backed the tractor up towards it, his father held up his hand for him to turn the engine off.

James and Dorothea stood in the doorway and watched in fascination, as they had done for the entire three days, longing to run in and explore. However, they had been threatened with total banishment if they did, so now they hovered, exasperated and wildly excited.

Seth slid down from the tractor seat and walked slowly over where his father tap-tapped with the rake-handle.

'What's up?' he asked.

Judd tapped again, first here and then there, listening carefully.

'You'm heard them stories 'bout this place, ent yer, boy?' he asked at last.

Seth frowned, brushing his thick, black hair from his forehead with grubby hands.

'What stories?' he said as Judd tapped again with his rake.

'About that there well?'

Judd was generally a man of few words, but it was astonishing that everyone always seemed to know what he meant.

Seth was immediately conversant now.

'What, that the chapel were built over a holy well?' he said. 'Well, of course I heard the stories, Pa, but they'm only myth, surely? I mean we've found no steps, nor no hole in the floor nor nothing; have we?'

'We ent,' Judd agreed slowly, 'but you listen, boy. Ent no earth floor beneath all of that. It's hollow up this end, 'less I ent hearing proper.'

This was too much for James. Being told to wait outside was all very well, but not when it was really getting exciting. With a little squeak of excitement he ran across the floor, his eyes shining.

'You mean there really *is* a holy well under here?' he demanded.

161

'Oh golly! D'you think we'll find treasure? Oh quick, let's get down there.'

He was hopping about from foot to foot and Judd looked down at him with a tiny smile playing about his lips.

'Got to get in first, though,' he observed in his long slow way. 'And the longer you're hopping about here, the longer you're gonna be waiting.'

James pulled his brows together furiously, pushing out his lips in an angry pout.

'Oh *Judd*!' he snorted, but it was evident he wasn't going to get anywhere so he slouched back to the door.

Judd and Seth began shovelling what was left of the rubbish from the floor, James knew it would be tea-time in an hour or so and was getting so impatient that he could have screamed with frustration. Then suddenly, hard against the wall in the top left-hand corner of the little chapel, Seth found what they were looking for. There was a stone, much the same size as the others which made up the floor, but into its top surface was sunk a large iron ring.

Now it was impossible to keep the children at bay, and within five minutes all four of them were scraping around its edges with anything thin and sharp that they could find, digging out the accumulation of centuries.

'Don't think it's going t'come up easily, will you, James?' Seth warned. 'We might have to wait till tomorrow to move it, 'cos it hasn't been moved for a bleddy long time, this stone. Ring could be rusted through f'rall I know.'

'Or it might not!' James retorted in exasperation. 'Oh come on, I *can't* wait till tomorrow . . . and I think you're teasing, anyway!'

Seth and Judd eyed each other and chuckled softly; teasing James was so easy because he fell for it every time, but for all that, when they tried lifting the stone it was in no mood to budge. Eventually Seth backed the tractor up and they ran a chain through the iron ring, then slowly inched the great machine forward until at last the stone loosened and began to come up.

It was obvious immediately why it hadn't wanted to move, for the underside was smothered in torn tree-roots. Bits dropped down from it as it lifted and when Judd had firmly secured it they all walked to the hole and peered down into the semi-darkness beneath.

The holy well, unseen by anybody for centuries, by the look of it.

A flight of steps, carved from the rock, led down into a small underground chamber and they went down cautiously, finding the stale and earthy smell getting ever stronger the deeper they went. The room was considerably smaller than the chapel which had been built over it, but evidently all the work done to it had been carried out at the same time, for it was not a natural chamber and had been carefully hewn out.

Three walls were smooth and had been lined with stone, the fourth held a complicated, but natural rock formation with a very old, cast-iron basin beneath it. Through this rock, at sometime in the long distant past, had trickled a stream which had now dried up. Nothing wet remained anywhere, but where water had dripped for centuries, small stalactites had formed and hung there like tiny, grimy icicles.

Above them, where the ceiling of the underground room joined the outside walls of the chapel, two half-moon-shaped openings had once let in fresh air and a little daylight, probably just enough for the well to look dim and impressive. Both apertures had been covered by intricate cast-iron grilles; one was still in place, though now so choked and twisted up with root systems that precious little light got in any more. The other was broken and lying in hundreds of shattered bits all over the stone floor.

It seemed to the four who stood on the steps and gazed down into this place that no one had seen for centuries to have formed a sort of pattern; to have cast an imperfect circle on the floor. Within the circle was its offering . . . the thing that had not been hidden in this secret place for hundreds of years. The thing that had come from the sun drenched world above to be forever buried in the dark.

All of a heap, and partially scattered, was a tiny skeleton. Long

163

dried-up leather sandals still encased the feet, both of which had become detached from the leg-bones at some point and fallen a few inches to the floor. The limbs and torso, or at least the bones that had once been the scaffolding of the flesh and blood, were even now clad in the ragged remains of brown cotton shorts and a yellow shirt, and close to the skull, which lay at an odd angle to the neck and had a sizeable hole in it, was what was left of a small red ball . . . and some clumps of pale hair.

Judd, Seth, James and Dorothea all knew precisely what they were looking at, and all stood, motionless, as they slowly took it in. Then, abruptly, Judd sank down on to his knees and put his calloused hands over his face, rocking backwards and forwards as a groan of despair escaped his lips.

'My Peachy . . .' he whispered, his voice sounding dull in the dark, musty place. 'My little Peachy . . .'

He began to sob as if his heart was broken; creating a muted, suffocating sound within this extraordinary place of death.

Seth, in a panic, caught hold of James's arm and began to drag him back up the steps into the daylight. He made a lunge for Dorothea, too, but he was too late and too far away, and Dorothea saw only Judd's terrible distress. She stepped down on to the floor of the room, and silently cast her eyes around. The roots of the trees and shrubs that hugged the chapel walls above them, had grown so far across the roof on the inside that it was like being in a dug-out . . . or . . . she bit her lip as she stared ... . or . . . yes, of course. . . .

'He thought it was Alice's rabbit-hole,' she said in a voice soft with wonder. 'He must have done. He must have found the hole and thought it was Alice's rabbit-hole and he could fall into it, like she did, and not be hurt. Oh Peachy . . .'

Seth, still standing on the steps half-in and half-out of the room, squeezed James's arm urgently as James struggled to escape from him. They were both white-faced, but whilst Seth wanted to get away, James wanted to go down to Dorothea and Judd.

'Let me *go*, Seth!' he hissed, but was dragged round to face the man, who glared fiercely into his small face.

'James, you got to get your mother!' he urged. 'Quickly. You got to tell her to come now, and don't tell her in front of your Aunt Bella. Quick, *please*!'

'And what are you going to do?' James demanded huffily, freeing his arm.

Seth hustled him across the chapel floor.

'Get Mrs B!' he retorted, setting off for the kitchens at a run.

Dorothea stood before Judd and quietly put her arms around his neck. His wrinkled, sunburned faced was wet with tears and they both stared at the small skeleton, lying where it had lain for almost twenty years now, but neither made any effort to touch it for there wasn't any point.

Eventually he wiped his face with his gnarled hands and then returned the little girl's embrace with great tenderness, holding her close against him as he gazed at the bones of the child he had once loved so much.

'I'm not much of a one for reading, you know,' he murmured at last. 'Never bothered to learn, 'cos there weren't any point, I thought. So you tell us about Alice's rabbit-hole, Dorothea, will you? 'Cos I dunno what it means.'

'Oh it doesn't *mean* anything,' Dorothea replied, seemingly unaware that she was talking quite normally. 'It's part of a story. You see Aunt Bella said *Alice in Wonderland* was Peachy's favourite book in the world, and, well there's this rabbit-hole, and ...'

She kept her arms around his neck as she told him the story of *Alice in Wonderland* and he knelt on the stone floor beside Peachy's remains, whilst James tore into the house, banging into room after room in a frantic search for his mother. He eventually found her alone in the morning-room. She was writing a letter and as he stumbled clumsily in through the door her pen skidded untidily across the sheet of paper. He had made her jump.

'Mummy ...' he whispered, staring at her wide-eyed and suddenly finding himself extremely frightened. 'Mummy, we've ... we've just found Peachy.'

Anthea snapped her writing-case shut furiously and spun round to face her son, her mouth drawn into a thin, sharp line. She had, in fact, been writing to his father putting to him Miss Forrester's suggestion that James and Dorothea be allowed to stay at Pengloss in the future. In the days since she'd had her conversation with the former headmistress she had actually relaxed her rigidity sufficiently to drop little hints into the conversation now and then and James had rewarded her enthusiastically. He had greeted the idea with great excitement and promised anything, but *anything* to be allowed to stay. So his mother had left it that they would have to see how things turned out.

Well, if this was some sort of ploy to get what he wanted, she decided, it was wholly unacceptable!

'Just found Peachy . . .' she repeated softly, snarling as she narrowed her eyes at him in a rage. 'James, I don't know what this is all about, my lad, but believe you me, lies like that won't win you *any* favours. Whatever game it is that you're playing, you've just gone much too far, so if I were you I'd back off, before you really make me angry!'

His face was chalk-white, almost grey in the hollows, and as his mother's voice rose to a shout of temper, his eyes filled with tears. Anthea's jaw dropped, as suddenly a thousand fears crowded into her head, and she reached out a hand to him quickly.

'James . . .?' she whispered and unable to stop himself he threw himself into her arms and began to sob.

They met Edna and Seth as they hurried across the lawns to the little chapel. Edna looked panic-stricken, and the sight of James's white, tear-stained face did nothing to still her fears. It seemed as if they all piled down the flight of steps in a disorganized shove, and both Edna's and Anthea's hearts were knocking so hard in their chests that they felt faintly sick.

But on the floor of the holy well, all was absolutely calm. Dorothea still had her arms around Judd and was still telling him about *Alice in Wonderland*. Judd was gazing upwards at the twisted tendrils snaked across the ceiling, and it was evident that to him it all made perfect sense.

Anthea found her hands were shaking uncontrollably as she stared at the pathetic little skeleton. In her mind the vibrant and beautiful Peachy simply did not equate with these pitiful remains, and yet it all made sense to her too as she thought about it.

'He must have fallen in when the metal grille collapsed, and broken his neck when he landed,' she whispered. 'And if he'd crawled through a gap under a bush or a shrub up there, the branches would have snapped back behind him, and no one would ever have seen it. Oh Judd, I'm so sorry. I'm so, *so* sorry.'

'All these years,' Judd said in a bewildered and broken voice. 'I looked every place I could for him, you know? I crawled around the estate on me 'ands and knees looking under bushes and trees. I looked all about up there . . .' he nodded his head to the chapel above, 'but I didn't know.'

'No, of course you didn't,' Anthea replied gently. 'None of us did, did we? Look, I'm *so* sorry and I know this is going to seem like adding insult to injury, but you do realize that we'll have to get the police? We can't just move him. You do understand, don't you, Judd?'

Judd turned his head and gazed at her dully, then with the actions of an old, old man he seemed to drag himself to his feet.

'Oh ay,' he said. 'That's all right, Miz Anthea. I got to tell Molly anyhow.' He touched Dorothea softly on the head and hauled himself up the uneven stone steps into the brilliance of the summer afternoon.

Edna held her arms out to Dorothea and the little girl flung herself into the safety of them. James went back into the sunshine with Seth, then Anthea, with one last desperate look at the awful secret of the holy well, climbed back into the chapel herself. Up there in the warmth, and beneath a canopy of unbroken blue sky, it seemed grotesquely unreal. As if it could be changed; that just by turning back and going down again, it could be gone and Peachy could still simply be missing.

As Anthea went to find Bella and phone for the police, and James went out of the chapel with Seth and his father, Edna held Dorothea back for a moment. They stared at each other in the flower-scented fresh air, then they hugged fiercely, Dorothea pressing her face deeply into Edna's ample bosom as she thought about what was coming.

'You was talkin' to Judd, sweet'eart,' Edna whispered softly. 'Talk to me now.'

Dorothea uttered a huge sob.

'I didn't mean to. . . .' she whispered, and Edna, not understanding because it could have meant anything, squeezed the child tightly in a rush of relief.

'Of course you never meant to,' she replied. 'No one thinks you *meant* to, my lovie. Oh Dorothea, it's so good to 'ave you back, an' I loves you so much.'

Dorothea knew that her deception was over: now she would have to tell.

Once she was alone she found *This Man is Death* in the library, and took it upstairs to hide in her little suitcase underneath her bed. Maybe, just maybe, if he was hidden away out of sight, he wouldn't know when she told and she would get away with it, she thought hopefully – but she doubted it. And she doubted it even more when she overheard Aunty telling Mrs Webb-Goring that Inspector Maltby had asked to come down to Pengloss in a couple of days' time, to talk to her.

'It's hard to keep track of what's going on just at the moment, isn't it?'Anthea observed to Edna, when the little chapel was swarming with the local police and the story was already finding its way out into the village. 'Just for a while I'd allowed myself to forget about that bloody trial, you know!'

Edna inclined her head slightly and then quickly looked away.

'I have to say,' she observed, 'that I wish they could've found little Peachy at some other time. It don't help, just at the moment, that's for sure . . .' She blushed and bit her lip, adding softly, 'Not that I've any right to say such a thing, of course.'

Anthea smiled grimly.

'You have every right, Mrs B,' she replied, 'and I couldn't agree with you more. It couldn't have come at a worse time . . . for everbody except, possibly, Bella.'

A police-appointed pathologist had come to Pengloss with the rest

168

of the police, and had spent a considerable time in the underground room examining the bones, wanting to make no mistakes and be able truthfully to answer the inevitable questions.

When at last he had finished he sought out Bella and Anthea, who were together in the drawing-room, aproaching the white-faced Bella with great compassion. He was a kindly man who had spent much of his life dealing with situations such as this, and his manner, when he spoke, was both professional and delicate.

Well, at least he would have all the right words, Anthea thought, as her compassion for Bella filled her heart; but her fear of her sister going off into one of her ghastly 'episodes' terrified her. Just please, *please*, let him know how to use them with care and consideration!

'I just need to know if he suffered!' Bella demanded, staring at him with dark eyes that were full of pain and anxiety. 'I just need to know if we could have done something.'

The elderly pathologist sat down opposite her and smiled at her gently.

'Mrs Rosenthal, I will be as truthful as I can,' he promised. 'As truthful as it is possible to be. Your son appears to have fallen head first approximately fifteen feet from the aperture in the ceiling of the underground room. When he landed he broke his neck. He also suffered a severe fracture of the skull. The force of these two injuries would have been more than sufficient to cause death within seconds, and he wouldn't have known anything about it.'

Bella pressed her lips together, they were white and pinched as were her fingers, clasped savagely in her lap.

'But if we'd found him immediately? I mean that day?'

'You could have done nothing. In my opinion he died instantly.'

'And you promise he didn't suffer? You *promise?*'

'I promise he didn't suffer. He was never conscious again. He never moved.'

She nodded and for a moment there was a deep and painful silence in the room as both she and Anthea thought about the beautiful, smiling Peachy. About his pretty pink mouth and bright-blue eyes, his throaty chuckle and golden curls. And for that moment he was there, in the room with them . . . and finally free to go, for the pain of not knowing was at last at an end.

Bella stood up and shook the pathologist by the hand. She had not seen her son's bones, nor would she do so. They would be taken to the mortuary and fairly swiftly released for burial, and she had chosen, rightly, to remember her little boy as he had been twenty years ago. Anything else would have been destructive and painful.

When he had gone Anthea poured them both stiff drinks and then sat down again, giving Bella as much time as she needed to talk. Or not, as she chose.

Bella gulped her drink and then took a deep breath, closing her eyes wearily as the alcohol seemed to burn down to her stomach. In her mind she conjured Peachy and then waited, allowing the pain to roll in . . . but already, in the couple of hours she had known the truth, her feelings had begun to change – or perhaps not change so much as clarify.

'In my heart I've always known he was dead, you know,' she murmured at last still sitting with her eyes shut, the lines on her face showing so bluntly her twenty years of suffering. 'I knew right from the moment when no one collected the ransom money. He had to be dead. Nothing else made sense.'

Anthea gazed down into her drink, swilling the ice around with her finger as she absorbed her sister's words. Twenty years Peachy had been gone, but it was not easy, even now, to know what to say . . . and there were so many unanswered questions.

'Well,' she said eventually, 'if you always knew he was dead, Bella, then what were the psychics and private detectives all about, if you don't mind me asking?'

Bella Rosenthal's face was washed with sadness.

'Hope, Anthea,' she replied. 'What else? I took my eyes off my beloved little boy and he vanished. In my dreams I heard him calling out to me, and in my waking hours I was persistently racked by thoughts that someone was holding him, maybe even torturing him somewhere. My God, you should understand now. You've seen the photographs of little Rosemary Archer's mother in the papers. You saw Mrs B's face, before James brought Dorothea home to her. Not knowing is the worst kind of agony of all. And then David went away and was shot down and I had no one, not really, just a house full of ghosts.'

'But you always had me,' Anthea whispered.

Bella reached out a thin hand and touched her gently.

'And you had Charles, my dear, and then James.'

It was true. They had lived separate and different lives. Anthea the social animal, always going to parties, joining committees, racing through life because there was never enough time, and Bella buried in Cornwall in a beautiful house that had stood still in time. She hadn't understood at all, Anthea realized with a cruel jerk of pain. She hadn't even *begun* to understand Bella's suffering, and her compassion for her sister's wild mood-swings, and at times almost frightening behaviour, had worn thin very quickly.

'Oh Bella,' she whispered miserably, 'I haven't done the right thing by you, ever, have I.'

Bella Rosenthal smiled gently.

'Oh yes you have,' she replied. 'Maybe not consciously, but I promise you you have. You've let me share James and Dorothea, and that's meant more than I can tell you. I know they've had a shock today, but I'd like to see them before they go to bed, if I may. Would that be all right, do you think?'

Anthea thought afterwards that she almost lunged for the drawing-room door – and she wasn't certain whether her haste had been to fulfil Bella's wishes, or get out of her company; for out in the hall, which was silent and warm and reflected the evening shadows in the rich, dark wood of the panelling, she burst into tears!

When James and Dorothea came to Bella, half an hour later, James, anyway, was refreshingly normal, and not suffering even a suggestion of awkwardness or guilt. He did not feel the need to apologize, for he viewed the momentous happenings of the day with child's logic. It could only be good that Peachy had been found, and he was proud of being one of those to find him. He had great compassion for Aunt Bella, but he didn't feel the need to creep in, and he looked her full in the face.

She patted the sofa beside her as they came in, but before they could reach her Juno and Cyrus had intervened and Dorothea was on her knees between the two dogs, hugging them close to her. She was pale and looked frightened and Bella didn't miss it.

'You know, sweetheart,' she said softly, holding out her hands to the little girl. 'If you ever have a secret which worries you, you should tell them about it. They're excellent listeners and they never split. I've been talking to them for years.'

James looked at her thoughtfully as she spoke, and tried to imagine her talking to the dogs . . . and he could, quite easily, he realized. Aunt Bella was the kind of person who would talk to dogs, but that wasn't bad. In fact nothing Aunt Bella did was bad and he loved her very much. She might have been different from his mother, but 'different', he'd long ago decided, didn't mean odd – well not odd like he'd once thought, anyway.

He snuggled against her warmly, welcoming it as she slid her arm around him . . . and just for a moment – because he was only eleven and still saw the world through child's eyes – he wondered if finding Peachy might somehow count in his favour when it came to staying at Pengloss for ever. He even decided that he might ask, at an appropriate moment . . . before fetching up short, suddenly guilty for his thoughts!

'Now then,' Bella said, when both the children were snuggled against her, and happy to be in her arms. 'I want to ask two big favours of the both of you, which I know you won't mind at all. Firstly, you do know that Inspector Maltby is coming to see you in a day or two, don't you?'

James nodded, but she saw Dorothea's head go down, and tightened her grip on the child's skinny little shoulders.

'Do you want to tell me something?' she asked softly, and felt more than faintly concerned when Dorothea hurridly assured her: no. 'Well then,' she continued, kissing each of them, 'I want you to be very strong, and tell him the absolute truth. Don't be afraid, because no one here is going to let anything happen to you. Do you understand?' Both children nodded again and she went on:

'Because telling the truth is the right thing to do. So I want you to be truthful with him, and then I want you to be as brave as I know you are, and tell the truth again in court next month. Once you've done that you won't have to think about the awfulness of it ever again. You'll just be able to remember your friend Rosemary, and tend her memorial garden whilst you do so.'

James and Dorothea looked up at her, and both their faces were tired and rather wary. They were tanned from the sun and sea air, but they were grey beneath the eyes, and perhaps a little pale at the lips. It was not over yet, she thought, and was fiercely determined she would keep them at Pengloss for as long as it took.

Suddenly James's bottom lip began to tremble slightly and he lowered his gaze. He was thinking something out, Bella thought, and she must be honest when she replied to his questions, no matter what they were.

'Aunt Bella . . .' he whispered at last, and his eyes were suddenly full of uncertainty. 'Peachy didn't look like . . .' he threw a swift glance at one of the photographs in the room. 'He looked . . . different. Will Rosemary be like that, too? Just bones, and not Rosemary . . . at all . . . ?'

Bella hugged him tightly, and would have liked nothing more than to burst into tears but knew that she couldn't. This was her new role in life; this was, she supposed, the compensation she had been given for her beloved little boy, and she was not allowed to make mistakes.

'Yes, James,' she replied quietly. 'Eventually. And so will you, and so will I. So will everybody. What you have to understand is that what you found today wasn't Peachy, it was just the . . . left over bits, if you like. Peachy is with his daddy in Heaven, the *real* Peachy.'

'But Rosemary's mummy and daddy are still in Hampton,' Dorothea murmured. 'So who's Rosemary with now?'

Bella smiled and then kissed her softly.

'She's with Peachy I expect,' she replied, and liked the way it neatly dovetailed, both in terms of helping the children and – oddly – helping her at the same time. True, it was a romantically simplified and comfortable explanation, but it was what they needed. All of them. Something 'nice', to smooth over the top of all the awfulness. 'Which brings me to the other great favour I want to ask of you,' she went on after a moment. 'I was wondering whether there might be a possibility that you two could see your way clear to sharing Rosemary's garden with Peachy? What do you say? Do you think you could?'

Suddenly Dorothea's eyes sparkled and she looked at Bella in astonishment, as if even having to ask was absurd.

'*Of course* we're going to share Rosemary's garden with Peachy!' she cried. 'I mean . . . well . . . it's Peachy's *place* really, isn't it?' She paused then, wondering if she'd been tactless, but Bella was smiling at her warmly, so she decided to go on. 'And as we're planting a rosemary bush, for Rosemary, then we shall have a peach-tree for Peachy, and . . .' She stopped abruptly as the memory of the pathetic little skeleton floated into her mind. Peachy's place. The place where he'd lain undiscovered and neglected for so many years. Suddenly she threw her arms about Bella and pressed her little face deep into her neck. 'I'm so sorry,' she whispered.

Bella hugged her tightly.

'I know you are, sweetheart,' she replied. 'And thank you.'

Chapter 12

Detective Inspector Maltby stopped at one point on his long drive to Pengloss, and bought a couple of presents for James and Dorothea. He wondered, as he climbed back into the car and put them on the passenger seat beside him, whether strictly within the meaning of the act this constituted bribing the witnesses – but decided a bag of juicy red grapes and some sweets was probably not going to make a huge difference!

It certainly was an absurdly long way to travel to interview a witness, he thought, as his car ate up the miles and left the stink of the big city behind him, but this case – well this case had been different from the beginning. And surely this was the breakthrough he had been waiting for? He could hardly ask the local force to do the interview.

He was much impressed with the house when he arrived, and impressed, too, by the warmth of the reception he received, but as they went up to the old schoolroom, where Anthea and Edna had decided Dorothea would probably be most comfortable talking to him, he was immediately alarmed by the expression on the child's face. Maltby was trained to read expressions, and was very good at it. Quite evidently the adults around her were simply so delighted that she was talking again that they hadn't paid full attention. Dorothea might be talking, but something was terrifying her.

'You don't have to be afraid of anything, Dorothea,' he promised her as she gingerly sat at the table beside him. 'Nothing can hurt you any more, you know, I promise you.'

So *he* said! Dorothea thought sourly. *She* knew differently . . . but she also knew that this was the moment when she must put her courage to the test. She had to tell the truth – how could she not? Only . . . once she had told – what then, she wondered bleakly.

Obediently she gave a full account of everything that had happened on that black afternoon in February, from the moment Aunty had failed to arrive at school on time to collect her. She didn't ramble, she didn't cry and she didn't keep contradicting herself. Furthermore, her story dovetailed exactly with James's. It was enough, Maltby thought exultantly. If she would give her evidence like that in court when the time came, there could be no doubt of a conviction.

When they had finished he stayed on in the schoolroom making notes for a while, then Anthea invited him to join them for lunch and took him to meet Bella.

On the way she said:

'I can take you to see this underground room after lunch if you're interested? You know, the one James was on about?'

Maltby smiled at her.

'I'm very interested,' he replied, 'and I'd like time for a talk, if possible, too. Perhaps we could walk along the cliff path for a little while?'

She smiled back at him graciously.

'I'd be delighted,' she observed and led him into the huge drawing-room.

There, for half an hour or so he stopped being a policeman and comfortably appreciated the finer points of what being 'the other half' really meant in terms of luxury. He then ate a hearty and extremely tasty lunch, had a last chat to the children, and went to his car to fetch the presents he had bought for them.

'Ooo, grapes!' James exclaimed in greedy delight. 'I say, thanks a lot, sir.'

Maltby chuckled and glanced at Dorothea.

'You make sure you get your fair share, won't you?' he said and watched as a meaningless smile touched her fairly pretty little face. You're worried, he thought. Extremely worried about something.

But what can I say to make you feel better, I wonder?

'Dorothea,' he murmured and her dark, frightened eyes looked into his face. 'I know nothing can bring Rosemary back, my dear, but nothing further can harm you in any way, you do know that, don't you? Mr Johnson will never hurt you again; he'll never hurt anybody again, so try not to be so worried, I beg of you.'

Dorothea nodded and smiled at him again, then ran off out of the room behind James. From the back, he thought, she looked just like a normal, pretty ten-year-old, but from the front she carried the cares of the world in those haunted eyes. Damn and blast Arthur Johnson, for the miserable bastard he was!

He saw them just once more, when he went with Anthea to the ruined chapel. They were sitting on the stone altar in the sunshine, swinging their legs and stuffing grapes, as around them Rosemary's garden was beginning to take shape.

It was a lovely place and perfect for the project in hand . . . but how much nicer, he thought sourly, for the beautiful Rosemary, so full of promise, to have been sitting there beside them in the sunshine, sharing their grapes and vibrant with life.

So was this a place of wasted children then? A memorial garden for a child callously cut down just as she was about to blossom, revealing the pitiful end of another child destroyed by fate and left to rot in the darkness for years.

Bella had been only once to the underground room where her beloved Peachy had finally been found. His remains had long since been taken away and Molly and Edna had swept away the bits of the broken wrought iron grill; so that now, as Anthea and the policeman stood in the earthy-smelling dimness, all there was to see was a bunch of flowers, laid in memory of her son by his mother.

'How pitiful,' Maltby murmured as he gazed at the flowers and thought about the photos which decorated every flat surface in the drawing room. 'And it has to have been a one in a million chance that such an accident could have happened. Poor little boy. In my experience as a policeman coping with a vanished child is harder even than coping with a murdered one. At least with a dead child there is an ending; there's nothing but endless suffering and guilt with a vanished one. I'm glad for your sister that after all these years she does at last have an answer.'

Anthea glanced around the little room and shivered slightly.

'It's going to be filled in,' she observed, 'this place; to make absolutely certain nothing like that can happen again. Judd reckons the well dried up when the river that runs through the village was re-routed during the early part of the last century – and we always take it that if anyone knows about these things, Judd does. As far as I'm concerned the sooner they bury the damn place the better!'

Maltby glanced at her and saw her distress, saw too the goose-flesh standing on her arms despite the heat of the day.

'Shall we go up?' he suggested and they did, emerging into the sunshine where James and Dorothea were still filling their mouths as fast as they could go.

'Hollow legs!' Anthea remarked and steered him out, towards the gate which would take them on to the cliff path.

It was summer, but not yet the school holidays, so though there were plenty of people about, the carpark above the bay was not overflowing.

Anthea bought ice-creams at the café, and she and Maltby sat on the rugged grass above the cliffs, gazing down towards an azure-blue ocean which lapped lazily beneath them, whilst sharp-eyed gulls hung on warm currents of air.

'This is all so perfect,' he murmured, feeling faintly incongruous sitting on a tuft of grass in his business suit, licking an ice-cream. 'Like a slice of unreal life. Tomorrow, when I get back to my stuffy little office, with all the traffic noise outside, I'm not sure I shall believe I was ever here.'

For a moment Anthea paused, and then to her great surprise all her violent misgivings seemed to swim to the surface like a vast shoal, and burst out of her in an uncontrolled rush. Dorothea was talking again and this policeman had got everything he could out of her, so how much more did they want, for heaven's sake?

'And will *they* remember, do you think?' she demanded. 'When they have to stand up there in court: two little children; and be muddled and confused by men in black robes and white wigs asking them incomprehensible questions? Have you any idea what it's been like these past weeks, with the nightmares and the suffering?'

'Mrs Webb-Goring, I know,' he replied quickly, finding her anger perfectly understandable, but not really wanting to be on the receiving end of it. 'But the law says everyone is entitled to a fair trial – and I'm afraid Arthur Johnson is no exception.'

She drew her mouth into a thin, sharp line.

'So he still might get away with it, then?' she enquired.

Maltby shook his head firmly.

'Oh definitely not,' he answered. 'Not after what I've heard today. If little Dorothea gives her evidence in court as neatly as she gave it to me this morning then he hasn't got a prayer. But I do understand your misgivings, and I feel much the same as you do about it. Which is why when I get back my first visit will be to Johnson himself. He had a key for the padlock on that hut door, he used it when he took Dorothea in there, but none of the official water board keys fitted. He knew Rosemary's body was in there, because according to Dorothea he showed no fear or surprise at the sight of it, in fact he used it as a threat. He killed Rosemary, of that there can be no doubt. But since he did *not* assault her I am firmly convinced he killed her by accident – and to plead guilty now would be to his advantage, to my mind.'

'*Advantage!*' Anthea echoed. 'You mean he wouldn't hang?' The moment the words were out of her mouth she wished she could have bitten her tongue off and the blush which flooded her face showed Maltby exactly how appalled at herself she was.

'Oh God, I'm sorry,' she whispered, 'that was unforgivable. But it's a mother protecting her young thing, I'm afraid. I can't help it. I don't want James to suffer any more, and I don't want Dorothea to, either. They've had enough, and at long last they're getting better. For Dorothea's dreams to be forever more haunted by the thought that Johnson is out there, somewhere, and at any time she might run into him would be too much.'

Maltby smiled grimly and threw the remains of his ice-cream cone into the beak of a waiting gull, which swooped triumphantly upwards with its prize.

'Arthur Johnson is going to hang for the murder of Rosemary Archer, Mrs Webb-Goring,' he said firmly. 'Even if the death was an accident, he still hid the body while he tried to find a means of disposing of it. He still kidnapped little Dorothea when she stumbled on his guilt; there was no conceivable way he could have released her again so that makes him guilty of intent to kill, and he still lied continuously before the body was found. I'm afraid that on the morning James rescued Dorothea I suspect Johnson was in such a blue funk that, given the opportunity, he would have killed both her and James as well if he could, so he is *never* going to be walking the streets again. But if I can persuade him to plead guilty, James and Dorothea won't have to go to court.'

Anthea turned her face away from him and stared, through narrowed eyes, at the brilliant blue of the ocean. The air smelled fragrant and deliciously salty, the sky was a cloudless blue dome above their heads, and the memories of that cold, wet and windswept February morning were suddenly faintly unreal and discomfortingly sinister.

For no apparent reason then she felt the need to confess.

'I don't approve of hanging,' she whispered. To her surprise she heard him utter a little snort of agreement.

'Neither do I,' he replied. 'At least I don't approve of the ritual of hanging, anyway. Arthur Johnson has a wife and three little girls who are having the most appalling time of it at the moment, and when he's dead will have an even worse time. And for him, on the day, there's the awful waiting between breakfast and the appointed hour, and then the final walk, still desperately hoping for a last minute reprieve – it's a ritual and it's grim. But Mr and Mrs Archer won't see it like that; their lives are collapsing under the strain of their suffering. Maybe you and Mrs Buddry wouldn't have seen it like that, either, if James hadn't found Dorothea that morning, don't you think?'

Anthea smiled and suddenly she liked this man very much. A

hardened policeman he might be, but he had deep and sensitive feelings.

'Miss Forrester,' she said, 'the retired teacher who's been giving James and Dorothea lessons over the past weeks, thinks that they should be allowed to stay here for good, you know. That they should be given a completely new start in life once the trial is over, in a place where they won't keep tripping over painful memories.'

Maltby thought about James, the really quite super-polite little boy whose future had almost certainly been mapped out for him on the day of his birth. He was a nice child, with a childlike and yet peculiarly adult sense of his duty in life.

'James isn't quite twelve yet, is he?' he enquired. 'And yet he has already been confronted with two dead bodies – both of them children. Unless I'm much mistaken he's lived a pretty sheltered life up till now – unlike Dorothea, whose life was precarious to say the least until Mrs Buddry found her, but who has suffered very visibly since Rosemary's death. James has struggled to be very grown-up about everything; to not show his fear and to give a good account of himself, and I wonder if it has ever occurred to you that you just might be trying him a wee bit too hard, to expect him to go back to the way things were as if nothing has happened.'

Anthea lowered her eyes quickly and chewed the inside of her lip. When she said nothing, he frowned at her slightly comically.

'But your problem is?' he enquired and watched her blush. 'Well you do have a problem, so what is it?'

Abruptly her head came up and she stared at him fixedly.

'My problem, as you put it,' she retorted sourly, 'is that I am an extremely selfish woman, and if I have to spend the rest of my life buried in all this timeless beauty I shall go stark raving mad, frankly! It might be enough for James and Dorothea to sit on a stone altar and stuff grapes without any clear picture of the future, but I want to go home and get on with my life. I actually happened to like it rather a lot, before I left it!'

Maltby burst out laughing. As he gazed at her, he saw yet again what a remarkably attractive woman she was, and how different from her sister, with her perfect grooming and wonderful dress-sense. She was a socialite to her toe-nails, and it wasn't remotely surprising that this sedentary life at Pengloss was driving her nuts.

'Good Lord alive!' he exclaimed. 'How many adoring adults do they want, those children? They have your sister spoiling them rotten, Mrs Buddry, who growls occasionally but not very convincingly, Judd and Seth ready to drop everything for them and Mrs Newby feeding them non-stop. You go back to your life at Hampton Court and let them get on with it. I would!'

For a second Anthea stared at him in astonishment, then she cheerfully joined in his laughter and they hauled themselves to their feet. He must be on his way, he knew, so it was time to get back to Pengloss.

'Thank you,' she murmured as they started back. 'You've been very kind, and a big help as well. Well, at least Dorothea's talking again, that's something, I suppose.'

'It could be everything, so keep hoping,' Maltby replied with a smile.

He had been right, Pengloss did seem like a dream to him as he sat in the prison interview room the next afternoon opposite the unkempt, unhappy Arthur Johnson and his overweight solicitor. Flies buzzed stupidly against the window and the room smelled of unwashed bodies and disinfectant as they went wearily over the old ground yet again.

To Maltby a sudden minds-eye view of James and Dorothea playing in their old chapel brought a strange yearning within him. He would never have been rude enough to say so to Anthea, but it was his lifetime dream to live in the country. To play golf and walk the fields – and never be obliged to look another criminal in the face as long as he lived.

Oh one day, he thought, one day . . . and struggled to bring his attention back to what he was supposed to be doing.

Arthur listened as the policeman probed all his deepest, darkest fears, dragging them to the surface without mercy. Edna Buddry's wretched little niece might not have been able to speak for nigh on five months, but having got her voice back she was accurate to the letter, and spitting it all out with venom apparently!

Desperately he struggled to bluff his way out.

'She's made a mistake,' he insisted. 'Oh, I whole heartedly admit it was me who found her and her little boyfriend on the water board property the next morning, but it wasn't me who shut her in the hut. She's made a mistake!'

Maltby shook his head slowly.

'Arthur, she's eleven, not three,' he replied. 'She doesn't make mistakes like that. Good God man she knew you better than any other father from the school, you'd been meeting her and Rosemary on the corner of Acacia Road every morning for months. Why don't you tell us the truth? It'd make it so much simpler.'

Arthur rubbed his hands across his pasty, sweaty face and the bags under his eyes were blue ridges. His skin was bad and his whole frame gave off an aura of defeat . . . as if, Maltby thought, his terror of what he knew was coming was eating him away bit by bit.

'He says I've got a very good chance,' he observed defensively, pointing at his solicitor who was contributing nothing whatever to the exchange. 'That the evidence against me is a lot thinner than you'd like.'

'Not since Dorothea Sprake began talking it isn't,' Maltby retorted. 'And she's not a little shrinking violet, you know, anymore than young James is. They'll stand up in court and say their bit, if they have to . . . I just thought you might like to spare them the ordeal, and spare yourself and your family some of the hatred. And there will be hatred, and a lot of unpleasantness too, just like there was when Rosemary was buried, but it'll be your charming wife and innocent daughters who bear the brunt of it. You'll be safely locked in here each night. So what d'you say? Time to come clean?'

But it was not yet time, not for Arthur.

He went back to his cell without anything but whining repeats of the lies he had been telling all along, lies that he had come almost to believe until he had suddenly been uncomfortably forced to face the truth.

Maltby went home to his wife wearily and sat in an armchair nursing his frustration, half-dreading a phone-call to say that Dorothea had stopped speaking again, to save herself the ordeal of the trial. But Dorothea was too young and too truthful to dream that one up – though her agony was worse than anyone else could imagine.

At Pengloss she checked on *This Man is Death* regularly, waiting in terror for the retribution she knew was coming. The adults were faintly surprised when, for a couple of nights, the nightmares returned with a vengeance, but when, after five days, James and Aunty were apparently quite well and happy, Dorothea allowed herself to begin to believe that maybe she was safe after all. Oh certainly, Inspector Maltby had promised no one could hurt her, just as had Aunt Bella and Aunty and Mrs Webb-Goring – but they didn't know what she knew. They didn't know that Mr Johnson could be in two places at once if he chose. He had threatened her and she had told – only she had expected retribution to be swift, and nothing had happened. So cautiously she lowered her guard, and things began to calm down again.

Two weeks passed and the approaching trial grew close; they were counting down to it day by day. For those at Pengloss the details of how the trial days would be handled were reasonably simple: Anthea and Edna would accompany James and Dorothea to the Old Bailey when they were required, and make sure that in-between times they had some diverting pastimes; something to take their minds off it.

For Edith the decisions were much more difficult, because to attend the trial each day would mean leaving the children in Balham, and Phyllis had made it abundantly clear that this was going to put her out considerably.

But Phyllis would do it, she agreed graciously, for she supposed it *was* a necessity.

Edith wasn't sure it was a necessity at all, and yet nothing would have kept her away. Deep down inside, though she had been ruthlessly cutting the ties with her former life for ages, the last nugget of 'dutiful wife' clung on tightly and refused to be shifted. The trial stood in the way of the future like a tightly closed door, and she had long since stopped trying to see beyond it, but one way or another there must be a future, and she wanted it, whatever it was, very badly. She wanted release.

She wanted, she thought, on the rare occasions when she was completely honest with herself, to walk away from Arthur for the last time and leave him and her guilt behind, and when he was found guilty and condemned to be hanged – which she was absolutely certain he would be – she could do it. Whether he was guilty or not would be of no matter. He had put them through hell and could not be forgiven, but she had stood by him in his hour of need; she had been the obedient wife; she had fulfilled her contract.

When Maltby received a call from the prison – exactly one week before the trial was scheduled to begin – to say that Arthur wanted to make a full confession, he was never more surprised in his life. It was what he'd hoped for certainly, but my god, the man had taken them right to the wire!

Arthur had been growing steadily more listless and introverted as the grimy, London summer ground on, but to the officers who had charge of him that was nothing remarkable, it often happened to a prisoner facing a life or a death verdict. He didn't sleep well, certainly, and he had been sending back his food half-eaten for some weeks, but he had given no real indication of his inner hauntings to those around him.

When Maltby arrived he found that he was not expected to ask any questions, but simply to sit opposite the white, cadaverous-looking prisoner and listen, whilst Arthur, with tears pouring down his cheeks, gave the whole story of beautiful Rosemary's cruel and untimely death in stunning detail.

'But as God is my witness it was an accident!' he sobbed when he was finished, wiping his congested face with a grubby handkerchief. 'I *loved* Rosemary, I *adored* her, I wouldn't have hurt her for the world. I only wanted to give her a little gift but she wouldn't stop screaming . . . and the noise in that hut, the noise of her screaming . . . I couldn't bear it . . .'

Maltby found no gratification in the fact that he had been right – but he had no sympathy for Arthur either, or very little.

'You knew she suffered from asthma,' he pointed out. 'Surely you knew that if you put your hand over her mouth she might very well suffocate?'

Arthur shook his head.

'I didn't think about it,' he replied truthfully. 'Why should I have done? I just needed to stop her screaming. She shouldn't have screamed, I wouldn't have hurt her, she knew that. God I was always kind to her, gave her sweets and things, walked home with her from the bus . . . I wouldn't have hurt her . . . I *wouldn't*!'

Maltby eyed him cynically.

'Umm, but she was eleven years old,' he observed. 'What would *you* have done, at eleven years old, if a grown-up who should have known better had enticed you into a brick hut and then asked you for a kiss . . . no don't answer that, it doesn't matter. So, what about little Dorothea Sprake?'

All at once Arthur's face was touched with anger and bitterness and he stared, unseeing, at the world beyond the grimy window of the interview room.

'Bloody little brat,' he muttered, 'poking about where she had no business being. She looked so bloody frightened when she ran into me, and I *knew* she'd seen me buying that scarf and gloves – her and that posh bloody boyfriend of hers.'

Maltby nodded. 'And were you going to kill her?'

At that Arthur showed the whites of his eyes. It haunted him as much as anything, the knowledge that Rosemary's death had been a pitiful accident, but Dorothea's wouldn't have been. God almighty, had he been *so* frightened, so bloody *panic-stricken* that he could truly have contemplated killing a second child . . . and a third too . . . James?

'I was . . . going to tell her she could go, and then hit her over the back of the head with an empty bottle,' he murmured miserably. 'I couldn't have faced her and killed her. I couldn't have done that. I'm not a monster!'

Which is a matter of opinion, Maltby thought sourly.

'And James?' he enquired. 'Supposing James hadn't hit you first, were you planning to kill him too?'

Arthur closed his eyes and felt suddenly very sick.

'They'd knocked her over, you know,' he whispered, horrified by the memory. 'They'd knocked her out of the deckchair and she was sprawled on. . . . It took me ages to get her back . . . and her skin was all . . . loose . . .'

Maltby thrust the memory from his mind, for he had seen it too. He had seen the beautiful child, ugly in death, and dead children were always a painful memory.

'So,' he said, when Arthur had finished all he had to say, 'you asked to see me, and you told me in the beginning that if you told the truth then you wanted something in return from me. Come on then, let's have it.'

Arthur's eyes flickered nervously, and Maltby saw his fear. He thought he knew what was coming, and kept his eyes firmly on the man as he waited.

'Don't let them hang me!' Arthur suddenly begged in a tight voice. 'It was an accident, for god's sake, I never meant to hurt her. I never raped her or anything. Make them see that. I'll say sorry, I'll beg forgiveness of Mr and Mrs Archer if that's what you want, but let me go home to my wife and children, please. You know I'll never do such a thing again!'

Maltby gazed at him for a moment in faintly surprised silence, then he shook his head very slowly and began to gather up the notes and papers on the desk in front of him and pack them away, ready for departure.

'You haven't stolen biscuits from the pantry, you know, Arthur,' he said at last. 'You killed a child and planned to kill a second one. What happens now is called punishment, and whatever it is, it doesn't include going home and starting again as if nothing's happened. Sorry, but if that was what you'd hoped for then you're out of luck, I'm afraid. This confession will stand in your favour, certainly, but I don't think you'll find it will make any difference to the outcome.'

But he left the prison feeling no sense of elation – only a sense
of relief that James and Dorothea would never have to hear these
details spoken aloud in court. They had seen and would never
forget. All through their lives, often when they were least
expecting it, a sudden vision of the greying, week-long dead
Rosemary, sprawled in a heap on the floor of the hut, would fetch
them up with an agonizing jolt. And that was quite enough.

Now there were three families to talk to. Relief for the
guardians of the two at Pengloss but – what for the mother of
Arthur's three? And nothing for Rosemary's mother, he suspected,
not even an acknowledgement of the truth.

Doreen Archer spent most of these summer days in a deckchair
in the back garden now – only not out of choice. She was put
there of a morning and would sit under the blue sky without
comprehension. The sun warmed her skin: made it look quite
healthy really, but it truly was only skin deep. Beneath the surface
her heart was cold and dead . . . and for hours and hours, as she
sat there, she would watch the dancer in the white leather jewel-
box whirl and spin, as she continuously fingered the string of blue
beads.

In Phyllis Brown's little front parlour Edith stood before Maltby
and listened to what he had to say without any recognizable
emotion of any sort. He had done his best to be kind, to break it
to her gently, and he didn't believe for one moment that she had
ever believed Arthur to be innocent, but he saw from her eyes that
this was the final betrayal.

'You should take your children and get on with your lives, Mrs
Johnson,' he murmured, trying to be as gentle as possible. 'It will
all be over very quickly now that he's changed his plea to guilty, I
promise you.'

Edith pressed her lips together.

'I don't need you to tell me what the children and I should do
with our lives, Inspector, thanks all the same,' she whispered. 'So
he killed Rosemary all along, and intended to kill that sweet little
niece of Mrs Buddry's into the bargain. And on top of that he's left

us here to suffer all these weeks, promising me this and that, and it was all lies?'

Maltby nodded, feeling uncomfortable.

'But you mustn't let it colour your lives any longer,' he insisted. 'You and your little girls have done nothing, and as you say, you've suffered enough.'

Edith stared at him and then, lifting her head proudly she walked to the door and opened it.

'Thank you, for coming to see me personally, Inspector,' she said stiffly. 'But if there's nothing more . . . ?'

Maltby left, stepping out on to the grubby, unimaginative Balham street, glad to be out of Phyllis Brown's grubby, unimaginative house. He wanted so much that Edith and her three little girls should find a niche; a way to distance themselves from their pain and begin to live again, but Edith had made it abundantly clear that she required no assistance from him in the matter; so he had done all he could.

He went home to his wife feeling better than he'd felt for some-time, and enjoyed a pleasant conversation with Anthea Webb-Goring on the telephone at Pengloss. Soon, he thought, he would have to divorce himself from this case and move on to something new.

But it hadn't quite finished with him yet.

Edith stood in her sister's shabby kitchen, making supper and as she washed up the cups and saucers from lunch-time, which Phyllis had pointedly left in the sink, she thought, with unspeakable rage, of Arthur. All his lying and his self-pity, all the meaningless promises. Well it was over now, that was for sure. Not once more would she lay eyes on him in this life, for any reason whatsoever. Not ever!

Phyllis wandered into the kitchen as Edith stood by the sink, and for a moment she said nothing, simply watched as the cups came out of the hot, soapy water on to the draining-board. Then, snatching up a tea-towel she began to dry – and Edith knew immediately that something portentous was coming, because if Phyllis had nothing to say she was perfectly happy to watch her sister work without conscience!

Phyllis rattled a pile of saucers down on to the green plastic tablecloth and drew her mouth into a sharp line. She seemed to be having some trouble finding the words she wanted to begin with, then without warning she turned on her sister fiercely.

'Me and Reg have been talking,' she announced abruptly, 'and we've a proposition to put to you, which we'd like you to seriously consider. He wanted it to be both of us talk to you, but I said I'd handle it. So you can stop doing that for a bit and listen, all right?'

Edith obediently dropped the mop into the sink and turned, reaching for a towel to dry her hands. Phyllis's kitchen smelled faintly unwholesome, the shelf above the cooker, upon which stood a clock and two emergency candles, was thick with dust and grease. Somewhere in the pantry something was going off, and a blowfly was looking for a way in through the keyhole. It was, she thought sourly, disgusting!

'Well?' she enquired wearily, sitting down opposite her sister at the table. 'Strike while the iron's hot, eh, before I've had a chance to get over what that policeman told me? Let's have it then, what d'you want to do to me now?'

Phyllis's mouth was taking on a cruel sneer as her resentment came bubbling to the surface. Bloody hoity-toity Edith with her 'the girls must have a bath every evening', and her complaints about food being left too long in the larder; well she wasn't in a position to make demands any more, was she, not after today?

'I said you never should've married him,' she snarled with a nasty note of triumph in her voice. 'Didn't I say that, at the time? He wanted you 'cos you looked like a kid; didn't have any tits; only *you* wouldn't see it, and now look at the mess you're in. Well, you've got your come-uppance, and you've only yourself to blame this time!'

Edith thought of a dozen answers to that, and offered none of them. She was so tired, so weary and – frankly – so indifferent that she simply couldn't be bothered. Even if Phyllis was right and she shouldn't have married Arthur in the beginning, it was still none of Phyllis's business, and she was not entitled to take any credit for what was happening now. She'd been jealous of Arthur in the

190

beginning because he'd had a bit of money to splash about, nothing else.

'So what's this proposition?' she enquired in a flat voice. 'I'd rather you simply told me than that we had to have the "I told you so" bits first. I was about to start on supper.'

Phyllis pursed her lips tightly, annoyed at the jibe.

'Very well then,' she replied crisply, 'I will. Everyone in London knows who you are, Edith; the wife of the child-murderer. You and them girls are never going to have a *normal* life all the while you stay round here, as well you know. So me and Reg think it would be best all round if you was to make a clean break. Leave the girls here with us and move up north somewhere. You'll get yourself a job in a place where nobody knows you, 'specially if you change your name; and if you have the girls' names changed to Brown at the same time, it's going to be much easier for them. We're not saying you can't see them, of course you'll be welcome to visit now and again, but you've got to start afresh, and this is the best way.'

Edith stared at her sister in blank astonishment, and realized, suddenly, that for the first time in ages she was actually registering a feeling that was not tinged with weariness. Even when Maltby had told her Arthur had changed his plea to guilty she had only really wanted him to go away and leave her alone, but now she was outraged! It was a relief. Comforting to know that she had not slipped through a gap somewhere into a two-dimensional world that simply threw things at her without arousing any emotion.

'Leave my girls with you!' she exclaimed. 'Leave them with *you*!' She uttered a snort of hysterical laugher. 'I wouldn't give you my girls if I was going to be hanged along with Arthur, Phyllis Brown! You're dirty, cruel and spiteful and I've had just about as much of you as I can stand! Well, we don't have to stay here any more, so tomorrow the girls and I are going home to Cheddar Close. What's more, I want *nothing* more from you, not even your opinions; so if you've said all you had to say, you can go back in the other room with your husband and leave me to go upstairs and pack. We're going home tomorrow, and we're going out to get some fish and chips tonight!'

In the shattering silence that followed, Phyllis stared at her little sister in wordless fury. This was Edith, the shrinking violet, the one it had been so easy to bully as a child because she could be guaranteed to show her pain. Driving a wedge between her and her children should have been quite simple. But now, when she was being offered a sensible way out of her troubles she had the gall not only to throw the offer back, but to be rude into the bargain.

Furiously she closed her hand over Edith's wrist, squeezing it painfully as she brought her face to within inches of her sister's.

'Listen, you stupid bitch,' she hissed, spitting in her rage, 'you'll do as you're told if you know what's good for you, because in the end you won't have no choice!'

Edith shook her off savagely.

'You watch me!' she snarled, and banged out of the kitchen.

Chapter 13

When Thelma Gregson looked up from the column of figures she was busy totting up, and saw the customers who had just come into the shop, she was never more surprised in her life. It was not much after ten in the morning, and only days to go until school broke up for the summer – and here, amid the community who were still muttering savagely on the subject of Arthur Johnson's final admission of his guilt, was his pathetic little family, looking like exhausted refugees.

'Mrs Johnson!' she exclaimed, as with a twinge of alarm she took in Edith's weary face and the unkempt appearance of the little girls. 'This is a nice surprise, dear. You've decided to come home, have you? I'm not sure you've picked the best possible time though, if you don't mind me saying.'

Edith was not capable of registering facial expression any longer, the last of that had gone on her sister the previous evening. She offered Thelma a weak, meaningless smile and her thin hands seemed to work nervously around the childrens' shoulders.

'We're just here for a few days, actually,' she replied flatly. 'Little break . . . you know?'

Thelma didn't know, and felt uncomfortable as they stared at each other. Edith Johnson had frighteningly lacklustre eyes – in fact they reminded Thelma of the look in Doreen Archer's eyes the last time they had met . . . and she hadn't seen Doreen now for weeks.

'And then back to your sister's?' she enquired as she bustled about rather pointlessly.

Edith shook her head.

'No, we're going on to somewhere new,' she answered. 'So we're going to have a bit of a treat for the next few days, aren't we, girls?' She tweaked her white-faced, dark-eyed little flock closer. 'No expense spared, eh?'

She began to ask for a number of items, and Thelma wondered where on earth the money was coming from to pay for them, but decided firmly that if it wasn't forthcoming then she would write it off. Whilst this was going on Thelma gave each of the children a small bar of chocolate and was aware that they ate them with almost ferocious delight . . . so there hadn't been many treats in the past months, she thought sadly.

The goodies piled up and disappeared into four different shopping-bags. Then, to Thelma's astonishment, Edith pulled out the money and laid it on the counter. She wouldn't have dreamed of asking where it had come from, which was just as well because Edith wouldn't have told her, but Phyllis Brown was due for a shock the next time she went to add a few bob to the savings she kept in her mother's old bone-china teapot in the parlour. There had been a tidy haul in there the previous day. It was empty now.

'Oh, and there's one more thing, before we go, Mrs Gregson,' Edith said as she divided up the shopping-bags between the children, managing a tolerably realistic smile as she did so. 'The girls and I would like to say a particular thank you to you. Back at the beginning when Arthur was first arrested you were the only person around here who was kind to us, and you were exceptionally kind. We would very much like to invite you to lunch on Sunday, if you could manage it. We . . . er . . . we won't be here much after that, I'm afraid, so please say you'll come.'

Thelma Gregson was astonished, but she was careful not to show it. It seemed such a very odd thing for Edith to do, to invite her to Sunday lunch, when they didn't even know each other well enough to be on first-name terms. However, just at this moment in time it was obvious that she desperately needed the hand of friendship from somebody, and since Thelma mostly always had her bit of Sunday dinner on her own, she was happy to accept the invitation.

'Don't knock at the front door when you arrive,' Edith said. 'It won't do your business any good for people to see you coming into my house. Come round the back, and if you don't immediately get an answer, you'll find the key on the ledge in the back porch. It's just that I might be up with the girls or something, when you arrive.'

Thelma frowned. It was an odd thing to say, but then, she reflected, it wasn't so very surprising that Edith was behaving oddly, with everything that was going on in her life.

'All right, my dear,' she replied, smiling warmly. 'I'll see you Sunday, then, and I tell you what, I'll bring along a nice rhubarb-crumble for pud, as a bit of a thank you.'

She thought Edith was going to refuse, but after a pause another meaningless little smile crept across Edith's lips and she nodded her head a couple of times.

'That would be lovely, thank you,' she murmured and turned to leave the shop.

As she walked up Acacia Road with the girls and the shopping, she reflected that what she had done wasn't really all that fair. Of everyone around here Thelma Gregson had been good to her. Still, beggars couldn't be choosers, not in her circumstances, she reflected and hurried the girls into Cheddar Close.

The little house smelled stale and unlived-in. Windows had to be opened – but only at the back – and the hot water turned on, then there were baths all round and the bliss of clean clothes. Oh God, it was good to be home.

At last, when lunch was over, Edith sent the girls into the back garden to play and sat down to make a list of what she had to do. She had three days. Everything must be done and finished by the time Thelma Gregson arrived for lunch on Sunday.

Everything.

Phyllis Brown had saved ten bob and would have put it in the teapot, except that she decided to blow it on something special for tea, to celebrate the fact that Edith had finally cleared out! So she didn't discover that the teapot was empty.

Arthur didn't bother to do anything any more as the days to his conviction dragged by. He didn't know that Edith and the girls had gone back to Cheddar Close, and he probably wouldn't have cared much if he had. Mostly he just lay on his bunk with his hands behind his head in a kind of torpor, as the hours and minutes crawled on interminably.

He wouldn't see Edith again as a visitor, of that he was certain, but he desperately hoped she might come to court, if only so that he might see her sitting there. Of his girls he thought little now, for he hadn't seen them for so long he wasn't certain he would recognize them immediately.

Even in these days when he suddenly knew his lifespan to be finite, when he knew he would never see a winter's day again, or the glitter of Christmas, he thought in agony of Rosemary more than of anyone. He dreamed, regularly, of her black, shiny hair and almond-shaped eyes, of her long legs that promised to be beautiful and of her little girl's body that would suddenly blossom into womanhood . . . or rather would *have* suddenly blossomed, if he hadn't snuffed out her life first, of course.

He found it increasingly difficult to think about her as dead – because the memory of her corpse was so awful, and knowing they were going to put him to death anyway, he found himself taking a perverse pleasure in fantasizing about her.

Arthur was sinking into a mire of his own making, and simply didn't care any longer.

At Pengloss, after everything was organized, the inhabitants of the manor held a carefully planned and beautifully arranged funeral for Simon David Rosenthal in the village church: a church set high on the cliffs, with a graveyard blown by the salt winds from the sea.

It was a very small and private laying-to-rest, and more a celebration of his life than an act of mourning for his death, for Bella had done all her mourning over the past eighteen years. Peachy's bones were laid in a tiny white coffin and he was buried with his father. James and Dorothea collected their own flowers to lay on his coffin, and the day was warm, fragrant and exquisite.

Judd and Molly attended, with Seth and his wife; Edna, Anthea and Charles and of course, Bella were there. Present, too, were Miss Forrester and a number of the village people who had known Peachy and had felt so wretched for Bella for so many years; *All Things Bright and Beautiful* was sung, because it seemed so appropriate. To Anthea's relief Bella had arranged for the occasion to be very simple; there were no enormous wreaths and there was no public outpouring of grief from her, but at the service, and at the sunny graveside afterwards, she stood firmly between James and Dorothea, hugging them to her frequently.

If they had been considered to be a bit young for a funeral by most of the adults up at the manor, no one had actually dared to say so, and on the day they behaved beautifully. Dorothea, at her own request, wore her maroon striped dress, the one Anthea had bought her for Rosemary's party, whilst James wore his first pair of long trousers, a shirt and tie, and a blazer. They carefully fulfilled what they saw as their duty to their beloved Aunt. They were there to look after her, and look after her they did.

But for Anthea to stand in the ancient, squat, stone church and watch her sister burying her son without tears, without the slightest sign of hysteria, was almost surreal. Bella, who so many times over the years had trailed about Pengloss like the first Mrs Rochester, mad, inconsolable and in agonized despair. It was astonishing.

It was also, if she needed one, a very forceful argument for James and Dorothea's continuing presence at Pengloss, and she knew she needed to speak to Charles about it. But Charles had taken a month off work to spend some time with his family, so it could wait a couple of weeks, she decided.

It wouldn't wait a couple of weeks though. It would be settled long before that, as it happened.

On Saturday afternoon, with food laid aside for a special evening meal and only enough milk left for their cocoa that night, Edith finished the last of the pretty dresses she had been feverishly making on her sewing-machine and triumphantly cut the last piece of cotton. Standing up to stretch her aching neck she held up the dress for a second, and then put it on to the ironing-board for a final press.

Three little dresses in matching material, red, with a pattern of big white spots, carefully made to measure and destined to be a perfect fit. Her eyes ached a bit and her fingers were quite stiff from working so fast, but she was highly satisfied.

She had told the girls the dresses were for Sunday, and they were delighted. They had bitterly hated the way they had been treated at their aunt's house, hated the long grey socks they had been expected to wear with black plimsolls; the second-hand skirts and ghastly jumpers bought at local jumble-sales. It would be wonderful on Sunday to wear new dresses, to have their summer sandals whitened and to pull on clean white socks . . . and Mummy had promised to spend time doing their hair, as well.

Edith had been obliged to cut the toes out of last year's sandals for them, because there wasn't any money for new shoes, but the girls didn't mind in the least, and Shirley, particularly, was loving having her hair curled and pinned at night.

Edith called them in from the garden to see their finished dresses and watched their pretty faces light with pleasure at the sight of them. They were dusty, because the garden was still a mess from all the police digging, but even the dust couldn't hide the warmth and colour that was already creeping into their faces now they were free of Balham, and with a sudden rush of love, Edith gathered them against her tightly, squeezing and kissing them.

'Ringlets for tomorrow, Shirley,' she promised, wondering how she was going to manage with the child's hair still so short from Phyllis's untimely hacking. 'And curls for you two, Monica and Katy, so lots of pins tonight, I'm afraid.'

Shirley laughed and Edith gazed at her. She was such a pretty little girl – amazing really, when neither of her parents had ever

198

had much to offer in the looks department. For all the world she had a look of Shirley Temple about her and was such a dainty little thing.

'Will Mrs Gregson like our new dresses, do you think?' Shirley asked and Edith kissed her cheek softly.

'She'll love them,' she replied. 'And when we go to our new place, you'll be able to wear them regularly, along with all your pretty clothes. It'll be nice to be pretty all the time again, won't it?'

Shirley gazed at her mother for a moment, then tipped her head on one side slightly as a serious, faintly bewildered look came into her eyes.

'Mummy, is Daddy coming to the new place with us?' she asked plaintively. 'We do miss him. When's he coming home?'

Edith felt her heart tear in her chest. They missed their daddy – and, bitterly, she doubted he even remembered he had had them all that often.

'Daddy's going to join us in a little while, sweetheart,' she said in answer to the question, and knew that to some degree she was telling the truth.

But she didn't know to what degree, exactly, for she was not a religious woman so she was not clear about matters of life and death and heaven and hell. She understood sin though, and deep down inside she had a strong belief that Arthur would suffer for his. Suffer in this life and the next – if there was a next.

When they sat down to dinner that evening the girls were astonished to find all their favourite food on the table, and the meal turned into an hour of delight. There was masses of giggling and everyone ate to their fullest. It had never occurred to the children to ask what was for lunch on Sunday, but then Edith had known it wouldn't, because they were much too small to be concerned about things like that – and that the cupboards were now bare did not enter their heads.

They were happy. They were in their own home, they could run about as much as they liked and they had new dresses to wear in the morning.

At six-thirty they all piled into the bath together, wriggling like eels and splashing each other cheerfully, then once they were in their night-gowns and Edith had pinned their hair, as she had promised, she left them to have a last game on the landing as she went down to make them some cocoa.

They were noisy; yelping and screaming and thumping about, having fun. She listened to them with her emotions separated into two entirely different dimensions, and not touching at any point. They were full of life, young and vigorous; and beautiful as only children can be, and her fingers did what they must do, knowing how the silence would be . . . She mixed cocoa powder with sugar and a little milk into three mugs and then put the rest of the milk on to boil. It would be enough for four mugs.

Then she fetched her handbag and took out of it three bottles of sleeping pills.

They were solid tablets, all of which she carefully ground to the consistency of chalk with the back of a spoon, and then tipped into the milk saucepan. It took longer than she expected and the milk was almost boiling by the time she finished.

Carefully she stirred the milk, then filled the three mugs and put the remainder on the side to be rewarmed later. The drinks were thick with chocolate and extra sugar, if what she had added tasted of anything it would not be noticeable, for sure.

As she reached the landing, carrying the tray with the three steaming mugs of cocoa, the girls were leaping about and laughing, playing with toys of which they had seen nothing since the beginning of March and were delighted to have found again. They groaned at being told it was time for bed and started begging for more time. Edith grinned at them cheerfully.

'I tell you what,' she said. 'How would you all like to sleep in Mummy and Daddy's bed tonight?'

'Yes! Yes! Yes!' replied a chorus of excited voices, and the three little girls burst into their mother's bedroom and dived on to the bed.

Edith had very carefully changed the sheets and removed all traces of Arthur since her return home, for to be in that room

200

with even the faintest suggestion of him, would have been unspeakable. Now it smelled of slightly cheap, very sweet perfume, the *Devon Violets* of which she was so fond, and of sweetly clean children with fresh nightgowns and talcumed bodies. To see her lovely girls all burrowing down between the sheets together did not even bring a brief glimpse of him to her mind. She had already pigeon-holed Arthur and he would never surface again.

She gave them each a mug of cocoa and sat on the bed reading them a story as they drank it. Not one of them suggested it tasted funny, but all remarked on how chocolatey it was. When they had finished she took the empty mugs, settled the girls down, kissed each of them very lovingly and prepared to creep away.

'And I don't want to hear any more giggling or whispering,' she told them as she reached the door. 'Otherwise I might have to come up and read the riot act. Clear?'

A burst of giggles erupted from the bed.

'Yes, Mummy!' Shirley sang out.

Edith closed her eyes as two tears escaped from under her lashes, then she closed the bedroom door and went slowly downstairs.

She spent the next four hours cleaning the house as outside the summer day closed into a warm, still night and a soft, glowing sunset became a diamond-studded, velvet sky. She made no sound and heard few. She had unplugged the radio, for she had no interest in the world beyond her little house any more, and only the sound of passing trains disturbed her deep silence.

She cleaned and polished, dusted and vacuumed and simply, didn't think. About anything. About Arthur's betrayal, or Rosemary's death, or what she had done to her beautiful girls, or even about how long it took to die. And she didn't think about tomorrow – because you couldn't think about what you didn't know.

At nearly midnight she took the new dresses upstairs to her bedroom and turned on the two bedside lamps. The white-faced little girls didn't stir, but then she hadn't expected them to. She fetched clean pants and socks and the newly whited sandals, then she pulled back the bedclothes and took each child in her arms in turn, removing her nightgown and beginning the process of dressing her for the day.

It was difficult to know if death had already taken them, or if they were still deeply and irreversibly in the dying process. She had an idea that both the twins had already slipped away, but she thought there just might be a tiny spark in Shirley. Whatever, it wouldn't last for long now. She propped them between her knees when it came to doing their hair, and had to counter the fact that their heads wobbled limply but she was gentle and loving at all times, allowing no pain or pressure. Last of all she laid them together on top of the bed, with a gap between the twins which was just big enough for one more person.

After that she sorted through the wardrobe until she found her favourite dress. She changed into it, putting on clean stockings and her best summer sandals. She put her dirty clothes carefully into the laundry-basket and then went down into the kitchen to make a last mug of cocoa. Afterwards, she washed the saucepan out and put it away.

Then she drank the cocoa and climbed into the middle of the bed, lying down on her back and spreading her arms to encompass her beloved children. She said nothing, but she held them close. She closed her eyes to finally free herself of the world and waited for sleep and with a mind empty of all thought she drifted away.

The hours of the night slid silently on towards dawn. The milk-train went through very early, but nobody in Cheddar Close heard it. At not much after four, for it was the height of summer, the sky began to pale in the east, and those people who kept chickens, hearing their cockerels singing to the dawn, turned sleepily, enjoying the fact that it was Sunday. In the little house in Cheddar Close there was only stillness.

A little later the sun came up, and because of the way the houses faced it pushed its morning rays in through the bedroom window and spread its warmth upon the bed. But it would never warm the little group who lay on it again, no matter how hard it tried.

Thelma Gregson felt oddly nervous the second time she rapped hard on the back door at a few minutes past noon, and received no reply. There was something strangely quiet about the house, as if it was empty. But it shouldn't be empty, because she'd been invited to lunch, hadn't she, and there was no way Edith Johnson would pull some sort of ridiculous stunt, she wasn't like that.

Somewhat reluctantly she found the key where Edith had told her it would be, and let herself into the house. She slid her rhubarb crumble on to the side, where there were no plates or napkins or knives and forks in evidence, in fact no signs of activity at all, and stood in the spotless kitchen gazing around at its extreme neatness in growing alarm. There was no delicious smell of roasting meat coming from the oven, no bubbling pots of vegetables on the stove, not the remotest sign of a Sunday lunch being prepared anywhere. The house smelled of bleach, polish and sweet perfume and not a sound disturbed the dust-free silence.

Thelma heard herself swallow uncomfortably in the awful quiet, and wanted like mad to turn around and take herself back home. Something was wrong here, and she dreaded discovering what it was, but she was not the sort of woman who could do something like that. She had to go on, it was in her nature. She called out, hearing her own voice floating back to her mockingly. Standing at the foot of the stairs she gazed up to the sun-splashed, carpeted landing as a horrible inertia crept across her, weakening her legs beneath her spitefully.

'Oh for God's sake, please, no . . .' she whispered, putting her hands firmly on the banister and beginning to almost drag her vast bulk up the stairs. 'Let them be out, just let them be out . . . please . . .'

And in a way, of course, they were out. But they would never come home again.

She looked at the four waxy-white faces for ages; smooth and beautiful, like faces etched on sleeping marble statues. She found herself thinking, absurdly, that the colour of the skin didn't go with the twins' lovely red hair and knew it was stupid, but she couldn't face the truth because it was too awful. She touched them with trembling fingers, touched each one of them and found rigor mortis, and still she couldn't wholly take it in.

Then tears of terrible grief flooded down her cheeks and she stood by the bed, rocking backwards and forwards in her despair as the little girls and their mother slept on in the firm grip of death.

Inspector Maltby stared at the four bodies and clenched his teeth together as a muscle jumped in his cheek. Illogically he wanted to scream with rage. How could Edith Johnson have done this? How could she? And yet why not, of course? Where had there been any chink of light in her darkness recently, or any hope for the future?

Thelma Gregson was down in the kitchen with a WPC drinking tea and still weeping into her handkerchief. Maltby could immediately see the logic Edith had applied to all this. No way could she have permitted the perfect bodies of her babies to begin to decompose, and with morning sunshine full on them each day, in the heat of July, they would have done so quite quickly.

And who else could she have asked to find them but Thelma Gregson? Nobody else in the damned village would even talk to them. Everybody shunned them because of what Arthur had done – so was *everybody* to blame then, for this tragedy? Everybody, including himself. Somebody had to be, he thought sourly, somebody had to be responsible for these pretty dead children.

Downstairs in the sparsely furnished, ultra-neat little sitting-room he had found a note. In small, rather childish handwriting Edith had asked for the funeral to be paid for from the sale of the house, and asked, too, that they be buried as they had been found, in their best clothes.

'All together in the same grave, please,' she had written. 'All together in the same coffin if you like.'

Maltby had felt sick.

Now, as he stood beside the double bed, he couldn't tear his eyes away and the image burned into his brain. Two mops of red, curly hair and one head of golden ringlets, faintly blue-tinged eyelids, collapsing pretty nostrils, bloodless lips and crisp, cotton, red-and-white spotted summer dresses. Four bodies, cosied together on the bed, stiffening inexorably.

His heart ached painfully, so painfully that he wanted to shout his agony to the world. Oh Arthur Johnson, he thought savagely, you bloody stupid bastard! You bloody, *bloody* stupid bastard!

During all the months of the children's stay at Pengloss, Bella Rosenthal had never heard her sister raise her voice once. Right from the very beginning, when they had crept into the manor on that February night like frightened mice, the rule had been strictly calm at all times, for James and Dorothea were to be presented with placid peacefulness no matter what. So when suddenly, on this warm, Sunday evening, a few minutes after Anthea had gone to answer the telephone she heard her shout a violent protest into it, she was on her feet in seconds and running for the drawing-room door.

Anthea was in the hall beside the telephone-table. She had just cradled the receiver and was leaning against the dark wooden panelling in an attitude of utter helplessness. As she saw Bella coming she closed her eyes and then put both her hands across her face as if to blot out the world.

'Oh . . . *God* . . .' she whispered. 'Oh no . . . no . . . *no*! This is too much! This is just too much, I can't believe it!'

Bella touched her softly, wondering for a moment if her sister was going to faint so unsteady was she.

'What on earth's the matter?' she asked, and felt Anthea rigid beneath her fingers.

From behind her hands Anthea blew out an agonized sigh and thought of the awfulness of Inspector Maltby's voice. Words dropping like heavy stones from his lips as he told her what he had seen. And suddenly it was as if she was sinking into quicksand and wanted to scream and scream for release.

'Mrs Johnson,' she said shakily at last, 'you know, Arthur Johnson's wife? She killed herself last night, Bella, and took her

205

three little girls with her. They were *so little* . . . babies, that's all . . .' She rubbed her face fiercely with her hands. 'Three tiny little girls, all dressed the same and lying there with their mother between them. Hell! How many *more* people are going to suffer in this tragedy, for God's sake? It's like some awful gaping maw, just getting wider and wider and sucking more people in!'

Bella put her arm around her sister and led her back into the drawing-room, then went in search of Charles and Edna. When they were all together Anthea repeated what Maltby had told her on the phone. She saw Edna's mouth tighten swiftly as the colour drained from her cheeks.

'Mrs B, do sit down, please,' she whispered wearily and suddenly they were opposite each other, either side of the fireplace but together in their shared distress.

Edna thought about Edith Johnson and her three little girls; they had always been so beautifully turned out and so charmingly mannered. Those two little red-haired twins, all curly and freckled, and the sweet Shirley, who had wanted to be a ballerina when she grew up. It was impossible to think of them as dead; their lives, full of promise, simply snuffed out before they had ever had a chance.

'They was ever such nice little girls, you know,' she murmured through quivering lips, to the silent little group in the drawing-room. 'And ever so pretty and well looked after. I can't believe Edith's done it, I really can't.'

'Mr Maltby said she'd reached the end of her tether,' Anthea said flatly. 'That they had no money and nowhere to go, and that no one in the village but the local shopkeeper would have anything to do with them. I think you know her quite well, don't you, the lady who serves in the shop?'

Edna nodded and thought of big Thelma of the ferocious face and kindly disposition. Poor Thelma, seeing those children would have broken her heart.

'I knew little Edith quite well, too,' she replied, 'and I liked her. I suppose like everyone else in the village I couldn't imagine what she'd bin thinking about, when she'd married *him* – but for all that you shouldn't judge folk by their looks, should you, and even if we didn't like him, no one ever thought he'd be ... well ... you know, a child killer.' Suddenly she pressed her fingers against her lips and her eyes became deep with concern. 'Look, I don't want Dorothea finding out about this if it can be helped, I really don't. She and Rosemary used to walk little Shirley to school of a morning, up until Rosemary ... disappeared.'

Anthea twisted her hands together and stared dully into the empty fireplace. Her heart felt heavy in her chest and she found herself haunted by Maltby's description of the little girls lying on the bed. All dressed the same, and their little limbs and faces white like marble. It was almost to hard to bear.

'I don't want James finding out either,' she muttered. 'Dear God in Heaven they've suffered enough, both of them, they just don't *need* any more. Certainly they don't need the horror of this.'

'Well,' Bella said with the air of calm command that had been creeping back into her voice lately, and reminding Anthea and Charles so much of the Bella they'd known before Peachy's untimely death, 'it will have to be very carefully organized then, won't it? No newspapers delivered to the house, and none to be left about anywhere. No radio news on when either James or Dorothea are in the house, and no going to the village on their own. Mind you, I'm not sure how we deal with that one, they didn't take any too kindly to being gated when they first came here, did they?'

'I wouldn't worry about it,' Edna observed, 'they don't hardly ever go to the village any more, anyway. Now they got their garden to plan and all them chickens to look after, they don't seem to want to do anything more'n go down to the cove for a swim now and then. I'll have a word with Judd and Seth, that should be enough.'

'And if it rains,' Anthea murmured, turning to her husband and taking his hand gently, 'Charles – bless you darling – has bought the train-set down, so they're bound to fall back on that, because you know how beloved the wretched thing is of James!'

She rubbed her temples wearily with her fingers and got up

207

slowly walking to the window to feel the warmth of the sun on her face as she gazed out across the lawns. As James and Dorothea appeared, tanned and beautiful, and squabbling cheerfully, she had a completely crazy desire to rush outside and hug them.

'Oh God . . . no more!' she shouted in frustration to the empty sky. '*No more!*'

Chapter 14

Keeping newspapers out of an estate the size of Pengloss might have been a good idea, but it was almost impossible to do, and stories about Edith and her girls, about Arthur and subsequently about Rosemary again, reared up in the press and dragged on for days. In the end the offending piece came in from the village shop, wrapped around a block of ice-cream, and was then placed in the pantry to become a receptacle for chicken scraps.

Molly Newby didn't think about it because it was her normal routine, and like most adults she tended to regard old newspaper as rubbish. The fact that it still contained its 'old news' didn't enter her head, it went out into the scullery and was simply used for something else until it got thrown away.

Shirley and her mother and sisters had been dead for a week.

Some hours later Dorothea collected the scraps from the scullery and then let herself into the chicken run – which was now big and roomy, with a lovely chicken-house and lots of space for them to scratch about – and began to distribute them.

They converged on her *en masse*, her family of chickens – they were nothing if not greedy – and she loved to squat down amongst them and feed them by hand. Charlie paced up and down like the lord of the manor, every so often scratching the ground and giving voice. Normally he could not be persuaded to take from anyone's hand – but Dorothea was patient, and in the end he would take from her if she was lucky.

When the food was all gone she went on squatting in the sunshine for a while watching her family happily. She was feeling so much better these days that for the first time for months she was beginning to 'look forward', and had quietly decided that if she managed to keep *This Man is Death* locked in the dark under her bed for ever, then she was going to be safe at last. Obviously Mr Johnson didn't know she'd told – and now everyone said he was going to be hanged, so surely she had nothing to fear any more? People *didn't* come back from the dead; that much she knew for certain – from bitter experience.

As she went on idly sitting there, enjoying the sunshine and day-dreaming pleasurably, a breeze, blowing in from the sea, caught the edge of the piece of newspaper, briefly gave it life, and blew it upwards, against the netting. It hung there for a moment, and Dorothea turned to look at it.

Looking back at her was a photograph of Shirley Johnson and her twin sisters.

Had it been anyone else it was unlikely Dorothea would have bothered to look any harder, but the sight of Shirley brought Arthur vividly into her mind, and reminded her – if she needed reminding – that he wasn't dead yet!

The tragic and pointless deaths of these three beautiful little girls . . . began the item beneath the photograph, and Dorothea felt her heart freeze in her chest as she read the words . . . Shirley, Monica, Katy . . . they were . . . *dead* . . . ?

She reached for the piece of newspaper with clumsy hands and read the item in full, as panic seemed to well up inside her like a great suffocating wave. She was much too young to grasp the implications of why Edith Johnson should have killed herself and her children; as far as Dorothea was concerned this was simply her warning. She had been complacent, thinking she had beaten Arthur at his own game. Well she'd failed, and now he had success-fully proved that he could do what he threatened whenever he liked.

So he *could* be in two places at once then? It didn't matter that they told her he was locked up in prison, he could obviously leave without anybody seeing him and do as he pleased – and he had done this to warn her. She was next.

White-faced and with trembling hands she folded the piece of newspaper and hid it amongst her clothes She crept unseen into the house, went upstairs and pulled out her little suitcase from under the bed. She flung the newspaper in on top of *This Man is Death* and slammed the lid shut violently, then she threw it back underneath the bed again as quickly as she could.

What to do? *What to do?* She sat on the bed with her hands clenched between her knees, rocking backwards and forwards in her agony. She had to get away, must put as much distance between herself and James and Aunty as she could, but where could she go? She didn't know anyone.

The answer to that one came immediately, creeping in like a monster in a nightmare. There was only one option open to her, and she knew it. She must go back to the orphanage and never come near Pengloss again. But the idea was so dreadful, and it was so far away, how on earth would she get there?

Miserably then, with big tears trickling down her cheeks, she counted her pocket money. Three shillings and fourpence; perhaps that would be enough for the bus-fare to Manchester – wherever Manchester was. She remembered quite well that it had taken almost all day to get down from Manchester to Hampton Court – and Cornwall was much further on than that.

Well, she would walk some of it, she decided, to save a bit. Cut through Tregennis Woods and pick up the road to Helston, and perhaps get a bus from there. She would leave before five the next morning, and wear her second-best dress and her sandals. Then in her little suitcase she would take her best dress, the maroon-striped cotton one, and her black shiny shoes to give to the governess as payment for her keep. Otherwise there was just her dolly, and she couldn't leave her behind – she had to have something to remind her . . .

Her packing done and her plans all made she went downstairs for supper later, but her eyes were heavy from crying, her face blotchy – and it was noticed at once.

'You all right, sweetheart?' Aunty said sharply. 'You'm looking a bit peaky.'

211

Dorothea felt almost grateful, because she knew she wouldn't be able to eat anything, her throat seemed to close over at the very *idea* of food.

'I feel sick . . .' she whispered, as her eyes filled with tears again.

Edna touched her head and pulled a quick face.

'Bit feverish,' she muttered to Anthea and then cast an enquiring eye upon James. 'You feeling all right?' she asked him.

James was ploughing into a huge plate of food, as happy as a sandboy. He smiled brightly and went on chewing, so Aunty gathered Dorothea up from the table and took her away.

Dorothea didn't know whether this was the worst thing or the best thing, having Aunty kiss and cuddle her, tuck her into bed and then sit with her until she was drifting off to sleep. Was it a memory to cling to when she was back in the orphanage, or was it almost unbearable because it would never happen again? She was so bewildered that she longed to tell Aunty the truth, but her fear was overwhelming, and when Aunty finally kissed her and crept away she thought her heart would break in pieces.

She sobbed and sobbed as warm evening closed into warm night, and was still awake and floundering about in her misery when she heard James come up to bed.

Dorothea had had a bedroom of her own, since Charles had brought the train-set down from Hampton Court, and James had set it up on the floor in the room they had been sharing. That was a good thing, because it meant she wasn't going to disturb him when she got up; she had even set the alarm on the clock that ticked away beside the bed – but she didn't need it. Sleep was not something she was granted a great deal of that night. Most of the night she lay awake listening to the familiar sounds of Pengloss and breaking her heart in the knowledge that the next night-time sounds she heard would be those of the orphanage. The prospect was truly appalling.

When at last she decided to get up it was still dark, but the sky was paling very slightly in the east and she knew it was time to leave. She had written a note to Aunty, which she carefully placed on her bedside table, and grasping her suitcase firmly she set off downstairs. However, the only way she could get out of the house was through the kitchen, which meant turning the key in the back-kitchen door; an act designed to bring Juno and Cyrus bounding in from the drawing-room no matter how quietly she performed it.

The three of them looked at each other briefly and then the dogs yelped softly in delight. A walk! And this early in the morning! Perfection!

She tried to tell them that they couldn't come, but they weren't listening, and anyway, she reflected, since she'd got to walk through Tregennis Woods on her own, it might be nice to have them for company. Oh well, she'd work out how to send them back later, she thought, and so, with the two of them bounding happily about her and the air full of the delicious and heady scents of early morning, she walked firmly away from Pengloss . . . and forced herself not to look back.

Tregennis Woods surrounded what had once been a fine estate which had fallen into ruin at about the same time as the fortunes of Pengloss had been turned around by the Rosenthals. Eventually the house, empty and full of gaping windows, had mysteriously burned to the ground and there had been no one to care any more. Surrounding farmers had quietly annexed any decent growing or grazing land, and David Rosenthal's father had bought the Tregennis woodlands – but hadn't bothered to do anything with them. So now they were a poacher's paradise, patrolled only occasionally by Judd – and, according to James, haunted.

It was daylight and full of the promise of an exquisite day when Dorothea and the dogs turned off the road and plunged into the woods. Everywhere the path before her was dappled with sunshine and, surprisingly, not nearly as scary as she'd been expecting, so she forged on, trying to keep as straight a path as possible, knowing that if she got it right she would come out on the Helston Road.

She found herself comforted by the presence of the dogs, despite the fact that they kept racing off into the undergrowth hunting after exciting smells, and she had no idea that she wasn't alone in the woods; but she wasn't. The man who saw her was one of the most disreputable poachers in the district, and not likely to report to anyone that he'd seen one of the manor children in the woods at half past five in the morning. But the sight of her had the effect of driving him out, which would eventually be to her advantage as it happened, because he was skulking sulkily home by the time she was missed, and would subsequently run into Judd Newby.

Judd and Molly Newby sat down to breakfast at six-thirty every morning, summer or winter. Molly would put a hearty breakfast on the table in front of her husband, and then nip across to the manor to let the dogs out. It was their routine.

They followed it this morning in the normal way, and Judd felt the breeze of the new day blowing in from his open kitchen door as he ploughed into his plate of bacon and eggs with delight, thinking about his plans for the day. He was going to do some work on the garden after early milking, he had decided, and knew he needed to speak to James and Dorothea at some point, but he'd see them after their breakfast, he thought, as he spread butter lavishly on a slice of toast, and that would be soon enough.

When Molly came breathlessly back into the kitchen a moment later, the look on her face made him forget his breakfast in an instant. She was white to the lips and barely able to speak. Her hands trembled and clutched in one of them was a sheet of school-room paper with some writing on it in pencil . . . and the fear that Judd had known all those years ago, when Peachy had inexplicably vanished, crowded back upon him like a cunningly familiar enemy.

'What?' he demanded. 'What, Molly? *What*? Where's the dogs for God's sake? Speak to me!'

At last she found her breath, for she had run full tilt from the manor and running was not something Molly Newby did much at her age.

'She'm gone, Judd!' she panted, staring at him wide-eyed with panic. 'Dorothea. She'm gone.'

Judd felt his nerves begin to sing, he felt sickness rise in the pit of his stomach as waves of rage and panic shivered through him.

'Tell me, woman!' he snarled, and Molly plunked herself down into a chair, smoothing out Dorothea's note beneath her trembling hands.

'I went to let the dogs out,' she said miserably, 'and they was gone. Well, I knew no one but one of the kids would've let them out so I crept upstairs. Her room was empty, and she'd left this note for Edna. Oh God . . .' Suddenly her eyes filled with tears, because it was all so inexplicable. 'She'm run away from us, Judd!'

For Judd those words brought such a flood of relief surging down through his body that he almost fell back into his chair. Run away. If Dorothea had run away at first light, and had Juno and Cyrus with her, then she couldn't possibly have reached anywhere where she might come to any harm, and she was as well protected as if she'd had her own personal army with her. Run away was not vanished. It was not happening again after all. He put his hand on his wife's arm gently and then began to pull on his jacket.

'Read us the note, Mol,' he begged her politely, 'and then do us a favour, if you will. Put together a couple of slices of your lovely homemade bread and jam, wrapped in a bit of greaseproof, and fix us up a nice flask of cold milk. She'll not have had any breakfast, I'll be bound, and she'm going t'be starving. I'll get the pony harnessed.'

Dear Aunty, Molly read, as her heart was wrenched by the loving care the child had taken in writing what she supposed would be her last note to her beloved Aunty.

> *I have gone back to Manchester because Mr Johnson told me that if I told he would hurt you and James and I told and now he has killed Shirley and Monica and Katy and I don't want him to hurt you. I will come back when I am grown up. Your loving Dorothea.*

'We ent bin listening, have we?' Judd murmured when his wife had finished, and was blotting her tears with the edge of her pinny. 'None of us. We ent bin listening, Molly, and we should've known better!'

And so saying he went out of the cottage towards the paddock.

Dorothea had come right through the woods and on to the Helston Road by seven o'clock. The morning was warm now, and she was desperately hungry – because she hadn't thought to put anything to eat in her little case. She was thirsty, too, and had not the remotest idea how long it was going to take her to walk to Helston.

Juno and Cyrus walked behind her, but the road was metalled, and boring, and they were anxious to get back into the woods; they didn't like walking on the road.

Dorothea kept telling them they ought to go home now, but each time they simply wagged their tails cheerfully and kept on following her, so in the end she just accepted their company and kept on trudging. But the little case, which held the book, the newspaper, a dress, a pair of shoes and her dolly, suddenly seemed to be incredibly heavy and she was getting very weary.

Judd ran into Ezra Munt just outside the gates to Pengloss and pulled up the pony sharply, gazing down at the disreputable old poacher who stood on the grassy bank beside the road looking disgrunted, and like something nasty on a new carpet.

'Don't you start a-picking on me, Judd Newby,' Ezra snarled. 'You ent caught me doing nothing . . .'

Judd silenced him with a look.

'I don't care what you been doing,' he retorted. 'I just need to know if you've seen a little girl in your travels this morning, that's all.'

At that the old poacher's face broke into a sly smile and he showed a mouthful of rotting teeth.

'So it *was* her,' he exclaimed. 'I thought it must be, 'cos she had them bleddy dogs with her – feckin' brutes! Well, well, run away from home, has she? Naughty girl. She's on the Helston road by now, complete with her little suitcase, I thinks you'll find, and you makes sure you gives her a good beating when you catches up with her, eh Judd?'

Judd sneered and flicked his whip at the pony, leaving Ezra

Munt chuckling after him. Well, he'd keep, he thought. Oh, he'd keep all right!

Dorothea heard the clop of hoofs on the road some time before she saw anybody coming, and in those minutes she actually caught herself begging for it to be Judd, which she realized was pointless and wicked, since she was supposed to be running away. Then Juno and Cyrus pricked their ears, barked a couple of times and ran like the wind towards the sound. It stopped, started again, and round the corner, with both dogs leaning over the back of the pony-cart, came Judd.

Dorothea sank down heavily on to the grass verge and clutched her little case between her knees. She was exhausted.

'Can I give you a lift anywhere?' Judd asked calmly, gazing down at her. 'You've got a long walk, afore you gets to any place at the moment.'

Dorothea gazed up at him and her eyes filled with tears. She hadn't, she realized, thought about how much she was going to miss him when she'd gone, she'd been too busy thinking about Aunty and James, but she was going to miss him. Dreadfully.

'I'm going to Manchester,' she replied quietly. 'You don't know how long it'll take me to get there, do you?'

Judd shrugged his shoulders, and then rolled and lit one of his strong cigarettes, puffing smoke into the morning air. It smelled so familiar.

'Ent never bin to Manchester,' he answered truthfully at last. 'Mind, I never bin to London neither. You had breakfast?' Dorothea shook her head and he opened the little door on the side of the trap. 'Hop up, then,' he said, 'and you can have a bite to eat while we'm talking about it.'

Molly had not only put in breakfast for Dorothea, but a bacon sandwich and a flask of tea for him, too. He unscrewed the cap from one of the flasks and gave her a cup of ice-cold milk, which she swallowed down thirstily. Then he unwrapped her bread and jam, his bacon sandwich and poured himself some tea.

'Good spot for breakfast,' he observed, and they ate in companionable silence.

217

When every scrap was gone, Judd tapped the reins lightly and the pony began to move along at a fairly lazy walk. They were still heading in the direction of Helston, so Dorothea went on sitting beside him, saying nothing . . . and they covered a mile or more, without seeing a house, a turning, in fact anything at all other than the hedge.

'Long road, this,' Judd remarked eventually, and gently halted the pony. 'And now,' he said, turning slightly, to face Dorothea, 'I think it's time you told me what this is all about, young lady, 'cos I'm not taking you to Manchester if I don't know why.'

Oh, it was such a relief to tell. Even as the words came tumbling out of her mouth, as she took out the awful paperback book and the crumpled sheet of newspaper, as she talked about Arthur whispering to her in the hospital, it was such a relief that it just poured out and wouldn't stop. And Judd listened in silence, nodding occasionally, but never taking his eyes off her once.

When she'd finished he took up the book and looked at it thoughtfully.

'My Molly bought this,' he observed slowly. 'I remember her bringing it home – bleddy lurid nonsense. Sometimes I'm glad I can't read good you know. Took it to the village fête last summer and then Miz Anthea bought it. Lot of nonsense, I reckon.'

Without a second thought he chucked it on to the floor in the back of the trap and it slid under the seat.

'Burn that when us gets it home, we will,' he declared. 'And now, about your little friends. I'm afraid it weren't their pa killed them, my lovie, it were their mother, 'cos she got sick in the head, poor woman. There was a girl in the village like that when I was young, had her baby out of wedlock an' killed it, and herself. Bad, bad business, 'specially when children die . . .' He paused and looked steadily at Dorothea, seeing a look of doubt creep into her eyes. 'Listen,' he murmured quietly, 'you know I wouldn't lie to you, don't you?' She nodded. 'Then I got something to tell you, to help you understand.'

Without warning he suddenly snapped the reins and turned the pony smartly in the middle of the road, then they began to trot back towards Pengloss at a cracking pace. The sky above them was the newly painted blue of morning with a mere suggestion of high altitude cloud, the sun beat down and warmed the little road and a blackbird set up a rumpus as they clopped by.

'When I went off to fight in France in the war,' Judd said, after they had travelled some distance in silence, 'not the last one, the one before, that was; there was another fellow from Pengloss went with us, a chap called Frank and Frank and me had been friends since we was lads. Well we fought, and ran about, and somehow never got shot, and then one winter it started raining and it just never stopped. In the end we was having to use duck-boards to get too 'n fro anywhere, 'cos there was mud pits ten feet deep. Well one day Frank and me was crossing one of they duck-boards, when he slipped and fell in. It was so quick I had no time to grab him and he never had a chance even to cry out. He just vanished. Gone. I yelled for help, of course, and I clawed about in the mud for ages, but I never found so much as a trace of him, and never saw him again, till they dredged up his body, by which time he was dead and cold. Well that night, we was on the duck-boards again, Frank and me; and this time when he fell he grabbed hold of the side. But I couldn't pull him up. No matter how hard I tried I couldn't pull him up – and to this day I still can't pull him up, but I'm still trying, regular as anything. Do you understand?'

Dorothea was silent for a moment as she digested the story, and suddenly she thought about Arthur Johnson leaning over her in the hospital. She thought about Rosemary in the bed next to her, about the darkness and the silence . . . and she did understand.

'It was a dream,' she whispered. 'In the hospital. It was a dream.'

Judd nodded and smiled down on her with great warmth and love.

'The man Johnson,' he said quietly, 'was in police cells that night, so I'd heard, and he's never seen the light of day again since. He's a prisoner, locked up with keys and padlocks, and what's more, in a couple of weeks they're going to hang him. He can't hurt you, my lover, and he can't hurt Aunty nor James, neither.

And if you wants me to be really honest, I don't think he *wants* to hurt you. He's sorry for what he done in killing your little friend; he said so in the papers. So let's get you back to Pengloss afore you're missed, shall we, and then you can have another breakfast!'

Dorothea leaned against him and felt him slip his arm round her protectively. Suddenly all her fears melted away. James and Aunty were safe, because Judd had said so, and that meant she really, truly didn't have to go back to Manchester and throw herself on the mercy of the governess. She drank in the fresh, faintly salty air, listening with pleasure to the sounds around her, and safe now, to do it, she remembered the mingling, awful smells of the orphanage with a tiny thrill of disgust. She didn't have to go back. She was safe.

She was sleeping soundly against Judd by the time they reached the manor.

Later that afternoon, when they realized the damage they had done in trying to keep secrets, the adults at Pengloss decided enough was enough and it was time to make amends. Seated in the drawing-room, they told James and Dorothea all they knew about the deaths of Shirley and her sisters. Then they listened to what the children had to say in return.

They talked about it and about Rosemary. They talked about hanging and punishment, and eventually went away feeling a bit less bewildered. But Edna, Anthea, Charles, even Bella would never know exactly what James and Dorothea's feelings were – for they didn't know *exactly* how they felt themselves.

'I suppose,' Anthea observed when they had gone, 'that had they been born ten years earlier than they were, violent death in the midst of life would have been just an everyday occurrence for them, with the bombing and the dreadful things that came out of Europe and so on?'

'Yes, well be grateful that they weren't,' Bella replied. 'I can't see that that was to anybody's advantage. Now what's important is healing their wounds and giving them the freedom of life.'

And so they were eventually asked whether, instead of going

back to their old lives, they would feel happier to remain at Pengloss and begin new ones. Predictably their answers were enthusiastically in the affirmative.

But James, who at all times tried to be a little grown-up, and who also hated the idea of hurting anybody's feelings, was careful to temper his enthusiasm with consideration as he talked to his parents, for the last thing he wanted was to disappoint them. He knew what tradition meant to his father – in fact he thought he recognized that a considerable sacrifice had been made on his behalf.

'It's not that I wasn't looking forward to going to Marlborough in September,' he told them, slightly pompously, 'I was. Very much. It's just that – well – I think I *should* stay here with Aunt Bella and Dorothea, don't you? Be the man about the place, you know?' It was almost as much as Charles and Anthea could do to keep a straight face; and then, suddenly, he was a little boy again as he looked quizzically at his mother, knitting his brows in astonishment at the follow-up of his thoughts. 'Are you staying here for ever, as well?' he asked.

Anthea's eyebrows shot upwards in alarm, but her heart leapt with relief. His words had not been longing or wistful, just surprised, and she knew that she could go without the slightest worry.

'Not likely,' she retorted. 'I'm going back to Hampton Court with Daddy – in fact I'm going as soon as his holiday is finished. Chickens and milking-parlours don't have quite the same attraction for me as they do for you. In fact they don't have any attraction at all, if I'm honest. You two, however, will be resuming lessons since you've elected to stay, because Miss Forrester will need to coach you for your entrance exams into the grammar school. Life always has its problems, I'm afraid!'

A look of alarm sprang up in Dorothea's eyes and she turned quickly to Edna, who had been standing quietly by, listening to the conversation without comment.

Reaching out a thin, slightly nervous hand she whispered:

'Are you going back as well, Aunty?' and received a wonderfully familiar baleful glare for her pains.

'*Me!*' Edna echoed. 'I'm not going anywhere, I assure you. The way you two gets fussed and spoiled round here, *someone*'s got to be handing out the punishments, otherwise you'm going to wind up horrible. The both of you!'

Dorothea threw herself into Aunty's arms, hugging her fiercely, for at last it was safe to feel confident. Safe to feel . . . safe, she thought.

On the morning of 6 August Arthur Johnson was up early and dressed for the last time. He hadn't asked for anything special to eat the previous evening, and in the tense quiet of this final morning of his life, he drank a cup of tea but refused any toast, and smoked a cigarette as he waited his appointed hour to die. He had not slept during the night, so he had not faced his ghosts in his dreams. Perhaps today he must face them for real?

He had left a carefully thought-out and painstakingly written letter for Inspector Maltby, in which he had repeated his declaration that Rosemary Archer's death had been a terrible accident, but in this, the last words he would ever write in this world, he begged Dorothea's forgiveness for what he had done to her, and begged Tim and Doreen Archer's forgiveness, too . . . although he knew that was something he would never get.

The Archers knew his execution was that morning, but it made little difference – Rosemary was still gone, whatever happened, and Tim knew his life could never be repaired, not by an act of revenge. Tim thought it was all pointless. Doreen was past thinking in any capacity any more. Doreen didn't even apparently notice that she lived at all any longer, she had retreated into the world of the dead with her beloved daughter, and Arthur's death would touch her in no way at all.

As Arthur waited in his cell for the appointed hour he did not hope for a last-minute reprieve, because he didn't want one. He felt sick with fright, but that was the fear of dying, not of being dead, for he longed to be dead. There was just that last moment to be got through, and then he would be free, and he found the waiting intolerable.

The chaplain came to pray with him as the minutes ticked away, and in those last prayers he thought of Edith and his beautiful girls and of Rosemary . . . of how he had destroyed so many lives and never meant to hurt anyone, and at a minute to nine they came to collect him for the final short walk to the gallows. There, in silence but with a brave determination, he stepped firmly on to the trap door and permitted the hood to be pulled down over his face . . . and Maltby winced as the trap snapped open.

Winced and turned away, anxious to get out of this place of death and back amongst the living. It was over. At least it was over for Arthur Johnson. Maltby doubted it would ever be completely over for the survivors of this tragedy, and wondered if he would have felt differently had Arthur Johnson been a cold, vicious killer, rather than a man firstly obsessed with what he couldn't have, and then driven by fear. Would that have made it harder or easier, he wondered, and didn't know the answer.

At Pengloss the clock on the mantelpiece in the drawing-room busily tinkled out the hour of nine, but nobody was there to hear it. Outside, with a gull calling mournfully overhead and the summer sun already warming the grey stone walls of the chapel, Bella, Judd, Molly, Seth, Edna and Dorothea stood amongst the new flower-beds in the garden and sang *Happy Birthday* to James. He was twelve years old.

They put his presents on the stone altar for him, and after a while everyone but Dorothea drifted away. Only he and she were left, standing in the sunshine together in their special place.

James looked at his new watch, the one his parents had given him for his birthday.

'It's nearly half past nine,' he observed. 'So Mr Johnson's been hung now.' He frowned and stared at the stone altar and the warm grey, ruined walls around him, where there was no noise at all but the calling of herring-gulls in the sky above. 'But nothing's changed,' he murmured. 'I thought it would be, but it isn't.'

Dorothea pressed her lips together and gazed around her in a sort of haunted despair.

'I don't want anybody else to die,' she whispered. 'Ever. First there was my mummy and daddy and then Rosemary and Peachy and then . . . and I don't want any more. I don't!'

There were two slate plaques in the garden now, one for Rosemary and one for Peachy, and there was another one ordered for Shirley and her sisters. All these children who had been such a part of everyday life – except Peachy – where had they all gone, Dorothea wondered. Were they there really, playing in the streets at home as always, and it was she who was missing, not them? It was somehow easier to think of it that way than any other.

'I think,' James said, 'that we should make a pact, you know. That every day for the rest of our lives we'll come into this garden no matter what. That's what I think we should do.'

The rest of their lives. At eleven and twelve years old respectively it was not possible for them to look with any certainty into the future, for now this was the rest of their lives . . . and it was certainly a promise Dorothea was ready to make.

A shaft of sunlight shone through the missing roof of the chapel and played with glittering fingers about the gold letters on the polished black plaque above the altar. Dorothea gazed at it steadily.

Rosemary's Garden, it said, and in her mind's eye Rosemary's almond eyes smiled at her warmly.

'Goodbye . . .' she whispered, looking up into the wide blue sky. 'Oh, Rosemary . . . Goodbye . . .'